CRONIN'S KEY

By

N.R. Walker

Copyright

Cover Artist: Sara York
Editor: Erika Orrick
Cronin's Key © 2015 N.R. Walker

First edition: March 2015

ALL RIGHTS RESERVED:

WARNING
Intended for an 18+ audience only. This book contains
material that maybe offensive to some and is intended for a
mature, adult audience. It contains graphic language,
explicit male/male sexual content, and adult situations.

Dedication

For my readers.

CHAPTER ONE

Detective Alec MacAidan ran through the dark, wet back streets of New York City. The rain gave a silver-scape to the buildings, dulling the stench of garbage-littered alleys, and added an eeriness to what had been an already weird night. Shadows seemed to move and follow him as he ran, making the hairs on the back of his neck prickle, but he never quit running. Chasing.

He was one of the fittest guys in his department, and at only twenty-nine, he was younger than most. His jeans were wet to his knees, and water streamed down from his soaked brown hair to his coat. His senses alert, the only sounds he could hear were his own heart pounding in his ears and his boots striking the pavement.

He'd chased down ice addicts before, and this one was no different. Unnatural strength and speed, ashen faces and wide eyes, and manic highs and lows made these people unpredictable and dangerous. But as he navigated his way, chasing the guy through the back alleyways, around corners, over fences, barely catching glimpses of the guy's dark coat before it disappeared again, the shadows got closer. Alec had the creeping realization he wasn't chasing someone at all.

He was being chased.

Followed. Hunted.

Despite the burn in his lungs and legs, he pushed himself harder, faster. As he rounded the corner of a building, the guy he was chasing approached the eight-foot brick wall that fenced the back of the alley.

The assailant didn't stop; he didn't even balk. He simply used the alley wall to his right to launch himself up onto the top of the brick fence, where he paused for just a second, long enough to stop, turn, and look at Alec. And he smiled before disappearing onto the other side.

Two things flashed through Alec's mind: speed and teeth.

Neither of them human.

Alec did as the assailant had done. He ran to the dead end, then stepped onto the alley wall and used it to propel himself up enough to get his arms up on top of the brick fence, pulling himself over it.

He swung his legs over and jumped down into another shorter alley that met a main road just a hundred yards away. Cars passed and Alec thought for sure he'd lost the chase, but a lone figure stood in the alley. Alec thought for a moment that the man had simply given up running, but something flashed near the street—a coat, Alec realized—before disappearing around the corner.

The lone man just stood there. All Alec could see was a silhouette, lit only from a streetlight behind him at the end of the alley, the man was completely shrouded in shadow. Alec pulled his gun and aimed it at him. "NYPD," he huffed, out of breath. "Hands where I can see 'em."

The man fell to his knees, then slumped to his side on the wet pavement. Alec ran to him, and when he was close enough, he could see a dark pool of blood seeping through the man's shirt. Alec hadn't heard any shots fired, nor any confrontation. Was he shot? Stabbed?

Alec pressed his hand against the man's chest with one hand and radioed for backup with his other. "This is MacAidan. I need a paramedic."

It was only now that he was close enough that Alec could see the man's face. He was pale with dark eyes, but he was smiling. He was oddly beautiful and serene despite having what looked like a bullet wound in his chest.

"What's your name?" Alec asked him.

The man laughed. "He missed my heart."

"We'll get you to the hospital," Alec said. "Just hang on."

"No." He shook his head slowly, still smiling. "It's you. It really is you."

Alec was sure the man was seeing someone that wasn't there, as most people taking their last breaths often did. "What's your name?"

"He will come for you. Tell him it's started, they're coming." His voice was wispy, fading. "It's not one, it's both."

The man was making no sense. "Tell who?"

The man on the ground reached up and put his hand to Alec's chest. He smiled again, his eyes glazed over with something akin to wonder. "I touched the key."

"Detective MacAidan." Alec's radio cracked to life, startling him. He didn't know how long the operator had been calling his name. "State your location."

"The key to what?"

The dying man laughed. "You must tell Cronin what I said. He'll find you, Ailig."

Alec's blood ran cold. *Ailig? How the* hell *did he know...?* Then the man on the ground took his last breath and crumbled to dust.

* * * *

Alec had seen some pretty weird shit in his life, but nothing quite prepared him for what he'd seen tonight.

If it weren't for his still-wet clothes and hair and the blackened bloodstains on his hands for proof, he might even think he'd imagined the whole thing. If it weren't for the small wooden shard on the table in front of him, he might actually think his colleagues were right: he'd finally lost his freakin' mind.

They didn't believe him, and Alec didn't really blame them.

He'd always been the odd man out in the NYPD. He preferred to work on his own, which helped because no one really wanted to stay his partner for

4

too long anyway. And that's how he liked it. Alec loved his job, and he'd moved through the ranks quickly, not only because of his dedication but also because of his photographic memory. He was renowned for it: the smallest detail, the briefest glance, he saw it all.

His captain at the 33rd, a large second-generation Italian man by the name of De Angelo, sat across the desk from him in the interrogation room and shook his head. "You mean to tell me you chased a guy who leapt over an eight-foot wall, then bled all over you before he crumbled to dust?"

"No," Alec repeated, not caring how frustrated he sounded. "I said I chased a guy over the wall, then *another* guy bled all over me before he crumbled to dust. It was not the same man." Obviously it wasn't *a man* at all, but that was not something Alec wanted to add to the discussion at this point. As it was, half the division was sitting on the other side of the windows watching him, not even trying to hide their amusement. Alec wondered idly what jokes would come of this.

"Crumbled to dust…?" De Angelo repeated.

"Yes. Clothes and all," Alec said. "The man I was chasing fled the scene. He went left on Wadsworth Avenue. You can check surveillance cameras of the area. He was wearing a long coat."

"And this man that… crumbled to dust" — De Angelo made a face — "did he say anything to you?"

5

"Yes. He said some guy would find me, that it was happening. I don't know what he was talking about," Alec said. "But then he said I had to tell Cronin what he said, and no, before you ask, I don't know who Cronin is. He said he touched the key."

"The key?"

Alec nodded. "That's what he said. And then he… um." Alec wasn't sure how to say this.

"Then he what?" De Angelo prompted. "Turned into dust?"

"Before that," Alec said, ignoring the patronizing sonofabitch. "He called me by name."

De Angelo blinked. "He called you by name?"

Alec nodded again. "Yes. But he didn't call me Alec. He called me by my birth name, the old Scottish name only my father calls me. He called me Ailig. There is no way he could have known that. *No one* knows that."

Alec was sure De Angelo was torn. Alec could tell he wanted to discredit him—what he was saying was ludicrous, after all—but the division captain also knew Alec would never lie. He was honest to a fault. Plenty of other men would just say the perp had got away, too bewildered to mention inhuman speed and bodies that turned to **dust, but not Alec MacAidan. It wasn't the first** time something bizarre had happened.

"Weird shit just seems to follow you, don't it?" De Angelo said, not looking at Alec but at the far wall instead. "Kinda like the time that bullet went around you instead of through you, huh?"

It wasn't like Alec could hardly tell the man weird shit had been happening to him all his life. Instead he cleared his throat and said, "Actually, that bullet got me."

"You got shot in the leg," De Angelo said. "Hardly as bad as it could've been."

What De Angelo didn't say was it was hardly the head shot it was supposed to be. Alec and his then-partner Cavill had been caught in the crossfire of a drug heist gone wrong, and there were nine other people, six police, three civilians, who had seen a bullet literally bend from Alec's head to his leg.

Alec shrugged. "I, uh... when I was running through those alleyways, I had the distinct feeling of being followed."

"Did you see anyone?"

Alec shook his head. "No. Just shadows."

De Angelo shook his head again and sighed deeply. "When the patrol cars and paramedics got to the scene, they only found you. No dust, no clothes, no witnesses."

"The rain washed the dust away," Alec said.

De Angelo eyed the small wooden shard on the table. "They just found you, MacAidan, holding that. What do you think it is?"

Alec looked over the small piece of polished wood. It was maybe two inches long and reminded Alec of a pencil that had been sharpened at both ends: pointed, smooth, and sharp. He'd never seen anything like it before, but he had no doubt what it was. "It's a bullet."

De Angelo's eyebrows shot up, and he snorted out a laugh. "A bullet? Made from wood? What are you trying to kill? Vampires?"

Alec remembered when the man he was chasing sat on the brick fence and smiled at him… all he could see was teeth. Even the memory of those pointed teeth sent a cold shiver down his spine.

De Angelo was still laughing. "MacAidan, that's the most ridiculous thing you've said yet."

Alec lifted his chin, and oddly enough, he thought of his father. His dad never questioned the weird shit Alec claimed he saw, never thought less of him, and would probably have told Alec to punch his commanding officer in the mouth for laughing.

The other cops watching through the glass partitions were laughing now too, looking at Alec and snickering. Alec looked back at De Angelo and smiled tightly. His clothes were still wet, his boots and socks soaked through. He just wanted to go home and get warm. "Are we done?"

De Angelo sighed, long and loud. "Yeah. But do yourself a favor. Don't mention any of this in your report." Then the captain leaned across the table and reached for the wooden bullet.

"Don't touch it," Alec snapped.

De Angelo, despite being the ranking officer, immediately retracted his hand, leaving the bullet in front of Alec. From the look on his face, it seemed De Angelo's reaction surprised even himself. He stood up and opened the door, not for Alec's benefit, but for the other cops in the department. "Why don't you take a day or two of leave, MacAidan. Clear your head a little."

The other cops laughed again, and De Angelo puffed out his chest as he walked through the department toward his office. Alec pocketed the wooden bullet and walked to the door, just about to tell the other cops to fuck off when a man walked into the middle of the department floor.

He was impeccably dressed in an expensive black overcoat with the collar up. He had pale skin, dark eyes, and rust-colored ginger hair, short and messy. He was looking right at Alec.

"Can I help you?" one of the other cops asked him. The general public never came into this part of the department.

The man smiled at Alec, ignoring how about twenty cops were now staring at him, obviously not liking the fact he'd taken it upon himself to just walk into a restricted area like he owned the place.

De Angelo, who hadn't quite made it to his office yet, barked across the room. "How the hell did you get in here?"

It was something Alec couldn't explain. Despite the growing agitation in the room, the noise, the flying questions, and movement, all he felt was calm and quiet.

The other cops had guns drawn, but Alec didn't care. He walked over to this strange, beautiful man, like his body wouldn't let him go anywhere else.

The man smiled at Alec. "It is you. Finally." There was an accent, Alec thought. Scottish? He wasn't sure.

Alec paid no attention as the cops in the room barked orders to *show us your hands* and *get on the ground* at this man. The room was in a flurry around them, yet he didn't move. Alec couldn't explain it; what had been confusing before now was crystal clear, everything that Alec didn't even know was wrong was right. And he knew, he just *knew*, this man's name was Cronin.

Cronin smiled. "Will you come with me?"

"Yes."

"Put your arms around me and hold on."

Alec did as he was told, feeling the man against him as he slid his arms around his waist, so perfect and so right. The last thing Alec heard was a soft sigh in his ear.

Then both he and Cronin disappeared into thin air.

CHAPTER TWO

Alec felt like he was being pulled apart at a cellular level. A pain, so absolute, so blinding, tore at his body. He could feel every nerve ending; every receptor, every synapse in his whole body was on fire. Bones, muscles, cells felt as though they were being shredded.

Pixelated, his brain registered. It felt as though his body had disintegrated into a million pixels, tiny dots, held together only by raw nerves.

Then as quickly as it started, as quickly as it burned him, the impossible pain was... gone.

Alec pushed the man who held him away and sucked back a gasping breath. He staggered, still gulping for air. "What the... what the hell was...?"

"It's called leaping," the man said softly. "I apologize. I forgot what it was like the first time."

Alec looked at him. The beautiful man with pale skin and ginger hair... Jesus, just two seconds ago he was standing in the middle of the department floor, surrounded by fellow cops all pointing guns at him... Earlier, he'd chased down some inhuman creature, then he tried to stop a man from bleeding out, only to have him turn to dust... God, Alec couldn't think straight. His mind was still reeling, still scattered, from being pixelated or — what did he call it? *Leaping*?

This man... Alec couldn't quite remember how he knew his name, but he knew it with absolute certainty.

"You are Cronin?"

"Yes."

Alec spun around to take in where he was. It looked almost like a museum, complete with white walls, marble floors, expensive minimalistic furniture, and artifacts on the shelves, but the skyline out the glass wall told him it was a penthouse. A New York City penthouse, over Central Park, no less. Jesus.

Despite the extravagance, it was warm at least, and Alec was grateful for that. His clothes and boots were still wet and heavy, and he shivered.

Cronin put his hand out, then pulled it back, as if unsure. "I will find you dry clothes."

Alec was sure the accent was indeed Scottish, but his head was still a little fuzzy. "No," he said adamantly. "Answers first. Where am I? Who are you? Where are you from? And what the fuck is leaping?"

Cronin fought a smile. "You are in my apartment, 157 West 57th Street, New York City, to be exact. I am Cronin, and I am originally from Scotland. And leaping is the quantum removal of matter from one space and replacing it in another."

"Of course it is," Alec mumbled. His head began to swim again. Maybe it was because it was three in the morning, or maybe he needed to eat something or get some sleep. Or maybe, just maybe, he was losing his fucking mind. "I think I need to sit down."

Alec half stumbled to the leather sofa, not caring that his wet clothes weren't probably good for it. He sat forward with his head in his hands, trying to make sense of everything, anything, when a warm blanket wrapped around his shoulders. When Alec looked up, Cronin was kneeling in front of him. His eyes were dark and imploring, his skin was a near-flawless alabaster with just a few freckles on his nose, his red hair was still perfectly messy, swept up off his face, and he smelled so damn good... Alec was transfixed by the man in front of him, unable to look away.

Then Cronin tentatively raised his hand to Alec's forehead and brushed his damp, shaggy hair from his eyes. He stared at Alec, seemingly as captivated with Alec as Alec was with him. Without any conscious decision to do so, Alec leaned forward as if to press his lips to Cronin's, but he stopped himself just a half inch short of contact. He wanted to kiss Cronin; God, how he wanted to kiss him...

Alec pulled back quickly and made himself look away, embarrassed and confused by his reaction to this man he just met. The same man who made him disappear in front of a room full of cops. Alec leaned back on the sofa and covered his face with his hands. "Jesus."

"You've had quite a night so far," Cronin said, speaking softly to the floor. "And I fear it will only worsen yet."

Alec's hands fell heavily to his lap and he stared at Cronin. "Worse?"

Cronin looked at Alec then, and Alec swore he'd never seen eyes that dark. "I will tell you everything," Cronin promised. "We have much to discuss. But the others are expected to join us soon, so if you will—"

"Others?" Alec interrupted. "What others?"

Before Cronin could answer, an elevator dinged, and Cronin smiled as he stood. He moved fluidly, Alec realized, as he watched him walk away. Not a moment later, Cronin came back into the room with two people behind him.

People. Well, they were the least normal people-looking people Alec had ever seen. A man, Japanese, with his hair shaven underneath, a bun on top, and strikingly beautiful. The woman had long straight white-blonde hair and the bluest eyes Alec had ever seen. Both of them were pale, and he was unsure who was more attractive.

It was a natural beauty, Alec thought. Just not an entirely *human* beauty. Yet he felt no fear; in fact, he felt totally at ease.

Alec stood, his tired body protesting, but his manners wouldn't let him stay seated for introductions.

"Alec," the Japanese man said with a nod and a smile, as though they were old friends. Alec had never seen this man before — surely he'd remember him — but a sense of déjà vu crept over Alec's skin like a hundred baby spiders.

The woman smiled at Cronin for a long second before walking over to Alec and touching his arm. "We have waited a long time for you," she said. Then she glanced at Cronin. "Some a little longer than others."

Cronin was suddenly between the woman and Alec, smiling, but Alec saw a look of warning pass between them. "Alec, this is Eiji"—he nodded toward the man—"and this is Jodis," he said, introducing the woman. "They are my oldest and dearest friends."

Alec gave them a smile but then, looking at the three of them in turn, asked, "Can someone please tell me what the hell is going on? Because I get the feeling that I was expected to be here, but I don't know any of you. I mean, it's great that you guys are friends and all, but I've had one helluva night where not a great deal is making sense and I'm pretty sure the whole NYPD is in lockdown right now, given what they all saw. I'm either on their MIA list or their most wanted list. And quite frankly, neither is good."

"What has Cronin told you?" Eiji asked.

"Uh, nothing," Alec answered. Ignoring the way that both Eiji and Jodis glanced at Cronin, he continued. "I had a rather weird night at work, for the lack of a better word, and that was before Cronin here turned up and said, 'Will you come with me?' Which I did, by the way. If anyone here would like to explain what the hell *that* was about? How did I know his name without being told? How did I know, I mean *really* know, that I had to go with him? The entire police department had their guns pointed at him. I should have had my gun pointed at him, but oh no, what did I do? I put my arms around him and did this leaping thing—which hurts like a bitch, I have to tell you. It felt like the cells in my body were being ripped

15

apart, then we turn up here, just like that." Alec snapped his fingers. "Then you two show up, and I'm going out on a limb here, but I'm guessing from the shit I've seen tonight, that the three of you don't exactly fit neatly into the human box, and for the life of me, I cannot figure out why that doesn't bother me. Because it should. So that's been my night. Now excuse me if I sound a little fucking crazy." Alec knew he was ranting, but he couldn't seem to stop. "Oh, and Cronin also told me that the worst is yet to come, which is awesome. Can't wait for that, because I can deal with weird—I've been dealing with weird my whole life—but tonight's been… well, it's been a whole new definition of fucking weird, and he tells me it's going to get worse? Because I can't see how that's even possible!"

Cronin flinched, as though Alec's words physically wounded him.

"Okay," Jodis said calmly. She put her hand on Cronin's arm. "Alec has obviously had a stressful night. He's seen things which are… difficult to define rationally."

Alec snorted. "Difficult to define rationally. That's one way to put it. I saw a man turn to dust. There was nothing rational about it." Alec shivered.

"Are you cold?" Jodis asked. She turned to the red-haired man. "Cronin, have you offered dry clothing?"

"He refused," Cronin said quietly.

"What about something to eat or drink?" she asked him.

Cronin looked horrified, quickly turning to face Alec. "Forgive my manners," he whispered. "I'm out of practice in such things. Can I offer you something to eat or drink?"

"Uh, coffee?" Alec asked. "Coffee'd be great."

Cronin took a step back toward what Alec presumed was the direction of the kitchen, but stopped. He seemed torn between wanting to cater to Alec's needs and not wanting to leave.

With a quiet laugh, Eiji said, "I'll go. You stay here. There is much to be said."

Everyone watched him leave through the elevator. "Is the kitchen on a different level or something?" Alec asked. Jodis led him to the sofa, sitting down gracefully beside him. Cronin sat opposite. He was clearly agitated, Alec realized, and he wondered if his little rant had offended him. "If you don't have coffee, a glass of water will be fine," Alec said.

"Oh no. It's not that," Cronin said quickly. "The kitchen is through there," he said, pointing to a door on the far wall. "Though it is empty. I apologize for not having anything you require. I don't eat... here."

Jodis fought a smile, and before Alec could question Cronin's phrasing, she said, "Alec, if you would, please start at the beginning. What happened tonight?"

Alec pulled the blanket over himself and sighed. He recounted the ordeal from the beginning: chasing the guy in a long coat, the unnatural speed and agility, the mouthful of teeth, shadows that moved and followed him, then, of course, the guy who was injured and bleeding who became dust that washed away in the rain.

Alec held up his hands, still slightly stained black. "His blood was too dark for a chest wound," Alec told them. "He said the bullet missed his heart but he could feel it moving. He said, 'It's you. It really is you,' which has happened a lot tonight, just so you know." Alec shook his head. "Then he said, 'He will come for you. Tell them it's started, they're coming. It's not one, it's both,' just like that. Those were his exact words. He said I must tell Cronin that. That it's started, they're coming, and there's not one, but two. Now I have no clue what that means," Alec said, looking at Cronin. "But I assume you do?"

Cronin looked at Jodis with wide eyes, her expression much the same.

"Oh," Alec said as he remembered, "then just before he turned into dust, he looked at me all excited and said he touched the key."

Both Cronin and Jodis now stared at Alec, their intent stares unsettling him.

"He said what about a key?" Cronin whispered. "What were his exact words?"

"He just said that," Alec answered. "I touched the key."

Cronin and Jodis turned to each other again, and although neither of them were actually talking, Alec could have sworn they were having a conversation.

The elevator pinged, and Eiji walked into the room holding a takeout drinks tray with four cups on it plus two brown paper bags of what Alec hoped was food. He obviously sensed something was not right between Jodis and Cronin, but still gave Alec a small smile, though it was strained at best. "I didn't know which coffee you preferred, so I brought you a range. There is also a small selection of foods," he said.

Alec grabbed the closest coffee, not caring what type it was, and took a mouthful. Then he riffled through the brown paper bags and pulled everything out, sprawling contents onto the coffee table. Sandwiches, chips, fruit, deli pasta salad, brownies, and a can of refried beans. Alec picked up the beans, blinking, wondering what on earth had possessed Eiji to add those to the collection.

"Are those to your liking?" Cronin asked.

Alec looked up to find the three of them were watching him. He put the beans back on the table and picked up the sandwich. "Perfect, thank you." He nodded toward the other three coffees. "You guys want one?"

They each shook their heads. "No, thank you," Cronin said quietly.

Jodis gave Alec a smile. He liked her. Sure, she was beautiful—even if women weren't his type, he could appreciate beauty when he saw it. But she smiled at Alec as though she was truly happy he was there.

Eiji seemed happy as well, though more amused than pleased. Alec noticed he watched Cronin a lot, looking for what, Alec had no clue. A sign? A reaction?

Cronin, on the other hand, seemed agitated, scared almost. He glanced at Alec often, sometimes smiling, sometimes not. It was confusing. The whole night had been confusing, yet what was most absurd was how Alec felt about a man he didn't know. It wasn't rational. This Cronin, whoever he was, made Alec's whole body thrum.

Alec put the coffee and half-eaten sandwich on the table and pushed them away.

"You have questions," Cronin said. It was a statement.

Alec laughed. "Ah, just a couple."

Jodis smiled at Alec, Eiji smiled at Cronin, while Cronin looked like he was about to be executed.

"What happens now?" Alec asked. "What happens to me? I feel like I've stumbled into an episode of the *Twilight Zone* or something. How is that quantum leaping thing even possible? Not that I want to try it again, thank you very much. What the hell was the man who turned to dust? Or the one I chased through the backstreets? Not *who*. *What*. How does everyone know who I am? That guy said someone's coming for me. What did he mean? And what the hell is the 'key'?" Alec used quotation marks in the air. He looked at Eiji. "And where do I know you from? I've never seen you before, yet you're familiar... somehow."

Cronin's gaze shot to Eiji's, his dark eyes burning, and he was about to speak, but Alec put his hand up to stop him.

"I haven't finished yet. And you," Alec said, looking at Cronin. "How did I know your name? How did you know mine? Why did I say yes to leaving with you? Why do I get the feeling that I couldn't have said no? What the actual fuck is going on? I've said twice that I don't think you're human, and yet no one's corrected me. In fact, Jodis and Eiji here seem to think it's funny." Alec pointed his thumb to the two others next to him. "Why doesn't that scare me? Because I'm thinking after everything I've seen tonight, I should be rocking it out in the fetal position somewhere, but I feel oddly fucking calm. So, please, tell me, what the hell is going on?"

Eiji and Jodis looked at Cronin, giving him time to speak, but he seemed unable to find the right words.

Jodis spoke instead. "I think we should start at the very beginning." She smiled and her voice was soft and melodic. "You feel safe here?"

Alec shrugged. "Yes."

"And you're not afraid of us, are you?"

"No." Alec couldn't explain it, but no, he wasn't.

Eiji smiled at him. "We cannot harm you, Alec."

Well, that was odd. "Um, thanks?"

Cronin looked straight at Alec with a mix of fear and determination on his face. "What we are has been misconstrued over time. We've had many names in many cultures over many millennia: *vrykolakas, ubyr, strigoi*—" Cronin swallowed hard. "—vampyre."

Vampire.

CHAPTER THREE

Alec looked at the three faces who were now studying him. He had to push the air out to make his voice work. "Vampire?"

Cronin looked him square in the eye. "Yes."

A bubble of laughter escaped Alec. "Right. Sure. Yep, good one. I've seen this movie. Couldn't you think of something a little more original? Because, you know, the whole vampire thing got old. It's been done."

"Cronin speaks the truth," Jodis said softly. "It is no joke."

Alec blinked, then blinked again. Vampires. The rational part of his brain told him this was nonsense; there were no such things except in myths and fiction. But there was a cold, fluid realization of truth, like quicksilver through his veins that told him otherwise. He knew what they were saying was true, and whether he wanted to or not, he believed it.

Alec scrubbed his hands over his face. He was beyond tired, stressed, and it had been one helluva crazy day. He stared out the glass wall, seeing the faintest hint of daylight on the horizon. No one spoke while his mind processed and pulled in a thousand different directions.

Finally, Alec looked at the three of them, then settled on Cronin. "Aren't vampires supposed to have fangs or something?"

Cronin smiled, slowly exposing his teeth. His completely normal fangless teeth. Then, in what Alec thought was a silent snap, two perfectly pointed fangs popped down in the corners of Cronin's mouth.

Alec's whole body reacted. He recoiled, his heart hammered, his brain stopped working, frozen, and the hairs on his body stood on end. But most disturbing was how turned-on he was. Instant heat and desire flared in his belly and his groin. Alec shot to his feet and quickly put some much-needed space between them.

Fucking hell.

He'd never felt anything so intense, so pure.

Alec sucked in some deep breaths as he walked to the other side of the room. It was Jodis who followed him. She kept a few feet between them, but when he faced her, she smiled at him and spoke softly. "It is shocking when you first see it, yes?"

See what? Oh, the teeth. It wasn't the teeth that he found confronting. It was how his body reacted.

"So, what?" Alec said, looking at the three of them in turn. "You can just make them appear when you want? How does that even work?"

"We can. Like flexing a muscle," Jodis answered. "Though sometimes it is an involuntary reaction, such as when we are threatened, when we feed, or when we are sexually aroused."

Cronin stood up. "Enough."

Alec stared at him. "No. It's not enough." He looked back at Jodis. "This is good. Tell me everything now; get it all out in the open. No one's answered any of my questions, so let's have it, huh?"

Cronin lifted his chin. "You have just learned that humans are not the only people to walk this earth. You've leapt with me, you've seen vampiric teeth, you're sitting in a room with three vampires, yet you are not afraid?"

Alec turned to Eiji. "Does he always answer questions with more questions?"

Eiji roared with laughter. "Oh, this is perfect," he said, earning a cutting glare from Cronin.

Alec ignored whatever was going on between them and spoke to Cronin. "I'm not afraid. I told you already I can deal with weird. What I want is answers."

"Fine," Cronin said. His teeth were now back to normal, and Alec wasn't sure if he was thankful or disappointed.

"So you're all vampires?"

"Yes."

"But that guy in the alley bled all over me. Vampires have blood?"

"Yes."

"That means you have a heart and a circulation system," Alec stated. "It also means you can die."

"We heal quickly" was all Jodis said.

Alec shook his head, trying to take everything in. "You can all do that leaping thing?"

"No," Cronin answered. "Different vampires have different skills. I have the ability to leap, as do some others."

"What other different skills?"

"Eiji can read DNA, and Jodis can turn objects into ice."

Alec blinked and stared, open-mouthed, at Jodis. "Of course you can."

Cronin continued. "Other abilities vary from vampire to vampire. Usually it is something one takes with them from their human life."

"You started out human?"

"Yes."

"Who were you?" Alec asked him. "I mean, you said you were Scottish…"

"I was born of the Dál Riata people in Dún Ad, what is now western Scotland."

"When?"

Cronin looked at him for a long moment. He swallowed hard and lifted his chin. "I was born, human, in the year 744 and reborn vampire in 768. I was twenty-four."

Alec blinked a few times. "744? As in the year seven hundred and forty-four?"

Cronin smiled. "Yes."

Alec looked at Jodis then. "And you?"

"I am Nordic. The year of my human birth is unclear, but I would estimate the same or similar to

Cronin." The blonde woman smiled at Cronin. "It was I who changed Cronin."

Alec stared at them. Both Cronin and Jodis were obviously okay with this development, and if there was any animosity between them, it was long forgotten. "You changed him?"

"Yes. It was not intentional," she said, almost wistfully.

"Oh, good," Alec deadpanned. "What's a bit of unintentional homicide between friends?"

Jodis surprised Alec by laughing. Cronin on the other hand, looked at Alec as though he was worried for his mental well-being. Maybe he should be, Alec thought.

Eiji stood up and bowed his head. "I am Eiji. The year of my birth was not documented, but my human life was ended in the year 261. I had lived approximately twenty-seven summers."

"Two hundred..." Alec was dumbfounded. "Are you shitting me?"

Eiji laughed. "No. No shitting involved."

Alec stared at the three of them, then closed his eyes and rubbed his temples. "You know, there's a joke in there somewhere. A Highlander, a Viking, and a Samurai walk into a bar."

"I was no Samurai," Eiji said, still grinning.

Alec looked at him. "Sorry." He sat back down on the sofa, or maybe collapsed was a better word. "Okay. So you're all ancient, and I'm twenty-nine."

"Well, that technically makes you the oldest here," Jodis said with a smile. Alec snorted and let his head fall back onto the back of the sofa. The events of the night were weighing on him. Jodis walked over to the sofas again, but this time she sat down next to Eiji, putting her hand on top of his.

Cronin stood at the end of the room, leaning against the wall. "You are tired. Would you prefer to sleep or ask more questions?"

"Questions," Alec said, trying to shake off his exhaustion. He picked up another coffee. It had gone cold, but he didn't care. He drank it anyway. "I have stupid questions, just for curiosity's sake. Mirrors? Can I see your reflection?"

Cronin smiled. "Yes."

"Does holy water hurt you?"

"No."

"Garlic?"

"No."

"Sleep in a coffin?"

"No."

"Sleep at all?"

"Yes."

"Sunlight make you burst into flames?"

Silence.

"Holy shit!" Alec said. "Really?"

Cronin held eye contact with Alec for a long second. "We cannot tolerate sunlight."

Alec looked at the wall of glass and the almost-risen sun. "Well, I hate to break it to you guys, but the sun's

28

almost up and these windows are great for the view—which is pretty spectacular, I will say—but you're gonna get one helluva tan in a couple of minutes."

Cronin laughed at that, a quiet sound that made Alec's heart beat faster. "Specially made ultraviolet-resistant glass. Completely safe."

"Well, that's good," Alec mumbled. The way Cronin was looking at him made Alec think he was enjoying this. "What about crosses or other religious symbols?"

Cronin shrugged. "Nothing."

Alec was happy with how this was going. He was finally getting answers. "So, my questions earlier..." he started.

Cronin answered. "The two men you saw this evening were both vampires."

"They weren't together," Alec stated. "I was chasing one. The other one, the one that... died... did he intervene to save me?"

Cronin shook his head. "I don't know."

"Yes," Eiji answered. Cronin and Alec both turned to him. "He was protecting you."

Cronin's jaw bulged. "And you know this, how?"

Eiji looked right at Cronin. "Because I told him to."

"You *what*?" Cronin asked, his voice was quiet.

Fatigue started to drag Alec under, and the coffee and shaking his head weren't fighting his exhaustion anymore. "Is there a bathroom here?"

The discussion—and tension—halted. "Sorry. Of course," Cronin said. He pointed toward a hall off the main room. "Down the hall, first door on your right."

Alec walked in the direction Cronin had pointed and found the bathroom. It was grand: dark marble floors and white tiled walls from the floor to the ceiling. Everything in this whole apartment, what he'd seen of it, spoke of opulence and an unfathomable amount of wealth.

Alec relieved himself and wondered whether vampires needed to piss, thinking he'd add it to the list of new questions he was formulating. The detective in him had to look through the cabinets. There was nothing except expensive hand soap, which had never been used. Even the towels looked brand new, and he wondered whether Cronin *lived* in this place at all. There was nothing personal to suggest he did. No products, no signs of life.

Alec washed his hands, the cold water making him feel better, then washed his face as well. It made him feel half-human, he thought, then snorted at himself, given the non-humans just a few yards away.

He stared at himself in the mirror, taking stock of all that he'd learned in the last twelve hours. He still looked the same; his shaggy brown hair was a mess, probably from running his hands through it a hundred times, and his hazel eyes were surprisingly clear despite the turmoil he expected to see. He didn't know why he presumed to see a change in himself. He had just learned the world was not as it seemed, that creatures not-human walked amongst them. Life as he knew it was fundamentally over, changed so completely, yet he still looked the same.

They'd answered a lot of questions, yet one remained: *Why him?*

What did any of this have to do with Alec MacAidan?

Despite how tired he was, Alec figured he'd find out how and why he was involved, and walked to the door. He cracked it open and stopped when he heard voices. They were talking about him.

"You knew!" Cronin whisper-shouted. "How could you not have told me?"

Eiji answered. "Because you wouldn't have let him live."

What?

"What?" Cronin hissed. "Of course I would have!"

"No, I mean *live*. A full human life. You would've risked everything following him, protecting him."

"Of course I would have!"

"He needs a human life! You can't spend a millennia with regrets, Cronin."

Huh?

"He needed protection!"

"I looked out for him."

"For almost thirty years without telling me! You are supposed to be my brother!"

"I am," Eiji cried. "Jodis first, then you. And now him. I would lay my existence down for him. You know that!"

Cronin growled. "He chased down a Seeker, Eiji. A Seeker! He could have been killed. One of us *was* killed protecting him. He should have had training by now."

Training for what? And what the hell is a Seeker?

"Was this the first time his life was in danger?" Cronin asked.

There was a moment of silence; then Eiji answered, "No."

An anguished growl ripped through the air. Alec should have run away, he should have been scared as hell. But he wasn't. It was Cronin, and the sound pierced Alec like nothing he'd ever felt. The growl snapped into a snarl, and Alec was in motion. Without meaning to, without any conscious decision to do so, Alec now stood in front of Cronin with his gun drawn at Eiji's head. "Back the fuck away from him."

Alec's own words stunned him. He couldn't recall the thought, the inclination that would make him say that. Or what on earth possessed him to stand between two vampires and threaten one of them? He only knew he had to protect Cronin. At all costs, he had to protect what was his...

Alec lowered the gun in his right hand and raised his left, palm forward, to Eiji in a sign of surrender and apology. He shook his head, still unable to process what he'd just done. He turned to stare at Cronin, who seemed as shocked as he was. "What the fuck was that?" Alec asked him. "Why would I do that?"

Cronin didn't answer, but a smile played at his lips. And when Alec turned to look at Eiji and Jodis to apologize, he saw that they were smiling too.

"Okay, someone needs to start explaining what the fuck is going on," Alec said. "I get the whole weird shit thing, even the vampire thing" — Alec shook his head — "or whatever. But *that*? Threatening Eiji isn't me." Alec looked at the Japanese man. "I wouldn't... I didn't mean... I just did it without meaning to." Then Alec realized something. He turned to Cronin. "Like when you showed up at the police station and I just *had* to go with you. That's what that was like. Why would I do that? Tell me, what is it about you? Why do I react to you?"

Cronin wasn't smiling anymore. In fact, he looked troubled.

Eiji stepped forward and put his hand on Alec's arm. "I'm not offended, friend. In fact, I am pleased by your reaction. It is normal, expected, and very welcome."

Huh? Alec slowly put his gun on the table and shook his head. He was so confused, and he wondered what it would actually take for him to crack. He felt like he was losing his mind...

"You need to tell him," Jodis said. She was looking at Cronin, so Alec presumed what she said was directed at him.

"He's had enough for one night," Cronin said, his voice was just a whisper.

Alec looked at Cronin. "Don't tell me when I've had enough," he snapped. Then he turned back to Jodis, seeing that she was fighting a smile. "Tell me what?"

"Cronin?" she pressed.

Alec was pretty sure Cronin had no intention of telling him anything, which, given how tired and mentally taut he was, just pissed Alec off. He let out a growl of his own and pointed his finger at the red-haired vampire. "You. Start talking. I have been ripped out of my life and thrown into this, told about fucking vampires—which I've handled pretty fucking well if you ask me—but I swear to Christ if you don't start talking right the fuck now, I will walk out that door."

Eiji and Jodis were both obviously amused. Cronin's nostrils flared. He glared at his friends. "I fail to see the humor."

"I like him," Eiji said. Cronin's jaw bulged.

"Fine." Cronin looked squarely at Alec. "The reason you knew who I was, the reason you feel so calm around me, is the same reason I knew who you were upon first sight alone. That feeling of calm and peace that you are unable to describe is new for me also. The reason you react to me and I to you is…"

"Is what?" Alec asked.

"There is not the word in my native tongue to describe it exactly." Cronin looked out through the heavily tinted windows, and when he finally made eye contact with Alec again, he was searching and vulnerable. "*Ionndrainn cridhe*. Or *dàn*."

Alec shook his head. He had no clue what that meant or what language it was. It sounded… *Gaelic*? He was still stuck on Cronin admitting he reacted to him…

Jodis smiled, her face was so serene. "Fate, Alec," she said. "You and Cronin are fate."

"Fate?" Alec repeated.

"Yes. Meant to be together," Jodis explained. "Like Eiji and myself. Two halves of the one whole. It is not conscious decision, Alec. Cronin called it *ionndrainn cridhe*, and that's a very close description. Longing of the heart, but it's not really a matter of the heart either. It is a predesign of the soul."

Alec blinked. Then he blinked again. "Huh?"

"You are meant for each other," Eiji added.

"So you're telling me," Alec said slowly, "that I have no choice? I am, for all intents and purposes, stuck in some arranged fucking… *marriage*?"

Cronin recoiled from Alec's words as though he'd slapped him. Alec smiled with satisfaction, yet his gut twisted and his chest ached when he saw the hurt on Cronin's face.

Alec swallowed hard. "You know what?" he said. "I'm done. I'm outta here." He didn't really know how to leave—he'd arrived by leaping, the unorthodox way of travelling—but he headed toward the elevator he'd seen Eiji use. He pressed any buttons he could find, hoping one of them would shut the doors.

Jodis followed after him. "Alec. You can't fight it."

The last thing he heard before the doors closed was Cronin's haunted voice.

"Let him go."

CHAPTER FOUR

Cronin watched the elevator doors close, watched Alec leave, and he felt like he was going to be sick. If such a thing were possible.

"He can't leave," Jodis cried.

"Well, he clearly doesn't want to stay," Cronin said, his voice barely a whisper.

"He won't get far," Eiji added. "He's just had a lot to take in, Cronin. He'll be back."

Cronin barked out a laugh. "He can chase down a Seeker, watch a vampire turn to dust in his hands, sit in a room with three vampires each over a thousand years old, and he doesn't flinch. Yet you mention what I am to him..."

Jodis put her hand on Cronin's arm; her eyes were kind and imploring. "Give him time," she said.

"Time?" Cronin laughed, though it was a bitter sound. Then he shook his head and swallowed down the nauseous biting ache in his chest. "Not a concept he can appreciate, I'm sure."

"You're feeling his absence," Jodis said softly.

Cronin pushed the heel of his hand against his sternum. "Ridiculous, is it not? That I can walk this earth for almost thirteen hundred years and not feel a thing. And now..." He shook his head again, and looked out across the city. The sun had risen completely. "I can't even go after him."

"He's on his way back," Eiji said, nodding toward the elevator. "He's strong, Cronin, and stubborn. He's very smart, and he has the ability to take in and see everything in a room. That's why he was a good cop. That's why he'll make an even better vampire."

Cronin hissed at Eiji, just as the elevator dinged to signal its arrival. "You know him better than I. I've still not forgiven you for keeping him from me."

Eiji laughed. "You'll be thanking me. Fate couldn't have picked a better match for you, my friend."

The elevator door opened and Alec walked slowly back into the room. He very deliberately didn't look at the three vampires who were watching him. "So I can't even leave, huh?"

"How far did you get?" Eiji asked with a toothy grin.

Alec glared at him. "Shut up."

Eiji snorted. "I tried to leave when I first found my Jodis."

"I frightened him," Jodis said with a smile.

"I got no farther than a furlong," Eiji said. "My feet refused another step, as did my heart."

Alec ran both hands through his hair, but then he swayed. He could barely keep his eyes open, and it looked like his mind would not process another thought. Cronin was quick to steady him, holding his arm. "Are you well?"

"Just tired, 's'all," Alec mumbled.

"You must sleep," Cronin said.

It seemed Alec was tempted to argue with the order, but perhaps the concern in Cronin's eyes stopped him. He nodded instead.

Cronin led him down the hall and opened a door, second from the end on the left. Alec didn't seem to care for the grand furnishings, he simply crawled onto the bed fully dressed, boots and all, closed his eyes, and slept.

* * * *

The sun was at its highest point in the sky, the filtered glass protecting Cronin as he stared across the skyline. He hadn't spoken in a while, though long stretches of silence between vampires were not uncommon. "He's human," he said, knowing Eiji and Jodis would hear him.

Jodis's voice was quiet. "He is."

Cronin never took his eyes off the city. "He was never supposed to be human."

"Do we not all start out that way?" she asked rhetorically.

"You cannot hurt him, if that is your concern," Eiji told him. "Your entire being will not allow it."

"Not on purpose," Cronin said, turning to face him. "Though the beating heart we can hear from three rooms away reminds me of his mortality."

"He won't stay human," Jodis said. "He will want endless days with you, Cronin. I know you don't think that right now, but he will."

"He called it an arranged marriage," Cronin said softly, sadly, "as though the idea disgusts him."

When Jodis spoke, Cronin didn't have to see her smile. It was in her voice. "That will change. Give him time to adjust. You've already seen how he cannot leave."

"Which he resents me for," Cronin added.

"He defended you, against another vampire," Jodis said. "Granted, Eiji was never a real threat, but he stood between you and pointed a gun at him." Jodis was amused by this. "A human threatening a vampire? Have you ever seen such a thing?"

"I should be concerned for his mental welfare."

Eiji put his arm around his oldest friend. "Cronin, he was born for this life. He was born to be yours. He won't fight it for much longer. He won't be able to. So enjoy it. You've waited a long time for this." Then Eiji chuckled. "Though I do believe he'll make you earn it. It shall be fun to witness the mighty Cronin being challenged at every turn by a human."

Cronin scowled playfully at him. Eiji had a wicked sense of humor, and Cronin soon smiled. "He's very handsome, yes?" The truth was, Cronin had never seen such a perfect man. Alec was tall and fit, his hair was a rich brown and his eyes... his eyes were the color of the moss Cronin had played in as a boy. It was a memory he'd long forgotten.

Jodis laughed, and Eiji clapped Cronin on the back. "Ah, so you noticed? And was it not obvious that he found you appealing? When you showed him your teeth, the pheromones coming off him were suffocating."

Cronin gave an embarrassed smile. "So you felt that as well?"

Jodis scoffed. "It was difficult not to."

"I know this is all exciting for you and a lot to take in. But we need to talk." Eiji looked at Cronin. "Not about Alec, but about what he saw and what was said to him."

"I know." Cronin said, now serious. "Who died protecting him?"

"I can't be sure," Eiji answered. "Not until I meet with the others to find out who it was. It was either Mikka or Jacques. Alec never mentioned an accent, so I would guess it was Mikka."

Cronin nodded sadly. "He saved Alec's life."

"Yes." Eiji bowed his head. "It was an honorable death."

Cronin looked at him. "Mikka said he touched the key. Before he died, that's what he told Alec."

"And that it had already started," Jodis added. "He said it was not one, but both. Do you think it's possible?"

Cronin sighed and nodded. "I have no reason to doubt Mikka. He was nothing but loyal."

Eiji nodded also. "It means the rumors are true. We've heard the rumblings and seen the signs. There is a war coming, my friend. Maybe the biggest yet. Mikka said it was both. The Illyrians *and* the Egyptians, Cronin. We cannot fight them both."

The three vampires stared at each other in a long, solemn silence.

Finally Cronin spoke. "We need to find the key."

* * * *

It was agreed that Cronin should feed. He was reluctant to leave Alec, even as he slept, but he also couldn't risk becoming thirsty in his presence. Cronin had spent a millennia around humans, and his self-control was one of his strengths. But Alec was different... he invoked a different kind of thirst in Cronin, a hunger. So being well-fed was paramount.

He stood at the closed door, listening to the steady heartbeat on the other side.

"Go," Jodis urged him. "We will keep him safe."

Cronin gave a resigned sigh and nodded. "Want me to bring you back something?" he asked with a smile. "I'm thinking French."

Jodis chuckled. "No, thanks. We'll head out after nightfall. I don't think Alec would appreciate our version of takeout."

Jodis and Eiji were limited to feeding at night—being unable to travel in the day—and Cronin had returned on many occasions bringing "food" back with him. He had the power of leaping, so it literally only took minutes for him to disappear to any country in the world where it was night and return with a somewhat bewildered human for Jodis and Eiji to feed upon. He could then leap to a different country, taking the drained human with him to dispose of.

No witnesses, no evidence.

"No, I guess he wouldn't," Cronin agreed. He refused to think of how Alec would perceive his dietary habits. Alec was a cop, no less, and no doubt believed murder was the grandest deal breaker...

"Go feed, Cronin," Jodis said. "Bon appétit."

Cronin gave her a half smirk, then disappeared.

He found it difficult to concentrate. The distance and time away from Alec felt like lead in his gut, but he leapt to an abandoned alley in Paris. The night was darkened with a color that did nothing to impede his sight and chilled with an air he acclimatized to quickly. Sometimes he would walk the streets, feeling the life in the city around him, or catch up with other vampires and discuss issues in their world.

But tonight he wasted no time. Cronin waited for just a moment, listening with his impeccable vampire hearing for the familiar conversation he sought.

He waited for the right words to slink through the air. Those words...

He didn't have to wait long. He never did.

He listened as the would-be attacker struck up a conversation with a woman as she walked down the dark street alone. She ignored him at first, hurrying along, quickly deducing that the man wanted neither the time, nor a cigarette...

The woman begged for him to leave her alone, and when he grabbed her arm, dragged her into the alley, and pushed her to the ground, she begged for her life. Cronin didn't really care about the life or death of humans, per se... but not like that. It was not supposed to be like that...

Half a second later, all the woman would have heard was a whispered "Run" and the weight of the would-be rapist was gone.

Cronin carried the putrid man to the rooftop of a secluded and derelict building. A fitting end, he thought. The man hadn't screamed, even as his confusion gave way to fear. Cronin could see the realization in the man's eyes, the usual look of shock and horror.

Cronin didn't bother with conversation. He rarely did. They always asked, "Why?" and "What are you going to do to me?", then lastly, "What the fuck *are* you?", though Cronin never replied. How big and brave these men always were when pitted against a weaker species. But when they *were* the weaker species? Oh, how the tables quickly turned.

None of it mattered. All Cronin could think about was getting back to Alec. So with a flex of his teeth, he pulled the man's head back and bit into his neck.

* * * *

Cronin appeared in his living room, scaring the shit out of Alec. He was putting a glass of water on the coffee table and suddenly having someone appear beside him made him jump, sending the water flying.

Jodis put her hand out, turning the glass of water and the spilled contents into ice before a single drop hit the floor.

Alec put his hands out in an everybody-stop motion. "Jesus! You" — he looked at Cronin — "just scared the bajeezus outta me." Then he glanced at the spray of ice and then at Jodis. "And how freakin' cool is that?!"

"Sorry," Cronin said with a smile. He was just happy to see Alec. The fact he wasn't glaring at him was an added bonus. "I'm not used to having company unfamiliar with me... just appearing."

Alec stared at Cronin for a long few seconds as if he'd missed him, and Cronin couldn't look away. Alec's heart rate spiked, which Cronin put down to being startled at his sudden appearance. Alec shook his head, as if to clear it. "It's fine," he said.

"I trust you slept well?" Cronin asked, sitting across from him.

"Yes," Alec said, then almost as an afterthought he added, "Thank you." He scraped up a shard of ice from the table and put it in the glass. "Jodis, that was seriously cool. I mean, I know Cronin said before you can turn things into ice, but to see it! Can you do it again?"

She laughed. "Of course."

"Can you just turn liquids into ice?" Alec asked. "I mean, what're the parameters? Are there limitations, or does it just need a molecular structure?"

Jodis glanced at Cronin and gave an approving smile. "Yes, anything with a molecular structure. There are limitations to quantities, nothing over a few cubic feet of water. And nothing more than a few feet away."

"Humans?" Alec asked. There was no malice in his tone, just curiosity. "I mean, we're made up of mostly water, so I guess you could. What about other vampires?"

Jodis was still smiling at Alec, her eyes a vivid blue. "Yes. I can freeze both humans and vampires."

"That's pretty cool," Alec said. "In a... weird fascinating morbid kinda way. Is that why your eyes are so blue?" Alec asked. "Sorry, that's so personal. I just have a lot of questions. And your eyes are blue, like *really* blue, and Cronin's are black." He looked at both of them in turn. "And Eiji can read DNA? How does that even work? I thought it was a way to determine heredity, like mitochondrial and nuclear DNA tells us of who we're related to, yes? But he can see lifespans, like the future?"

Jodis answered first. "Yes. Human DNA can be read both ways, past and future. It doesn't tell of events or which path one would choose, just the determined length and similarities to relatives."

"It's not an easy talent to explain," Cronin added. "But as Jodis said, DNA can be read in both directions. Humans have only discovered the past aspect so far."

"Wow" was all Alec could say.

"It is fascinating," Cronin agreed. "Though Eiji never understood his gift until the discovery of DNA pathways by human scientists. When he saw what they were doing and describing, he had a name for what he can see."

"DNA?"

Jodis nodded. "Up until then, he just assumed he could see some version of a lifespan."

Alec sighed. "I guess that makes sense." He pressed his hand against his chest and shook his head, then looked at Cronin. "I feel better now you're here," he said softly.

"As do I." Cronin's chest flooded with warmth at Alec's words, and he smiled. Cronin was so out of practice with human needs, in particular sleeping habits. Alec had been asleep for a few hours, and Cronin wondered if that was enough. "Have you been awake long?"

Alec shook his head. "About five minutes before you got here."

Cronin looked at the clock. He'd only been gone for a total of twenty minutes, at most.

Alec swallowed hard. "I think that's what woke me. I wasn't feeling well. I was just going to sip some water when you frightened the shit out of me and made me spill it."

"I'm sorry for leaving," Cronin said.

"Did you…" Alec cringed. "You know…?"

"I told him the reason for your absence," Jodis added without apology. "There's no point in hiding what we are. It is a fact of our existence. And something Alec must come to terms with."

Cronin studied Alec's face, looking for some sign of disgust. There wasn't any. "Yes. I left to feed," he told Alec. "Given you're human, I thought it was best to keep as well-fed as possible."

Alec's brow furrowed and after a long beat of silence, he nodded. "I get it. I do. I just don't... like it. And for what it's worth," he said, now looking at Cronin, "I feel safe around you. I don't know why. Everything in my head should be telling me to run... but it's not. It's telling me to stay."

Cronin smiled at that, and Alec put his hand up. "I don't pretend to understand what the whole *fated* thing means. But I do know that something in me is different." Alec pointed his finger at Cronin. "And just so we're clear, with the fated thing, whatever the hell it is, it doesn't mean you own me.

"And," Alec continued, his voice lower, "I probably should apologize. I said some less-than nice things to you earlier. I tend to get grumpy without sleep."

Cronin let out a laugh. Alec was nothing if not confounding. "You have no need to apologize for anything. Your reaction was warranted, and I'll admit, more accepting than I could have dared hoped." He smiled at Alec. "You need sleep. Duly noted."

The two men stared at each other, each unable to look away. Cronin's chest tightened and his whole body heated. He could taste desire on his tongue and feel it pulse in his groin. Alec's breaths grew shallow, his pupils dilated, his heart rate spiked, and Cronin opened his mouth, feeling his teeth ready to flex.

"Right, then," Jodis said as she stood, startling both men and breaking the tension between them. "You two need to take it down a notch. You rival Freyr." She smiled as she walked gracefully to the kitchen.

One corner of Cronin's lips curved upwards, while Alec struggled to catch his breath. "I, uh, I might grab a shower, if that's okay?" he asked. He stood and wiped his hands on his jeans nervously, seeming to look everywhere except at Cronin.

"Of course," Cronin answered, standing as well. "Please treat my house as your own. You don't need to ask permission to do anything here." Then, because he found it amusing, he said, "You're free to do as you wish. I don't own you, remember?"

Alec shot him a glare, which only made Cronin smile as he walked down the hall. "So," Alec said, following him. "Is that you trying to be funny?"

Cronin opened the door to the bedroom Alec had slept in, but stood in the doorway so Alec would need to brush past him. He ignored his question. "You will find towels and soaps in your en suite bathroom."

Alec stopped near the door so there was barely a foot between them. He was taller than Cronin by at least three inches, and probably a little broader too. Cronin liked the fact that Alec was bigger than him. It was more challenging…

Instead of looking into the room, Alec glanced at the closed door opposite them, then back at Cronin. "Is that your room?"

Cronin's smile faltered. "Yes..." He looked at his bedroom door, hesitated for a moment, then stepped across the hall. He pushed the handle, letting the door swing open, but didn't walk inside.

Alec stepped up to him, closer than was strictly necessary, before brushing past him. The room was dark, too dark for a human, and Alec only made it a step. "Have you got lights?"

Cronin flipped the switch. The room was furnished similarly to the other bedroom: large bed, luxurious black and gray bedcovers, matching drapes. Alec seemed to inspect the drapes, but they were of no use. The large window had been blacked out.

Not a sliver of light, a perfect seal.

Alec touched the covered glass. "Not a morning person, I take it?"

Cronin, who was nervous at Alec being in his private quarters, relaxed. "Is that you trying to be funny?"

Alec chuckled, seemingly pleased at having his own words repeated back to him. He looked again at the window. "I bet the window people who covered that thought you were mad," Alec said. "Obscuring one of the most sought-after views in New York City."

Cronin shrugged. "They believed, as do my cleaning and laundry staff, and the concierge and doormen, that I'm a financial broker. I travel a lot, and keep unusual hours, trading mostly in the London and Brunei time zones." He smirked at the look of surprise on Alec's face. "Not that it matters. I pay them enough to not ask questions."

Alec nodded. "Makes sense." Then he walked over to the far wall. It was a huge master bedroom, bigger than most Cronin had ever lived in. The far wall was bare except for one shelf at chest height. It was only five foot long, small in comparison to the vast blank wall, but it commanded presence. Because on the shelf, on little stands so they stood in perfect view, was an ax and a helmet.

Alec inspected the iron ax. Banged-up and crude, the blade curved, with a reverse spike on the head of it. The oak handle looked almost petrified now, and Alec raised his hand to gently touch one finger to it. Next to the ax, the helmet was made of a similar quality of iron. Merely an oval in shape, bent and held with an iron band to mold around a skull, it was dented, with a strip of iron that protruded downward to protect the nose, which was almost comical, Cronin granted. Protecting the nose did little good when the ax had gone through his chest.

They were fascinating, rudimentary, and Cronin could see Alec was in awe of them.

Cronin watched all of this in silence, as a wide-eyed Alec turned to face him. He was sure the human had a hundred questions—the man had questions at every turn—but yet he said nothing. He just blinked and shook his head, took a deep breath, and let it out slowly.

Cronin didn't have to tell Alec that these weapons were his, that they took pride of place in his private bed chambers because he'd used them in war when he was human. Somehow, it seemed, Alec already knew.

Cronin assumed it had been one thing to be told of his age, but to see such relics, such human artifacts — well over a thousand years old — made it very, very real. Alec swallowed hard and licked his lips. "Um… shower," he mumbled, walking distractedly out of the room.

After a few minutes, when Cronin heard the water start in the shower, he laid a change of clothes on Alec's bed. He wasn't sure if they'd fit exactly, and made a mental note that getting some personal effects for Alec would be in order.

He walked back out to find Jodis in the kitchen. She beamed at him. "My dear friend, I cannot tell you how happy it makes me to see you with him finally."

Cronin took a sharp breath and let it out with a laugh. "Today is a better day. He seems able to stand me, at least."

"Stand you? Is he not smitten already?" Jodis laughed musically, and Cronin ducked his head. "Eiji and I will leave you in peace tonight."

Cronin pretended he wasn't embarrassed by what she implied. "Where is Eiji?"

"Downstairs in the lobby. He wanted to make contact with a few of our friends to see if anyone knows anything of Mikka's death or that of the Seeker. He thought it best if Alec were not privy to his conversation." Jodis sighed. "He also has one of your credit cards."

"Do I want to know what for?"

Just then the elevator pinged and the doors opened. Eiji's usual chuckle came from behind the several boxes and grocery bags he carried. "I bought your human some human things," he said, walking in with his burden. "Of all the things we've witnessed throughout time—inventions, developments, advances—I do believe the credit card, Internet, and home delivery may be my favorite. I didn't even have to leave the lobby."

He slid the boxes and bags onto the kitchen counter. "Though I found out little information. Only that yes, it was Mikka who met his fate. There was rumor of more than one Seeker in the city, though no proof. Only rumors."

"Any word on the key?" Cronin asked.

Eiji shook his head. "No. Though if there is more than one Seeker, I would believe that whatever this key is, it is here in New York City."

Cronin frowned. "We need to call a council meeting."

Jodis and Eiji both nodded and answered in unison. "Agreed."

Alec walked into the kitchen. Freshly showered and wearing Cronin's clothes, and he did a double take. Alec's scent, washed and warm, filled Cronin's senses, making him feel lightheaded, if such a thing were possible.

Oblivious to his effect on Cronin, Alec stood beside him. "Oh, I forgot to show you this," he said, holding out his hand. On his palm was the small wooden bullet. "I had it in my pocket and forgot all about it. It was in the ashes of that vampire. I think it was what killed him…"

Alec's words trailed off when it was obvious the three vampires had gone stock-still. They looked at his hand, wide-eyed.

Eiji's voice was eerily quiet. "It's hawthorn."

Cronin nodded. He knew what that meant.

"The Illyrians are here."

CHAPTER FIVE

The three vampires were more than alarmed, talking so fast and quietly that Alec couldn't understand them, so he left them to it.

He stood in the kitchen and ate the food that Eiji had bought for him. It was takeout from a French restaurant, which Eiji found funny, saying something about it being a night for French. Alec didn't ask for details. With the way Cronin scowled at the Japanese vampire, Alec thought it best not to know.

Eiji had even bought him a coffeemaker, which Alec was most grateful for. And seeing how happy it made him, Cronin had thanked Eiji. Though from the assortment of different groceries he'd ordered, it was very clear that the man hadn't eaten human food in a long time. It was a nice gesture all the same, but Alec really just wanted to go home.

Cronin's apartment was clearly the most lavish place he'd ever been in, but it wasn't his. Nothing here was familiar, nothing was comforting. It felt like a grand hotel to Alec: beautiful, opulent, but sterile.

When evening settled over the city and the sun was finally set, Eiji and Jodis said their goodbyes with promises to be back the next night. Jodis had put her hand on Cronin's arm and whispered something Alec couldn't hear, though by the way her eyes flickered to him, he was certain she was talking about him.

Cronin ducked his head, and Jodis and Eiji disappeared into the elevator.

And Cronin and Alec were alone.

Cronin seemed nervous, and Alec wanted to go to him. He wanted to touch him, he wanted to wrap his arms around him. But he knew he shouldn't. It was too soon, it was all too much, and Alec admitted to being a lot of things, but a pushover wasn't one of them. So his mind warred with his heart and won. He shoved his hands in his pockets and anchored his feet to the floor.

"I'd like to go home," Alec said.

Cronin's eyes shot to his. "You can't."

"Why not?"

"Alec, your police friends are looking for you. And not only that, but the city is not safe right now."

"You don't have a problem with Eiji and Jodis going."

"They can look after themselves."

"I can look after myself," Alec barked, offended. "I chased down a vampire, remember?"

"I know," Cronin replied, the fact obviously still a little raw. "You could have been killed."

"But I wasn't."

"You can't even walk out onto the street, Alec. The police are looking for you, and they are no doubt monitoring your place."

"And whose fault is that?"

Cronin sighed. "I don't wish to argue with you."

"And I don't want to argue with you," Alec conceded. And he didn't. It was the last thing he wanted to do. "Look, I just want to go home. I wanna grab some clothes and some toiletries and then I can come back here. I miss my things." Then Alec remembered something. "Oh, man. What about Sammy?"

Cronin's reaction was immediate and serious. "Who is Sammy?"

Cronin was jealous, and Alec liked that more than he should. Alec smiled. "Someone I live with."

Cronin's nostrils flared. "I can leap there and get whatever you need."

Yeah, right. More like go there and scare Sammy to death. "You're not going through my stuff without me."

"And you can't go there alone." Cronin was quiet for a moment. "I could leap us there, though leaping was unpleasant for you."

"Unpleasant?" Alec asked. "Is that the medieval term for hurts like a bitch?"

Cronin tried not to smile and failed. "Medieval?"

"Is that not correct?" Alec asked. "Is ancient more appropriate?"

Cronin laughed and gave a nod. "Possibly." Then he compromised, something he didn't do often. "How about we wait until a later hour, and we'll both go. I'll leap us, you get what you need, and I'll leap us back. It'll take a few minutes at most."

Alec weighed his options. He wasn't too keen on experiencing leaping again anytime soon, but he wanted to go home even more. He nodded. "Deal." Cronin was seemingly pleased with this plan, so Alec figured it was a good time. "Can I ask you something?"

"Of course."

"Who are the Illyrians?" Alec licked his lips. "Well, I know from history class in high school who they are. Am I right to presume we're talking of the same people?"

Cronin gave him a small sigh and nodded. "I suppose I should explain from the beginning, and the Illyrians are a good place to start." He waved his hand at the sofa. "Though you might want to sit down. It's a long story."

Alec sat on the sofa and folded one leg under himself. He waited for Cronin to sit on the opposite sofa. "The Illyrians inhabited what is now Bosnia and Croatia. Is that correct?"

Cronin nodded. "You remember well."

"I have a photographic memory," Alec told him. "If I see something, read something, even once, I retain it." He shrugged. "It's why I made detective five years ahead of my academy peers."

Cronin smiled at him, but continued with his story. "The Illyrians to which you refer also inhabited Albania and Serbia, and into parts of Hungary. South of the Celts, North of the Greeks. They were large in numbers."

"Did you fight them?"

"This will go a lot faster if you leave your questions until the end," Cronin said with a smirk. "I have no doubt your inquisitive mind will have a few. Or a lot."

"Questions are highly likely, yes," Alec replied. He liked Cronin's formal phrasing and found himself replying in similar wording. He particularly liked how it made Cronin smile. He ignored the no-question rule. "Why did you say 'the Illyrians to which *I* refer'? Were there others?"

Taking a deep breath, Cronin continued. "Yes. These were the Illyrians that came before them. Ancient Illyrians, to be exact. Their precise age of origin is not known, but somewhere around 5000BC."

Alec blinked slowly. "Ohhh-kaaaay," he said. "And these are the Illyrians to which *you* refer?"

"You keep asking questions."

"Sorry."

"I don't believe you are."

"Because I'm not."

Cronin sighed again. Alec smiled.

"Yes, these are the Illyrians to which I refer," Cronin said. "Now please refrain from interrupting with questions."

Alec resigned himself to listening, even though he felt like a reprimanded child.

"The Illyrian coven were powerful and many in number. But as the vampire histories are told, their hunger for power and greed was their downfall. The more land and wealth they accrued, the more of a threat they were and, as it quite often happens, more of a target.

"They lived in the mountainous caves, mostly in what is now Bosnia and Croatia. There were no grand castles or palaces in those times, but the caves afforded protection from the sun during the day.

"They took what they wanted, doing little to hide their vampire nature, believing themselves to be unstoppable." Cronin sneered ruefully. "If lore is to be believed, it was dissension within their own ranks that led to their downfall. Conflict among themselves—over who ruled, who owned what, and who was more powerful—eventually split the coven into factions, and they fought each other. The Egyptians only had to intervene in the end."

Alec pursed his lips together. He *really* wanted to ask questions.

Cronin smiled. "Yes, Alec. The Egyptians."

"Like Cleopatra?"

"Not her specifically. But yes."

Alec couldn't help himself. "How did this escape documentation? The Egyptians have been documented, studied over thousands of years, how did this not get out? How is this not known to the general population?"

"The one good thing the Illyrians did was set a precedent for what not to do. Every coven, no matter how large, has a governing body, or a president, if you will. Enforcing laws and accountability for felonies of vampire law was a logical progression."

Alec's head was starting to spin again. His voice squeaked. "Covens?"

"Yes. Vampire colonies."

"Are you in a coven?"

"Yes."

"With Jodis and Eiji?"

"Yes."

"How many others?"

"Four hundred and fifty-two."

"Jesus."

"No, he's not one of them." Cronin laughed and Alec balked. "I'm only joking."

Alec narrowed his eyes at him. "Is that vampire humor?"

Cronin still chuckled as he shrugged. "Shall I continue with our brief history rundown?"

"Please do," Alec said. "And warn me next time you're gonna try and make a joke, okay?"

Cronin ignored him. "To answer one of your many questions, vampire histories are not strictly documented in your history books but there is evidence if you know what to look for. Anything that was written or transcribed in any way in relation to vampires was made obsolete during the late medieval era. Common laws and religious books were rewritten across Europe, including England and Rome, around the twelfth century to rid any references to vampiric nature."

Alec nodded in understanding. "To stop mass hysteria."

"Yes. So the people would not live in fear. But to also give us anonymity."

Needing a little head-clearing space, Alec got himself a glass of water from the kitchen. When he came back to the living room, instead of sitting on the sofa opposite Cronin, he sat beside him. He tucked one leg up under himself again and turned a little so he basically faced Cronin as the vampire recounted histories of Europe, the Middle East, and North Africa and how, for a couple hundred years vampires were almost forgotten. "Then in 1347, hell was... unleashed."

"What happened?" Alec asked softly.

"What you would refer to as the Black Plague."

Alec stared at Cronin, unblinking. "The Black Plague..." His mind reeled as realization sank in. "It wasn't a plague at all, was it?"

Cronin shook his head slowly. "No."

"Holy shit," Alec whispered. "Over a hundred million people died."

"It was closer to two hundred million," Cronin said, his voice low. "A seven-year rampage of one coven, Alec. Seven vampires started it, changing humans as they went, making themselves an army that almost wiped out Europe. They called themselves Yersinians, dressed all in black. Hence where the term 'black death' was coined."

"Jesus Christ."

Cronin looked as though was going to joke again that no, Jesus wasn't there, but he didn't. Alec wondered if the look on his face made Cronin stop.

"How did it end?"

"We stopped them."

"You were there?"

"Yes."

"Fucking hell."

"Yes. Hell, indeed."

Alec couldn't believe what he was hearing. His mind was running around in circles. "You were there?" he asked again.

"Yes. Many of us died." Cronin looked out over the city skyline, and Alec could tell by the way Cronin flinched and his eyes hardened that he was reliving some horrors.

After a few long minutes of silence, allowing them both to get their thoughts in order, Alec asked, "So there are good vampires and bad vampires?"

Cronin looked into Alec's eyes, and he gave him a small smile. "Yes."

"How do you tell the difference?"

Cronin's dark eyes glittered. "The one that's vying for world domination is the bad guy."

"But there's no distinct markings," Alec asked. "Like in the movies where the bad vampires have red eyes?"

"Uh, no." Cronin tilted his head. "Red eyes?"

"Have you not seen... You know what? Never mind."

"I don't credit popular culture," Cronin said. "Though I did read Bram Stoker's *Dracula* once."

"And what?" Alec deadpanned, letting his head fall back onto the backrest of the sofa. "Friend's autobiographies a little too self-serving for you?"

Cronin roared with laughter, surprising Alec. "You're very funny," Cronin said, his grin huge and his eyes shining.

After such a deep and depressing conversation, Alec was grateful for the break, and hearing Cronin laugh like that stirred something in his chest. He found himself smiling at him. "You've seen a lot of things, haven't you?" It was hard to get his head around just exactly what Cronin had lived through. Not just technological changes in the last few decades, but fundamental changes that shaped mankind in general, like agriculture and industry. Alec was a modern man and took things like electronic communication and medicines for granted, whereas Cronin lived in times when people wore shoes made from animals they'd skinned with their bare hands. He shook his head. "Wow."

"It is a lot to take in," Cronin said soothingly.

"Yeah, just a bit." Alec looked up at the ceiling and puffed out a breath, then let his head loll to the side so he could look at Cronin. He looked at the shelves of keepsakes, artifacts, and antique pieces. No doubt, each had its own story, but for now he was dealing with enough information for his brain to handle. "Promise one day you'll tell me everything."

Cronin's smile was immediate and warm. "I will."

They sat in silence for a short while, Cronin allowing Alec the time to absorb what he'd learned. Finally, Alec spoke. "What other times have there been... *incident*s like the Black Plague."

"Evidence of vampires has been found from as long as seven thousand years ago, when humans were still mostly uncivilized. Though very little is known about them. The Illyrians and the Egyptians were the first that I know of. Then there were a few isolated events, though nothing that caused widespread carnage until 1347. After that, there have been some more *incidents*, as you call them."

"Such as?"

"There was another plague in London in 1665, then in Moscow in 1771. Only a few tens of thousands of humans were killed in those..." Cronin cringed, likely at how callous that sounded. "There's been *plague incidents* in Italy, Africa, Helsinki, Baghdad. They weren't as severe as the first time, and the Yersinians, what little remained of them, were finally eradicated after Moscow."

"Eradicated?" Alec picked out the one word. "You mean that coven is all gone?"

"Yes."

"Well, good," Alec said. Then he shrugged. "Sorry."

Cronin snorted. "There were also Mayan people."

"Yeah right. Now you're pulling my leg."

"No."

"The Mayans were vampires?"

"Not all." Cronin sighed. "Some villagers escaped, and the localized myth of blood-drinking demons spread like wildfire. There were many books and scribes about what happened, though the Spanish coven controlled the incident and burned all evidence."

"Jesus Christ."

Cronin smirked and before he could speak, Alec did. "Let me guess. He wasn't there?"

He chuckled. "No."

After a moment's silence, Alec furrowed his eyebrows. "Okay," Cronin said. "Your questions."

"I have many," Alec said. "But one thing doesn't add up. Saying works of literature were rewritten eight hundred years ago is fine, and agreed, quite plausible. Monarchs and churches alike did a lot of unthinkable things to suit themselves back then. But it doesn't explain recent discoveries. Archaeologists have been discovering tombs in Egypt as late as the last decade with inscriptions and hieroglyphs and they've found nothing to suggest what you're saying is true. Some of those hieroglyphs are thousands of years old. They can't have been rewritten—they've only just been discovered."

"You have a photographic memory, yes?"

"Yeah."

"And you can recall pictures, texts?"

"Yes."

"It is similar to how a vampire's mind works." Cronin obviously liked that Alec was gifted with clear recall, and he apparently found intelligence appealing. Alec's chest warmed knowing he affected Cronin in such a way. He liked it more than he should. "You studied histories in your schooling?"

"Yes."

"Proof of vampire existence doesn't need to be in the form of written words, Alec. Remember how I told you proof was there if you knew what to look for?"

"Yes."

"I want you to recall what you learned about the Egyptians, Illyrians, Inca, Mayans, and Aztecs, even the Chinese and the Nigerians. They each lived thousands of miles apart, over many centuries, yet they are inexplicably linked."

Alec was quiet for a moment, his mind flashing images and information, forging a profile on each culture. His eyes shot to Cronin's when he realized what it was.

"Pyramids."

Cronin gave a nod. "And?"

A cold shiver ran down Alec's spine. "They all mummified their dead."

CHAPTER SIX

Cronin couldn't help but smile, and a flush of pride filled his chest. Alec, on the other hand, looked horrified.

"What does that mean?" he asked. "The mummification. Why is that important? It was to preserve the dead for the afterlife, was it not?"

Cronin shook his head. "Historians would have you believe so, but no. Embalming is the process of what, Alec?"

"Draining the blood..." Alec started to answer. Then he whispered. "Oh."

Cronin shook his head. "Not for reasons you might think. Ancient vampires were embalmed so they could not be returned to life."

Alec's eyes went wide. "Returned to life? Jesus. This just keeps getting weirder." He scrubbed his hands over his face. "To a human life? Or a vampire life?"

"Vampire. The process of turning vampire from a human state cannot be reversed."

"But vampires can die," Alec said. "I saw that guy... he turned to dust! Now I'm no expert, but that looked pretty fucking dead to me."

Cronin smiled at him. "Yes, vampires can die one of three ways. Wooden stake or bullet to the heart, as you saw — though the bullet is a relatively new development. Sunlight will kill a vampire, though not

68

instantly. It may take up to five seconds for the ultraviolet light to penetrate the skin and pierce the heart. Then there is also embalming, a process that has not been used for millennia."

"How…" Alec's brows furrowed. "How does it work? I mean, if vampires have super strength and powers and… How did they not turn to dust before their blood was removed?"

It was a good question, Cronin conceded. And one many people wouldn't think to ask. "We don't know exactly — we can only speculate — though we believe the ancient covens had at least one member with the ability to paralyze. We assume the process needs to be done while the vampire is still alive."

"Jesus."

Cronin chuckled. "No."

"He wasn't there," they said in unison, both smiling.

"And the pyramids?" Alec asked after a moment of silence. "What's the significance?"

"Given the times and the resources they had available, pyramids were the logical choice. They are, after all, the strongest, most stable shape."

"So it's not some mystical powerful portal?" Alec asked, half-joking, half-not. "Because really, anything's possible at this point."

"There's no magical reason," Cronin said with an amused smirk. "They are burial tombs, that much is correct. But the historians were wrong about one fact:

the walls of meter-thick stone and sealed chambers were not to keep people out."

Alec concluded. "They were to keep vampires in."

Cronin stood up. "Enough talk for one night," he said with a smile. "It is getting late."

Alec looked at his watch. It was almost midnight. He had no idea they'd talked for so long. "I'm not Cinderella, you know. I'm not going to lose a shoe when the clock strikes twelve. I worked night shift for years."

Cronin rolled his eyes. "No, but you did warn me that you functioned better with adequate sleep. And I'd rather not argue unnecessarily."

Alec raised one eyebrow at him. "You're seriously sending me to bed?"

Cronin barked out a laugh. "Uh, no. You wanted to go to your apartment."

"Oh!" Alec said, embarrassment heating his cheeks. "I forgot about that."

"It will require leaping," Cronin reminded him.

"Ugh," Alec groaned. "Nothing like volunteering to have your body shredded at a cellular level."

Cronin frowned. "You don't have to go. I can order you anything you wish."

"No, no," Alec said, sounding resigned. "Let's just get it over with. Now, how do I do this again?"

"You need to put your arms around me," Cronin said softly.

Alec moved right in front of him and slowly slid his hands around Cronin's back. Jesus, it felt good. It felt so unbelievably fucking right. He'd never experienced anything like it.

With no more than a quiet gasp from Cronin, they were gone.

* * * *

The pain was just as Alec remembered. So complete and blinding, every fiber of his body screamed in agony. Every pixelated cell blurred and burned, and then... everything shifted, like Cronin changed course... and it was over.

The pain was gone, Alec realized, and he sucked back a ragged breath. And then in its place was immediate pleasure. Cronin was pressed against him, pushing him against a wall. Alec's bathroom wall. "Shhh," Cronin whispered followed by a quiet moan. "There are two people in your living room."

Alec couldn't move, not even if he wanted to. And he really, *really* didn't want to. He could feel Cronin against him, all of him. He was all strength and smelled like nothing Alec had ever smelled before, like earth and heaven. His face was against Cronin's neck, and Alec realized that Cronin's was against his.

A vampire's mouth was at his neck, and all Alec could do was stretch to give him more skin, silently urging him to do it, to sink his teeth into him. He wanted it, God, like he'd never wanted anything else.

"Alec," Cronin warned, a quiet rattle rumbling in his chest. "Don't move."

Cronin was hard, his erection pressed against Alec's own aching cock and it took every ounce of self-control, every conscious effort, for Alec not to groan and grind against him, to bring Cronin's mouth to his...

"Ah, come on," a voice said on the other side of the door, startling Alec from his Cronin-lust-induced haze. "He's not here. He hasn't been here since we were here last. I think De Angelo's as crazy as what MacAidan was."

"De Angelo didn't go all beam-me-up-Scotty like MacAidan did," the second voice replied.

The first cop laughed and there was a mumbled reply about leaving before the front door slammed, followed by silence. Cronin took a step back from Alec, then took a very slow, calculated breath.

Alec saw what he thought were fangs before Cronin shook his head and they were gone, his normal human teeth in their place. He also had a rather pronounced bulge in his trousers.

Jesus. He was as turned-on as Alec was.

Alec closed his eyes and leaned over, his hands on his knees, and took some deep breaths. It wasn't the effect of leaping that had him so breathless. It was Cronin... *God, I wanted him to bite me. I wanted him to fuck me.* Alec knew he would have let him do either. Bite, fuck, preferably both.

"That was close," Cronin whispered.

Alec, still leaning his hands on his knees, looked up at him. He wasn't sure if Cronin meant it was close that they'd almost leapt into a room where people were standing, or if it was close that he'd nearly bitten him. "Close for what?" he asked, still catching his breath.

"Exactly. Alec, I will say this once, and only once," Cronin said. He lifted Alec's chin with just a finger, bringing Alec to full height. His tone was deadly serious. "If you offer me your throat again, I will not refuse it."

Alec swallowed. "You... I... couldn't help it... your body..." Then anger flared in his belly. He pushed Cronin's hand away and pointed his finger at him. "Maybe if you didn't press me up against a wall and shove your face in my neck, we wouldn't have this problem."

Cronin made a sound that Alec could only describe as a growl, and the vampire took a step back from him. "I apologize."

Alec bit back a snarl of his own. He had to remind himself that this was new to both of them. Again, he took a breath and shook off his anger, trying to quell the intense and not-always-rational emotions he had around Cronin. He looked around his bathroom: the old blue and white tiles were popular in the 1950s, the shower curtain hid the stained grout in the shower, and his toothbrush was exactly where he'd thrown it into the cup. Everything looked the same, just as it did a day ago. Jesus. Was it just *one* day?

Then he remembered the sudden shift he felt when they'd leapt here. "You changed direction?"

Cronin's dark eyes shot to Alec's. "You felt that?"

"Well, yeah. It was a shift or a—" Alec jerked his shoulders to the right, then felt stupid for doing so. "—change in direction, or something."

Cronin's lips twitched as though he might smile. "Yes. I can leap anywhere, but it's not until I almost reappear that I get a sense of who else might be there."

Alec nodded slowly. "Hang on. How did you know where I lived?"

"Eiji told me."

"How did he know where I lived?"

"He's been following you your entire life," Cronin said simply. "Apparently."

Alec's eyes went wide. "He what?"

Cronin put his hands up, palms forward, in a don't-shoot-the-messenger notion. "I knew nothing of it." Then he corrected himself. "I knew nothing of you. Eiji did, and he kept you from me."

By the way Cronin snarled, it was pretty obvious to Alec the vampire wasn't happy with it.

"Well, it explains the déjà vu I get from Eiji," Alec said. "I've never seen him directly—I'd remember if I did. But he's familiar to me in a non-familiar kind of way, if that makes sense?"

Cronin nodded. "In your peripheral vision. In the shadows, never in plain sight."

"But he's followed me since I was a kid?"

"Yes. To keep you safe." Cronin shrugged, but made no apology for the invasion of privacy. "He knew what you were going to be before you were born."

Alec scrubbed his hands over his face. "He what?"

"He met your father when your father was just a boy," Cronin explained. "He read him, his DNA, and saw that he would father a significant child." Cronin shrugged again. "Significant to me, at least."

"My father? Oh Jesus, Dad."

"Your father was never harmed," Cronin said. "In fact, Eiji protected him as he did you. Or so he said."

"You trust Eiji?"

"With my life." Cronin stared at Alec. "With your life."

"But he never told you."

Cronin shook his head. "Though I don't agree with it, I can see why he chose secrecy. I would have… interfered had I known that you were even alive."

Alec took a moment to process what Cronin had told him. "God. He saw me as a kid? I had acne and braces, for fuck's sake. No wonder he never told you."

Cronin smiled at that. "I would not have cared."

Then he thought of something else. "Jesus. He's seen the guys I've—"

Cronin did that growly noise again.

"Yeah, I can see why he never told you."

"He also never told me you lived with someone."

"What?"

"Were you lovers with this… *Sammy* person?" Cronin asked. He said the name as though it tasted bitter.

"Shit! Sammy!" Alec said, and he pulled the bathroom door open. "Sammy!" Alec darted across the short hall and into the open living and kitchen area. "Sammy?" Nothing. There was no sign of him. He looked under the sofa, finding nothing. He went back to the hall and opened the bedroom door, scanning the room, and finally looking under the bed. "Oh, little guy, there you are." Alec went around to the far side of the bed, got down on his knees, reached in, and pulled out the tabby cat. He stood up, holding the cat to his chest and scratching under its chin. "Did those cops scare you?"

Cronin stood at the door, smiling. "Sammy is a cat?"

"Sammy is," Alec said, "though I don't tell him that. Sammy thinks he's human."

The cat looked at Cronin and turned in Alec's arms. At first Alec thought he was trying to run away—Cronin being a vampire and all—but the cat didn't want to run *from* Cronin at all. Sammy meowed like Alec had never heard and pushed away from Alec until he let him go. The cat jumped on the bed and padded across to where Cronin stood, meowing again.

Cronin smiled and walked over to the bed, and Sammy mewled until Cronin picked him up. The cat purred and nudged his face to Cronin's chin.

Alec was floored. "Cats like vampires?"

"Cats protect vampires," Cronin said, then he amended it. "Well, cats will protect a good vampire and deter a vampire with bad intentions."

"How...? You know what? Never mind," Alec mumbled. He still couldn't believe his own Sammy had betrayed him like that, still purring in Cronin's arms.

"What symbol is on most Egyptian hieroglyphs, Alec?" Cronin asked. "What animal?"

Oh. "Cats."

Cronin petted Sammy, making the cat purr even louder. "You have a photographic memory, Alec, you've seen symbols of cats everywhere. Have you not?"

Alec's mind scrambled through his memory banks to recall images of cats... Not just domesticated cats, but the biggest cats of all.

Lions.

National flags all around the world, monarchy symbols of European and Asian alike, dozens of coats of arms, on shields and crests of battle gear for most nations, statues at government offices, museums, and places of worship. There were lions on sarcophagi dating back to Greek mythology, and ancient Southeast Asian histories, South American lore, and medieval Europe showed lions on just about everything.

Lions were emblazoned on every continent. Every. Single. One. Hell, there were even flags of the British lion in Antarctica.

"Oh." Alec swallowed hard as realization settled in. "They're everywhere."

The lion didn't represent strength and bravery. It was a symbol to warn the evil and to protect the good, and it had been for thousands of years across the globe. Alec snorted in disbelief. "And I thought there was no documentation of vampire lore anywhere." He shook his head again. "Jesus. It really is *everywhere*, isn't it?"

"I told you it was there. You only had to know what to look for?"

"But cats?" Alec asked. "Seriously?"

Cronin smiled. "Where is the biggest, most famous of all?"

"Oh Jesus," Alec whispered. "The Sphinx."

"Yes."

"And they protect?"

"The symbols are to warn. They hold no protective powers as such."

"So if the biggest warning symbol is in Egypt, then it's fair to assume that's where the biggest... war will be?"

Cronin gave a small nod. "Well, that and the fact that the Egyptian covens are moving out, it seems most likely, yes."

"Was that sarcasm?" Alec deadpanned. "Were you always such a smartass in your human life or did it take a good twelve hundred years to work on that one?"

Cronin chuckled. "I see it's a skill you managed to master in just twenty-nine years."

Alec rolled his eyes and sighed. He watched Cronin with Sammy for a moment and shook his head again, still not quite believing what he knew to be true. "Cats?"

Sammy nudged his head against Cronin's chest, still purring loudly. Cronin smiled. "Yes, Alec. Cats."

"Why not dogs?" Alec asked. "Oh wait, is that because of the whole werewolf thing? Because I've seen those lycan movies..." Alec's eyes went wide. "Shit. Are there such things as werewolves? Who can tear through vampire flesh?"

Now it was Cronin who rolled his eyes. "Did you not want to collect some personal effects?"

"Oh," Alec said, remembering what they'd actually come to his apartment for. He grabbed a duffel bag from his wardrobe and started shoving clothes in it. It occurred to him—like he knew it in his bones—that he'd never be coming back, so he stopped packing clothes and started with photos instead.

CHAPTER SEVEN

"I need to speak to my father," Alec said. They'd collected everything he'd wanted from his apartment, including Sammy, without so much as another word between them and leapt back to Cronin's apartment. Alec ran his hands through his hair and leaned his head against the back of the sofa.

Alec knew police protocol. He knew his father would have been questioned and in all likelihood was now under surveillance from the NYPD. He would have been told that his son had disappeared and very probably shown CCTV footage of him vanishing into thin air with another man.

"I understand," Cronin said quietly.

"But?"

"But nothing," he answered. "I will speak to Eiji and Jodis and hear what they have to say." His brow furrowed. "Alec, I don't wish to take anything away from you. If there is a way we can involve your father without causing harm or attention to him, then we should."

Alec looked at Cronin for a long moment. "Thank you."

Cronin smiled. "Tell me about him. Eiji said he's a Scot?"

Alec snorted. "Yes. He was born in Callanish, Scotland but came to the US as a boy. I never knew my mother. She died not long after I was born. My dad and I are close. Well, I mean, we were. Growing up, he was cool with everything. He handled the weird shit right along with me."

"What weird shit?"

"Well, when I was a kid, there were a few times when things didn't quite add up. Like the time I was about four and I was climbing the bookcase like a ladder. It was six foot high and heavy as hell, and my dad told me a hundred times not to climb it. I did anyway and it fell. I should have been underneath it and it probably should've killed me, but I was pulled out before it flattened me. Dad came running back in and I was a good few feet from the bookcase. He swore I must've just fell farther than I thought, but I remember being pulled out of the way."

Cronin pursed his lips and his nostrils flared.

"Then there was the time I was supposed to be having a sleepover at Bobby Monroe's house, but we fought over some game or something stupid and I walked home. It wasn't too far, just a block or two, but it was nine o'clock at night and I was about eight years old."

Cronin's voice was quiet and methodical. "You walked the streets of New York City alone at night when you were eight?"

"Uh, yeah," Alec admitted. He cringed. "Just that once. Anyway, there was a man who asked me if I wanted him to take me home, but my dad had told me a hundred times not to talk to strangers so I took off. Well, he chased me, so I took a shortcut through the alley, but he caught me. He grabbed my jacket and I turned around just in time to see him get lifted off me in a blur. I heard him screaming, and man, I ran. I ran all the way home." Alec shook his head. "I scared the crap outta my dad. And holy hell did I get my ass kicked for that."

Cronin took a slow, deep breath. "I get the feeling there are a lot of these kinds of stories?"

"Yep. I almost drowned once, but got pulled out of the local indoor pool. My dad saw that one. He ran after the guy who pulled me out, but it was raining and he was gone. Like he literally disappeared."

Cronin nodded. "And?"

"Dad started to believe me then. There were a few times throughout high school. Some seniors tried to lock me in the storage lockers under the bleachers in my junior year, and the three of them ended leaving the school citing some crap about ghosts or some shit. I heard one of them was in therapy for years," Alec said with a slow nod as he realized something. "It was all Eiji, wasn't it? Every time?"

"I'm starting to think so," Cronin said. "Believe me, I'll be asking him." He tilted his head. "There was an incident with a bullet?"

"Oh, there sure was." Alec smiled. "It was the weirdest one of all. It was just two years ago, routine bust, just at sunset. The perp swung his pistol and it discharged. It was five feet from me, aimed right at my head, but the bullet kind of blurred and changed trajectory in midair, like it bent or something. It went from head-height straight down and got me in the leg instead." Alec touched the indent on his thigh. He could feel the divot through his jeans. "It went straight through. I had muscle damage and spent five months doing physical therapy, but I heal fast apparently. It's as good as new now. Well, it was better than being shot in the head."

Alec could have sworn that Cronin growled.

"Six other cops saw that bullet change direction. They all reported it but it just got written off as some freak anomaly." Alec studied Cronin for a moment. "How did Eiji do that?"

"From what you describe, I'd say he deflected the bullet," Cronin answered. "If his speed was that of the bullet or faster, simply brushing it would have made it appear to bend."

"Faster than a bullet?"

Cronin nodded. "Vampires can move very fast, beyond what the human eye can detect."

"Or what the human brain will process," Alec added. "What humans actually see and what they convince themselves they see are not always the same thing."

"Very true." Cronin looked at Alec's leg. "Does your leg hurt?"

Alec saw the set of Cronin's jaw and the way he failed to disguise his anger. "Why do I get the feeling that whatever pain level I admit to will be directly proportional to how much you yell at Eiji?"

Cronin laughed. "Because you almost being shot in the head is directly proportional to how much he deserves to be yelled at."

"Oh, leave him alone. He was doing what he thought was right."

Cronin raised one eyebrow at him. "Is that so?"

"Yep. And anyway—" Alec shrugged. "—my leg doesn't hurt anymore. He saved me plenty of times, or so it seems."

Cronin sighed loudly, angrily even, then was quiet for a while. Eventually, he said, "Your father…"

"Yeah? What about him?"

"Do you still talk often?"

"Yeah, kind of. Not as much as I should, though. It's just that life gets busy, ya know? I try to visit once a week. We have Sunday lunch together sometimes, but I was always busy with work."

Delaying those phone calls and postponing visits was something Alec was truly starting to regret. "I'd like to see him, not just talk to him."

Cronin nodded, then his brow furrowed. "I'd like to meet him also," he said. "If you're agreeable."

"If I'm agreeable?" Alec repeated with a smile. "You know, it's kinda cute the way you speak."

Embarrassment heated Cronin's cheeks.

"And vampires blush?" Alec asked, his smile smug.

Cronin barked out a laugh. "It is something I've not experienced in a very long time. Well, not before I met you." He was particularly cute when he spoke with a smile. "I have adapted over the centuries. It helps with blending in, though human traits remain. My accent is long faded."

"Your accent is sexy as hell," Alec said, unsure of what made him say something so brazen.

Cronin blinked. "Oh."

Alec cleared his throat. "I really have no idea why I said that," he said. "I mean, it's true. But I'm not usually so... I don't normally just blurt shit out like that."

Cronin laughed again, and there was nothing but warmth in his eyes. Alec couldn't believe eyes that dark could be so warm. "For what it's worth, Alec, I like the sound of your voice too."

Alec smiled back at him, their eye contact intense. It was the first time he realized he might actually be smitten with Cronin.

Smitten, Alec thought. *Who the fuck uses words like smitten? Oh, that's right. I do. Apparently. Since Mr. Suave-and-Sexy-Vampire here leapt into my life and informed me that we're fated to one another for all eternity.*

The more Alec thought about the whole fated-soul thing, the less he minded. He couldn't deny his physical attraction to Cronin. His heart rate spiked and his whole body flushed when he saw him, and dear God, when he was near him... But it wasn't just physical. He was so intelligent and learned, he'd lived through things Alec couldn't fathom, and Alec wanted to hear every story, every recount of every year he'd lived. Oh, and that rust-colored hair was so damn perfect, and he had the sexiest smirk. The kind that made Alec's insides flip.

Before Alec's thoughts could get away from him, Cronin said, "It's quite late. I hope you don't think it rude, but I will retire to my room."

Alec looked at his watch. It was four in the morning. "Oh yeah. Me too," he said, standing up. Then he realized how that sounded. "I mean, I'll be going to my room. Not yours."

Cronin stood up as well, leaving just two feet between them. Alec could have sworn the air in the room was suddenly thick and electric. Cronin's eyes seemed to darken, and his voice was softer when he spoke. "I knew what you meant."

Alec tried to laugh it off. "So, you *do* sleep? I mean, you said you did, but unless I missed something last night, I didn't think you had."

"I didn't sleep last night. I don't require as much as a human, and I can go for a few days without sleep, though I do need to eventually, yes, but only for a few hours."

Alec nodded slowly, their eyes locked on each other. "Right. Good to know," he whispered.

They didn't move, they didn't blink. Alec could hear his own heart hammering in his chest and he was sure Cronin could too. The vampire smiled and took a step backward, away from him, though Alec thought he saw a glimpse of fangs before he turned and walked toward the hall.

Alec took a deep breath as quietly as he could, though he knew damn well Cronin could hear that too. He followed Cronin to where the bedrooms were, and Cronin stopped at his own door. It was open and he pushed on it. "Oh."

"What is it?" Alec asked, looking around Cronin into the room. Sammy the cat was curled up and sound asleep on Cronin's bed. Alec laughed. "Wondered where he went to."

"Well, he can't..." Cronin started to say. "It can't sleep on my bed."

Alec opened the door to his own room and chuckled at the horrified look on Cronin's face. "He's a bed hog too. Sprawls out like he owns it." He walked into the room, and just before he closed the door behind him, he said, "Good luck with that."

All jokes aside, lying in bed, all Alec could think about was how much he wished he was in Cronin's bed, instead of the cat.

Smitten? *Yeah, right.* He knew he'd give in. He knew he'd get the chance to kiss him soon, to taste his lips, to feel his body pressed against his. He wanted it. He wanted Cronin.

The last thought Alec had before drifting off to sleep was to wonder just how much of the attraction was fated? Was it real? How would he know? If they weren't fated and he'd met Cronin in a bar, would he even be interested?

And the truth was, having all choice removed made the jittery smitten feeling taste a little like betrayal.

* * * *

Alec woke up tired. His watch told him it was almost 10:00 a.m. The smell of coffee dragged him out of bed and into the shower.

Alec tried not to think about how it must have been Cronin who made the coffee he could smell, Lord knew it wasn't on his list of dietary requirements.

He knew Cronin had to feed, and he knew vampires would be feeding all around the world and had been for millennia. Just because he now knew about it didn't change that fact.

Did Alec want people to die? No.

Did he want Cronin to starve? The thought twisted his gut and bothered him more than thinking about innocent humans who'd had their lives cut short to feed vampires.

And it was this to-ing and fro-ing between accepting the situation he found himself in and rejecting it that was wearing him out. One minute he found himself drawn to Cronin, then the next he was irrationally angry at him. It was emotionally tiring. He had to remind himself that Cronin was in the exact same position and he probably didn't want Alec as his fated partner either. And as Alec let the hot water run over his head and shoulders in the shower, he realized that it was *that* thought—how Cronin wouldn't have chosen him if it weren't for fate—that bothered him the most.

Looking at his reflection as he shaved after his shower, Alec knew he'd have to tell Cronin how he felt. If this was the forever thing they said it was, then it was also an honesty-at-all-costs kind of thing too.

When he walked out into the kitchen, he found Cronin frowning at the coffeemaker and five full cups of black coffee lining the countertop. He looked very human, and it made Alec smile. "Has the coffee offended you?"

"I tried to make it for you," he said, still looking at the machine. "There are various settings, so I read the instruction manual, but it was then I realized I wasn't sure which type you preferred. So I tasted it…"

Alec laughed at the look of absolute horror on Cronin's face. "Not a fan?"

"I've never tasted anything so horrid."

Still smiling, Alec picked up a random cup and sipped it. It was strong, warm, and bitter. It tasted expensive, not like the swill he was used to at the police station. "Mmm," Alec hummed. "It's very good, thank you."

Cronin seemed pleased. He smiled shyly. "You're welcome. I know you like coffee in the morning."

"You been up long?"

"Since before the sun," he answered. "I trust you slept well."

Alec sipped his coffee. "Not really. Can I ask you something?"

Cronin looked alarmed. "Of course."

"I have to be honest with you. I'm struggling with this. Not just the lack of free will in the whole fated thing or the fact I can't go anywhere for risk of being seen by police or killed by vampires," Alec said, not even shocked at how absurd his life had become in just three days. "But I'm struggling with how I feel. These highs and lows are doing my head in. Is it the same for you? I mean, you didn't choose me either, and yet you're stuck with me, like it or not. Does that piss you off?"

Cronin looked to the floor, then out the window and across the city, anywhere but at Alec, it seemed. He blinked a few times. His voice was quiet and hurt. "I am not angry, no. I have waited a long time…"

"Please don't be offended," Alec urged him. "I know you've waited, for a length of time I can't begin to understand. You've been alone for a long time, and I'm sorry if I'm not gushing about hearts and flowers, but I need to be honest with you. I don't know how any of this works. I don't know what's expected of me or what's expected of you. And I have these feelings that I don't even know are real. How do I know what's real or what's not?"

"Do you feel it?" Cronin asked softly.

"Feel what?"

"Anything. Nervous, happy? Do you get a warm thrill when you lay eyes upon me?"

Alec swallowed hard. "Yes."

A flicker of a smile played on Cronin's lips. "If you feel it, then it is real. Is it not?"

"I guess." Alec sighed. "What I mean is, if we weren't fated or destined or whatever you call it and we met at a bar or through mutual friends, would I still feel that way?"

Cronin's brows furrowed. "That is a question I cannot answer."

"See, what's normal for humans is to date and spend time together, getting to know the other person. And emotional involvement is a gradual thing," Alec explained. "I think that's what I'm struggling with. This instant thrown-together-forever thing is hard to believe. I don't know…" Alec shook his head. "I can't explain it properly. I don't want you to think I'm not… attracted to you, because I am, not just physically, but emotionally as well. And that's what I can't get my head around. The logical part of my brain—the part that says it can't be real in just three days—won't seem to let go, that's all."

"I understand your concern. It's very fast, immediate even, and that's a difficult concept," Cronin said.

Alec felt the need to apologize. "I'm sorry. I don't mean to hurt you by saying that, I just need you to know where I'm at."

"No, I thank you for your honesty," Cronin said. He smiled at Alec. "May I make a suggestion?"

Alec wasn't sure he was going to like this, but he answered anyway. "Yeah?"

Cronin hesitated. "Eiji and Jodis won't be back until tonight, so while privacy allows, how would you feel about treating today as a… date?"

A slow smile spread across Alec's face. "I'd like that."

Cronin let out a held breath and smiled in relief. "Given the custom is one from your generation, I'll let you choose what it is we do."

Alec was still smiling. "Well, normally we'd go out for dinner, see a movie, have a few drinks. But taking into account the no-public, no-sunlight factor, and not to mention we have slightly different ideas on what constitutes as a good meal, I think I have the perfect idea."

* * * *

"Netflix?" Cronin looked confused.

"Yep." Alec was certain. Cronin had admitted to rarely watching television, and Alec was determined to bring him up to speed on popular culture. "You have a home theater in your apartment, and you've never used it!"

There was also a study-cum-library and another living room that Alec hadn't seen before now through what he had assumed was an access door in the kitchen. Boy was he wrong. It opened up a whole other side of the apartment.

"The other apartment I looked at contained a gymnasium for which I had no need. Not that I needed a television screen as large as this one either, but to choose between the two, I thought this more practical."

Alec snorted. He couldn't imagine having the finances to have those kind of apartment decisions. His last apartment dilemma was to choose between a working elevator and an eat-in kitchen. He chose the apartment with an elevator and just ate in front of the TV most mornings when he finished his night shift.

"You've obviously accumulated some wealth over the years." It wasn't a question. Though Alec thought it was probably rude to ask, he said it anyway.

"Yes." Cronin smiled and watched as Alec hooked up his laptop computer to the projector. "It wasn't always so. When I was human, currency wasn't even really a thing."

Alec stopped what he was doing and stared at Cronin. "No currency?"

"Well, there was. Though my village was quite removed and rather poor. We tended to barter and trade goods or skills instead. My mother would sell baskets for fish."

Alec blinked. "Jesus."

Cronin chuckled. "No, he wasn't there."

Alec snorted out a laugh, still in shock at this admission. Cronin's age would never cease to surprise him.

"Then, as I… *happened* across personal wares, I would sell them for coins." Cronin cringed.

"Happened across personal wares?" Alec laughed. "You mean you took silver rings and watches from your—" He searched for the right words. "—dinner dates?"

Now it was Cronin who laughed. "If that's what you'd prefer to call them."

"It's nicer than saying 'the man you just killed'."

Cronin shrugged, completely not offended. "True. I've also been known to leap into bank vaults to take what I want."

Alec forgot about the computer cords he was holding and stared at Cronin. "Bank vaults?"

"On occasion. Not in a long time, though."

Alec finished connecting the cords between his laptop and the projector, and—using a skill learned during years of police work—he hacked into someone else's Netflix account. He assumed the NYPD were now watching everything he did, so he needed the anonymity. He'd also just wittingly crossed the cop/felon line but couldn't bring himself to care. It wasn't as bad as robbing bank vaults, but still, illegal was illegal. It did, however, make him think of something else.

"So how does one go about purchasing prime New York City real estate but avoid attention?"

"I did the deal from London. It was all done via email, phone calls, and lawyers, and I met with the agent and lawyer here once, at night of course, and signed the paperwork. You'd be surprised how discreet they can be when large sums of money are involved." Cronin smiled at Alec. "It's easier to be someone from out of town."

"What about identification?" Alec pressed. "I'm pretty sure your driver's license doesn't have your date of birth on it."

Cronin sighed wistfully. "Once upon a time and for many hundreds of years, identification was taken by name alone. You were who you said you were. Identification papers were only introduced after World War I, and photographic evidence much later. False identification is harder with the introduction of certain technologies, but really, money can buy a lot of things."

"I spent years as a cop hating that fact," Alec grumbled. "So what name is this apartment under anyway? I assume not your real name."

"I am currently, whilst in America anyway, Mr. James T. Furst." Cronin smiled when he said the name.

Alec studied him for a long moment and wondered what he found so amusing. "Wasn't James the First the King of Scotland?"

Cronin barked out a laugh. "Yes. Eiji thought it would be funny."

Alec shook his head and laughed along with Cronin. "I'm starting to think the sense of humor trait glitches out when you guys become vampires."

Cronin ignored the jibe. "To answer your question, my very first real estate purchase was done in England. I had taken some personal effects such as clothes and shoes from a... *dinner date* here in America.

I leapt back to London and pretended to be American. They took in my newly acquired American clothes, my fake accent, and my bankroll and the rest, as they say, is history. Then as decades passed, I posed as the son or grandson of myself and resold the properties for profit. It's best not to stay too long in one place."

"I guess not. You collect artifacts, though. Like the ones in your living room. Do you sell those?"

"No, they are my personal collection."

"Will you tell me about them one day?"

Cronin smiled. "Yes. Anything you want to know."

"Have you always lived in such nice places?"

Cronin shook his head slowly. "I'm fortunate that I can leap to wherever the sun is not, though most of my kind cannot. It was not uncommon in earlier times that vampires would have to bury themselves in dirt or sand to avoid sunlight. Most found abandoned houses or caves if they were lucky; some took any house they fancied by killing every inhabitant."

"Oh."

Cronin cringed. "We might prefer a more pleasant topic of conversation for our... date?"

"Good idea." Alec picked up the remote and jumped on the huge sofa. It was cinema-like but wrapped around the room with reclining seats and footrests, and came complete with drink holders. He patted the seat next to him. "Take a seat."

Cronin hesitated.

Alec rolled his eyes. "I don't bite."

Cronin smiled. "And you complain about my humor. Yours is questionable, more so than mine."

"Well, it's a bit difficult to have a *date* when you won't sit next to me."

Cronin chuckled nervously. "It isn't that I don't want to sit next to you. I want it very much, but" — he sat down beside Alec and slid back, trying to look relaxed — "I'm afraid I have no experience in such matters as human dating."

Alec held out his hand closest to Cronin. "Would you like to hold my hand?"

Cronin grabbed his hand quickly, only then seeming to remember Alec's question. "Yes."

Alec didn't bother trying to fight a grin and pointed the remote at the projector. "I picked a movie you might find interesting."

"What is it?"

"*Blade*," Alec said. "It's a vampire flick. I thought you might like to see how you're portrayed by society. And believe me, it's one of the better ones. There are some I wouldn't let you watch."

The movie had barely started when Cronin's cell phone rang. He pulled it out of his pocket and answered. "Eiji? ... Yes. And the location? ... Understood."

Cronin ended the phone call and sighed. "Alec, I'm afraid our date will have to wait. The meeting of our coven will be tonight, so if you wish to see your father, I suggest we do it today."

CHAPTER EIGHT

Cronin didn't want to rush Alec. He didn't want to expose him to the dangers that were coming any more than he had to. With every fiber of his being, he wanted to protect him, save him. But it was all happening too quickly.

Eiji and Jodis had left to scout information, to put together the pieces and rumors to see if there was a clearer picture of what the Egyptians and Illyrians were doing, and hopefully, by association, figure out what the key could be. Whatever it was, whatever the grand plan was, Cronin knew it couldn't possibly be good. But without any evidence, speculation and imagination were all he had to go by.

The meeting of the coven to be held later that night was paramount, and vampire representatives from other covens from all over the country and even Canada would be there. Cronin couldn't miss it, yet he didn't want to leave Alec unguarded for any amount of time. He certainly didn't want to bring him into the meeting—the only human amongst a few hundred vampires—but he feared he had little choice. He simply could not leave him.

"Okay," Alec said. "So you have the address and you just need to think 'hallway' or 'kitchen' and that's where we'll leap to?"

Cronin gave a nod. "Yes."

Alec pressed the call button and put the phone to his ear. It was a simple prepaid phone, untraceable, to be used only once, then replaced. It also meant Alec's father wouldn't recognize the phone number calling him.

The call was answered on the fourth ring, and Cronin could hear every word. "Hello?" The voice was gruff, older in years, and, as expected, Scottish. It made Cronin smile.

"Dad, it's me."

"Oh, Alec. Where the hell are you? Are you okay?" He spoke so fast his words ran into each other. "They're looking for you, son. The police. They're probably —"

Alec cut him off. "Dad, I need you to listen. Go around and draw all the blinds. All of them."

There was a pause. "Okay. Do you think they're watching?"

"Just do it for me, please," Alec said. "I'll explain later."

There were muffled sounds coming from the phone, which Cronin deduced was the man closing the blinds to the windows in his house. "Okay," his dad said. "I've closed them all."

"Are you there alone?"

"Yes."

"Do me a favor," Alec said. "Go look out through the front door and tell me how many cars are parked out front."

Alec didn't wait for an answer. He ended the call, threw the phone on the sofa, and put his arms around Cronin's waist. "Right. He's at the front door so if you could leap us into the hallway. I figured it's probably best not to give him a coronary."

With the address Alec had given him in his mind, Cronin pressed his hand to Alec's back, his whole body alive with energy at the feel of Alec's body flush against him. It took his breath away. And they leapt.

As soon as they'd arrived, Cronin knew why Alec had told him to leap into the hall: there were no windows. In the split second of leaping, Cronin took in the surroundings. The apartment was small and old, the carpets and furnishings were yellow and brown, and the air smelled a mix of human food and faint lemon disinfectant.

Then Alec flexed and recoiled against him. Cronin could feel the tension vibrate in his body when Alec groaned quietly through his clenched teeth as the effects of leaping rattled through him. Yes, leaping affected Alec, but it surprised Cronin just how well he endured it. He'd taken humans numerous times — dinner dates, as Alec had called them — and most had screamed and shaken violently, some lost consciousness, yet Alec contained the pain without much effort. It was a sure sign of his strength and determination, traits Cronin greatly admired.

Alec pulled away and found his bearings almost immediately. He turned and ran down the hall. "Dad?"

Cronin followed, but Alec's arm stopped him from entering the small living room. There stood a man, easily identifiable as Alec's father; despite the age difference, they looked alike. His father was slightly smaller, and where Alec's hair was dark brown, his father's was gray. Their eyes were an identical shade of hazel.

His father startled, the phone in his hand now forgotten. "Alec?"

"Yes, Dad, it's me."

"How did you get in here?" he asked, looking at Cronin, who Alec was shielding behind him.

Alec didn't answer him. He just strode over to his father and hugged him. "You okay?" he asked, pulling away.

"Yes, yes," his dad said, glancing around Alec at Cronin. "I'm all right. You scared me, is all."

Alec clapped his dad on the shoulder and walked over to the window, looked up and down the street, then pulled the curtains to the edges the best he could. His father had pulled the curtains across but strips of sunlight still framed the windows.

That was why Alec had stopped him from entering the living room, Cronin realized. He was protecting him from daylight.

Alec pulled at the curtains more thoroughly and when they'd been pulled as best as the material allowed and the room was void of sunlight, Cronin stepped into the room.

"Dad," Alec said, "I'd like to introduce you to someone."

His father still stared at Cronin, and eventually he nodded. "I know who you are."

Cronin returned the man's gaze, unsure of what he meant. Alec was obviously confused also, because he walked over to his father and asked, "What do you mean? Did you see him in the footage the other cops showed you of me disappearing?"

Alec's father nodded. "Yeah." He didn't take his eyes off Cronin. "But that's not where I know you from." He held out his hand for Cronin to shake. "My name's Kole MacAidan. I was wondering when you were gonna turn up. You're Cronin, yes?"

Cronin felt every hair on his arms and neck stand on end. This man, Alec's father, knew of him. He cautiously shook the man's hand so as not to be rude, though uncertainty wasn't a feeling he liked.

"Yes, my name is Cronin," he said. "I don't mean to offend, but if you would care to explain how you know of me."

"Yes, Dad, please explain," Alec said. He looked pale and his eyes were wide. "Because this is all new to me, so how the hell can you know who he is?"

Kole kept his eyes on Cronin, but he spoke to Alec. "I know he's the one who would come for you." Kole smiled, the same one-sided smirk his son had. "I know what he is. I know vampires are real. I've known for a long time."

Alec pulled at his hair and half turned away, visibly stunned. "You *what*?"

Kole looked at Alec. "You were born to be special, Alec. We knew that. My *seanair* told me when I was just a boy that our blood was special."

"Your grandfather?" Alec said.

"Yes, as did my father."

"And you're just telling me now?" Alec roared, anger rolling off him in waves, and Cronin was immediately by his side, his hand on Alec's arm.

Kole's voice was softer. "We didn't know it was you exactly. It's our bloodline, who we are, it's... significant. We don't know why or what for. But your mother was taken—"

"My mother died!" Alec hissed. "You told me that."

"Yes, she did. When you were just a baby. Some bad vampires killed her, Alec. She died protecting you," Kole said. He frowned. "That was when I knew. You've been protected by them ever since. All those times you should have died or been taken. I tried to deny it, Alec, I didn't want it to be you. I wanted you to be safe and just live a happy life."

"Why didn't you tell me?" Alec asked. His chest was heaving and his breathing labored.

"Because you would have thought I'd lost my mind," his father answered. "And as far as I knew, my *seanair* was just a crazy old man. And maybe I imagined the whole thing. Maybe losing your mother tripped some wire in my head. It wasn't until I got taken downtown and watched a video of you disappearing into thin air that I knew it was all *really* real."

Kole sat on the sofa and leaned back. The older man looked exhausted. "I thought you were dead."

Alec fell onto the sofa beside his dad and put his hand on his leg. "I should have made contact earlier, sorry. I've just had a lot to get my mind around these last couple of days." He shook his head. "I can't believe you knew about this all these years."

Kole petted Alec's knee. "I'm sorry I never told you. I wouldn't have known where to start if I'd tried."

"'S'okay, Dad," Alec replied with a quiet sigh, the anger obviously gone. "Can't change the facts now."

Cronin hadn't moved, and Kole smiled up at him. "So, you're the one for my boy, huh?"

Cronin nodded, though he was still alarmed by this man's knowledge of him. "Mr. MacAidan, I wish we could have met under different circumstances, and I regret not having a more formal introduction. If you'll please excuse my candor, but how do you know what I am to your son?"

Kole smiled. "The Japanese guy told me."

"Eiji?" Alec asked.

Kole shrugged. "Dunno his name. Kinda small and fast, moves too fluidly to be... ya know, human. Smiles a lot. Hasn't aged a day since I was a kid."

It was definitely Eiji. Cronin took a steady breath and spoke as calmly as he could. "He told you of me?"

"Not exactly. No details or anything. Just that I would have a son and he would be special. Nothing else, well, not then. I was about ten years old when I saw him the first time. He just kinda appeared outta nowhere, and maybe he was gonna kill me, I dunno. But he touched my arm and gasped like I was hot to touch. He laughed like a madman, and—I swear I'll never forget it—he said, 'Oh, finally' like he'd just heard the best news.

"I didn't know what he meant," Kole said. "I was just a kid. Then he told me not to be scared, that he'd protect me until my child was born. And I gotta say, to a ten-year-old that didn't make a whole lotta sense.

"I didn't see him again for years, and truth be told, I thought I'd imagined it. Until Alec was born. We'd just brought him home, a tiny newborn he was, and I saw that man again. Heather, Alec's mom, was in the nursery one night and I heard her scream. I raced into the nursery and there were two men with vampire teeth standing over the crib. My wife lay on the floor. Her head was at an odd angle and her eyes were staring blank. Then the Japanese guy flew past me—I've never seen anything move so quick—and when one of the others tried to take Alec, he stopped them. One minute there were two men and the next there was just dust. I didn't see what he did to them. But then he picked up the baby and handed him to me. He said the baby was special and that he would protect him, always, for Cronin."

Kole looked at Cronin and then Alec. "I didn't know who this Cronin was, until I saw that video. But the Japanese guy said Cronin would come for him, and that it was a very good thing. This special boy had been waited for, for a real long time. That was all he said. To be honest, with just having lost my Heather, I didn't think of it again until things started to happen to Alec when he was a boy. Strange things. Then there was the man at the indoor pool." He looked at Alec. "You remember that time some guy pulled you outta the water? I'm sure it was the same guy."

Cronin nodded. "I believe so, as well."

"You know this man?" Kole asked.

"Yes," Cronin said. "He's like a brother to me."

"And you're both... vampires?"

"Yes."

"They're good vampires, Dad," Alec said. "I mean, if there is such a thing."

Kole nodded slowly, then looked at Alec for a long time. "Are you okay, son? If this is not what you want, then we'll leave. Just you and me."

Alec smiled at his father, but his eyes flickered to Cronin, then back to his dad. "I can't explain it, Dad. But yeah, I need to be with him."

"That's not what I asked." Kole spoke like Cronin wasn't even in the room. It irked Cronin a little, but he realized Kole's only concern was for Alec, and that was reasoning he couldn't fault. "I asked if you were okay."

"I'm fine. It's been weird, I ain't gonna lie, but I'm okay." Alec looked back up at Cronin and a flush colored his cheeks. "I'm safe with him."

Kole looked between his son and Cronin, who still stood on the other side of the room, and back to Alec. "Well, I ain't seen you blush like that since you were a schoolboy and I asked you if you had a crush on that hockey player... what's his name?"

"Wayne Gretsky." Alec cringed. "But we don't need to talk about that right now, Dad."

Cronin smirked and Kole stood up and walked over to stand in front of him. "You wanna tell me what your intentions are with my son?"

Cronin blinked, though he was beginning to see where Alec got his brazen character. He lifted his chin and looked defiantly at Alec's father. "I am vampire. I've lived too long to apologize for such a fact. I feed on the blood of humans and have done for almost thirteen hundred years, but I *cannot* harm your son. My intentions with regard to Alec are honest, Mr. MacAidan. I want him only to be happy, and it is woven into the fabric of my existence to see him so. He was born to be by my side, and I at his. Whatever fate drew us together I do not know, but I am thankful."

Kole MacAidan stared at Cronin and blinked slowly. Obviously disregarding the parts about fate and happiness, he said, "Okay. So you kill people for food."

Cronin answered stoically. "Yes. Typically felons and those who intend to harm others, but yes."

Kole considered this for a moment. "But you're Scottish?"

"Yes."

Kole looked at Alec and smiled. "He's a Scot!"

Alec was still staring at Cronin, unmistakably mesmerized by the words of fate he'd just said, as though he'd never heard anything so beautiful. "I know, Dad."

Kole looked back at Cronin. "Thank you for being honest." He shrugged. "I guess." He shook his head, much the same way that Alec did. "And I was worried about him bringing home some tattooed punk or a Lakers fan."

Cronin gave him a smile, and Kole clapped his wide, hard hand on the vampire's arm. "Can I get you boys something to drink?" he asked, walking off to the small kitchen.

Alec's brow furrowed. "Ah, Dad. You understood the whole vampire thing, right?"

Kole opened the fridge door and stopped, then turned to face Cronin. "Oh, yeah. Sorry."

Cronin slowly walked over to the sofa and sat beside Alec. "Your father took the news better than you did," he said softly.

Alec smiled at him. "Told you we're good with weird."

"I don't know whether to be thankful or worried," Cronin whispered. "Your father seemed only concerned that I am Scottish. It pleased him greatly."

Alec snorted out a laugh just as Kole came back into the room and handed Alec a can of soda. "Okay, then," Kole said, sitting in the single seat across from them. He looked squarely at Alec. "So, all this happened three days ago? Start from the beginning."

Over the course of the afternoon, Alec told his father everything he knew. Everything that had happened from him chasing down the first vampire to leaping with Cronin and learning about vampire histories. Alec explained what had happened with the Yersinians—how the Black Plague wasn't really a plague at all—and how the pyramids found all over the world were ancient burial sites of vampires the world didn't want to see returned. He explained the recent development with a new breed of Egyptian vampire who was pushing out the old covens, and how it involved something called a key.

"Whatever they're planning is big, Mr. MacAidan," Cronin said. "The local Egyptian covens have left Cairo or disappeared, which is akin to rats abandoning a sinking ship. They're getting out while they can."

"There's a meeting of sorts on tonight," Alec said. "I guess it's to find out what we can?"

Kole shook his head slowly, the color drained from his face. He swallowed hard. "You said a *key*?"

"Yes," Cronin answered. "A key is the prophetic name given to an item that will see the demise of rogue covens. It is not always the same. The key that saw the demise of the Aztec coven was the Coyolxauhqui Stone. The key that saw the demise of the ancient Illyrians was the humble bow and arrow. You may have heard of the Egyptian 'nine bows'. As lore sees it told, it was effectively these nine Egyptian vampires alone who saw the Illyrians undone."

"So this key is not a living thing?" Kole asked. He was still pale, and Cronin wondered if he'd taken ill.

Alec leaned forward a little, clearly concerned by his father's reaction. "Dad?"

"Wait here," Kole said softly. He got up slowly and walked unsteadily out of the room. He came back with a book in his hands. It was large, and from the binding, Cronin could tell it was of a fair age. He handed it to Cronin. "You read Gaelic?"

"Yes," Cronin answered, looking at the book he held. It was of Gaelic mythology, folklore, and traditional Gaelic names and histories. He looked up at Kole questioningly.

"Do me a favor," Kole said gruffly. "Find the section on names."

Cronin flipped through pages until he found what Kole had instructed. Alec leaned over Cronin's shoulder to look at the book, and although he knew some Gaelic words, he was not fluent enough to read.

Kole sat down in his seat. He looked as though he'd aged a decade. "Our name, MacAidan, spelled with an *an* is the only one. All other MacAidens are *en*. The prefix of Mac means what?"

Alec answered that one. "Son of."

Kole looked at Cronin. "Look up the meaning of Son of Aidan."

Cronin turned the page and scanned down the lists of Gaelic definitions until he found it.

Key.

"My name," Kole said softly. "Kole with a K, not a C. It's not Scottish, but English. It means Keeper of the Key."

Cronin's eyes met Kole's. The old man swallowed hard. "We never chose the name for Alec. His mother and I had the same dream on the same night, the day before he was born. We were both told what his name would be."

"You never told me that," Alec said.

"We never told anyone that," his father answered. Then he looked back to Cronin. "We call him Alec, but his real name is the Gaelic adaption, Ailig."

Cronin turned back a few pages until he found the name and his blood ran cold. His eyes shot to Kole, and Alec's father nodded slowly.

Cronin turned to Alec. "We need to leave."

"Why?" Alec asked. "What does it mean?"

Kole answered him. "Ailig means Defender of Mankind. Your name literally means Defender of Mankind; Key."

"We don't need to search for information on the key, Alec," Cronin said quietly. "Because it's you. That's why you've been tracked down, that's why you've been protected. *You're* the key."

"Me? Protected?" Alec asked, standing up. "You mean Eiji knew? Is that why he protected me? Cronin, the vampire who got shot with the wooden bullet, he called me Ailig. And it was Eiji who put him on detail;

he had to have known my real name. Eiji must have known what it meant."

Cronin blinked. This thought or realization was terribly unsettling. His jaw clenched and he stood up. He threw the book onto the sofa and held out his hand for Alec. "I don't know, but I can assure you I will find out."

Alec took Cronin's hand, the two looking only at each other for a long moment, then Kole quickly stood as well. Alec dropped Cronin's hand and hugged his father. "Stay safe, Dad."

"Will I see you again?" Kole asked his son.

Alec opened his mouth, but closed it again. He clearly had no clue how to answer. Cronin answered for him. "Yes. Mr. MacAidan, I'll do everything in my power to ensure you see him again, but right now we need to leave." Cronin held his arm out and waited for Alec to slide in against him.

Cronin couldn't believe he didn't see this before. He couldn't believe he didn't know.

His fated one, his Alec — the one he'd waited a millennium for — was the Key.

Cronin tightened both arms around him, breathing in his scent and feeling the warmth of home against him. "When we get to the gathering, stay close to me at all times."

Alec nodded against him, and they leapt.

CHAPTER NINE

Alec gritted his teeth and focused on the energy of leaping rather than the pain. When they'd arrived at wherever Cronin had taken him, he surprised himself by only needing a deep breath to shake off the lingering sting.

Cronin kept his arm around him, though, and it took a moment for Alec to get his bearings and orient himself. That was when he saw where he was.

It was a large abandoned warehouse. The floor space was huge and there were few windows, but from what Alec could see through the grimy glass, he was still in New York City and it was just getting dark.

Then he saw who he was with.

Cronin kept his body in front of Alec at all times, and with the many dozen vampires in the room, Alec didn't mind at all. Cronin told him to stay close, and now he knew why.

The warehouse was rectangular and there were no lights, which Alec realized was because the vampires didn't need illumination to see. There was a table at one end, close to where Cronin had brought them, and Alec saw Eiji and Jodis sitting at it. But Cronin didn't address them, he faced the hundred inquisitive faces of his fellow vampires, who were clearly curious as to why he'd brought along a human. He had their full attention.

"I'll have you know," Cronin said lowly. "This human man is mine. Touch him, even look at him in a manner I do not care for, and I will kill you myself."

Right, then. That was one way to say it.

Alec didn't know what to do or what was considered proper etiquette, especially now that Cronin had threatened to kill them if they looked him. He wasn't sure how to come back from that. Did he wave? Did he introduce himself? He wiped the palms of his hands on his jeans and smiled at every single vampire who stood, stunned, staring at him.

It was then that Eiji laughed from his seat at the table. "Nice introduction, my friend."

Cronin spun to face him. His voice was quiet, eerily so, and seething. "I need explanations from you."

If the whole warehouse wasn't quiet before, it certainly was now. The mass of vampires took a collective step back, and the dynamics in the room were clear to Alec. Cronin was someone important, and given there was one spare seat at the only table at the head of the room next to Eiji and Jodis, he deduced the three of them were important.

Eiji stood up. "Explanations of what?"

"Alec. You knew. You had him protected. It was how he could chase down a Seeker, it's why Mikka died protecting him."

Eiji shook his head. "Of course I had him protected since he was born. I told you this. What circumstance has changed, Cronin? To which explanation do you refer?"

114

"The vampire who died for me—was it Mikka?" Alec asked. Cronin nodded. "He called me by name."

Eiji looked confused. "So? He knew your name. Of course he did!"

"He called me Ailig," Alec explained.

"I don't understand," Eiji said. "Your name is Alec."

The gentle rumble in Cronin's chest became a dull roar. "His name is Ailig, traditional Gaelic. Roughly translated, Eiji, his name means The Key." There were quiet gasps from the other vampires. Alec didn't dare look at them.

Eiji's mouth fell open. "The key...?" He shook his head. "No..."

"Tell me you knew!" Cronin demanded. The hundred or so vampires in the room scattered to the walls.

"I knew no such thing!" Eiji defended himself immediately.

Jodis was now beside her mate. Her eyes were wide and filled with concern. "Cronin, he couldn't have known. He cannot lie to you."

"Then explain to me how he didn't know," Cronin asked. "He sees life maps with a touch. It's encoded in their DNA. So tell me. How did he not know? It seems a lie in either direction."

"All I see from Alec," Eiji said quickly, "is that he's important and that your lives are inextricably entwined. I see he is your fated one loud and clear. If I have misread his importance, I apologize. I saw his significance in relation to you, that is all, Cronin. Because of the magnitude he would mean *to you*. That is what I saw."

Alec could feel the anger leaving Cronin. Eiji's response, his justification and emotional reaction, was honest, and it was clear Cronin believed him. "Then how did Mikka know his real name?"

Eiji shook his head. "I don't know."

"I told him," came a woman's voice from behind them. It was an old voice, feeble, yet determined.

Alec turned to see who the voice belonged to, but Cronin maneuvered himself to put his body between Alec and the woman who spoke. He had to look over Cronin's shoulder to see her. She was old, with wrinkled skin and gray hair, clearly the oldest amongst the other vampires, which was remarkable given that every other vampire in the warehouse looked under forty in human years. How old they were in vampire years, Alec had no clue. But that wasn't the most significant thing about her. What stood out the most was her eyes. They were a murky, milky white, and there was no iris.

"I told him," she said again. "This one, your fated one, Cronin, is the Key. I have seen it."

A low growl rumbled from Cronin. "Explain!" he snapped. Again, the other vampires flinched, though the woman did not.

"I am a seer," she said. "You know this, Cronin. I have seen many things, of what has happened and of what is yet to pass. Born to Gaelic blood, not unlike yourself, your Ailig is the defender of mankind. He was born to be the key, Cronin, and a subject to his birthright, he shall be."

"Why was I not told?" Cronin was furious.

The woman, whose name Alec still didn't know, said, "There is safety in anonymity. Is that not a law we live by? The human was safer shrouded in secrecy. If his presence was made known, his life would have been over before it began." She lifted her chin. "No one was to know, not you, not Eiji, not Jodis. I am sorry for the betrayal—a crime fitting of punishment, I am fully aware—but it was to keep Ailig safe. It was not to benefit you, Elder Cronin, but all of our kind."

"Mikka knew," Cronin said, his voice just a whisper. "I assume Jacques does also, given he was sworn to guard Alec. Who else? And if they knew, Eleanor, where is the secrecy in that?"

Eleanor kept still, her unblinking eyes unnerving as she looked at Alec. "Only those two," she said. "When Eiji had set them the duty of protecting Ailig, I took it upon myself to divulge the secret. Eiji had explained that the infant, as he was then, was important, but gave no other information. Both Mikka and Jacques obliged because of their loyalty to this coven and its leaders, but they had to know the weight of such a duty. They had to know it wasn't just to protect him, as Eiji had said. They needed to know the magnitude of their responsibility—it wasn't just to offer their lives for your mate. It was also to protect the key."

Cronin looked at the crowd of vampires. "Jacques. Step forward."

A vampire came from the crowd to stand beside the woman named Eleanor. Eiji and Jodis now stood on either side of Cronin, Alec still shielded by him. Jacques was young in human years, maybe eighteen, he had blond hair and dark eyes, and spoke with a French accent. "Leaders," he said, bowing his head slightly.

"You stand by what Eleanor has claimed?" Cronin asked.

Jacques kept his head bowed. "I do. I was set to detail Ailig when he was just a newborn baby, as was Mikka. Eiji ordered us to protect the child until the day you found him."

"You knew of his importance?" Cronin pressed.

"Yes, Elder. Eiji told us what he was to you, Eleanor told us what he was to our kind," Jacques answered, still not looking up.

"Did you divulge this information to anyone?"

Jacques looked up then. His eyes dark and piercing. "Never."

"And Mikka?"

"His loyalty remained to his cause, Elder. He died protecting Ailig."

"You were there?"

"Yes. Ailig chased down the Seeker," Jacques said, and there was a quiet murmur through the warehouse. "We ran with him, of course. The Seeker was luring him somewhere, so we followed to find out what we could. But the Seeker turned, held a blow dart to his mouth, and shot at Mikka. I've never seen anything like it. Mikka stopped, just as Ailig jumped the wall. I wanted to follow the Seeker, to chase him down and demand answers, but I could not."

"Why not?" Cronin asked.

Jacques looked a little confused. "I could not leave Ailig," he answered simply. "It was dark and raining. He was alone. Much faster than his fellow policemen. He held Mikka and tried to save him, but it was of no use. I watched over him until he was at the police station and you arrived." Jacques bowed his head again. "It was the next day when I got word this meeting had been called."

Cronin studied Jacques and Eleanor. "You have both withheld information and therefore defied the laws of this coven. Eleanor more so than Jacques, but defied nonetheless," he said firmly, "an act not taken lightly." Both accused vampires bowed their heads.

Jesus, Alec thought. *Was there about to be an execution?*

"However, in light of the circumstances," Cronin went on to say, "I can see your reasons were justified. You kept Alec alive, not just because of what he is to me, but what he means to our kind. And yet it is I who is most grateful. Though know this: any further deception to any member of this coven, be it blatant lie or omission of fact, I will not hesitate to see you tried for treason."

Both vampires nodded before looking up. Cronin focused on Jacques. "You have protected Alec well."

"Thank you," Jacques replied.

"You are familiar with Alec's father?"

My father? Alec thought. *What?*

"Yes," the French vampire replied.

Cronin's voice was strong and resonated like that of a leader. "I want him kept safe. Protect him as you would Alec. Choose two to help you, and choose them well. I am entrusting his life to you."

Alec let out a breath of relief and fisted the back of Cronin's shirt in thanks.

Jacques nodded, but couldn't help but smile proudly, as if it was a great privilege. "As you wish." Then Jacques looked directly at Alec. "If I may, it is an honor to finally meet you."

Alec smiled at him. "Thank you." Alec heard Eiji chuckle, and when Cronin turned his head a little, Alec could see he was pleased.

"Eleanor," Cronin addressed the woman. "You will tell us all you know, all you have seen." Then he spoke louder, addressing the whole congregation. "And that goes for anyone here. There is a great movement of covens leaving the Middle East and we've heard whispers of the ancient Egyptian and Illyrians rising once more, though we have nothing to substantiate such rumors. We believe the two Seekers were Illyrian. They were searching for or trying to steal the key, which we now know is Alec. We also believe whatever they're planning will not happen directly on these shores, though that does not mean we are unaffected. If anyone here knows anything—if you've heard anything, whether you believe it fact or fiction—please come forward."

Then, in front of everyone, Cronin turned to Eiji. "I apologize for my earlier accusations. With little evidence I should have not let my emotions rule fair judgment. I hope you can forgive me, brother."

Eiji gave him a slow smile. "Your apology is accepted, although not necessary. If I had believed someone threatened my Jodis, I'd take off his head first and ask questions later. At least you asked questions first." Eiji put his hand on Cronin's shoulder. "It is a sentiment between fated ones, Cronin. You will defend Alec always, as you should."

"I've never doubted you before," Cronin said to him. Then he turned to Jodis. "And if I offended you, I am sorry."

Jodis smiled at Alec first, then Cronin. "No offense taken, my friend."

It was then Alec noticed one vampire in particular standing at the side, closer to the table of leaders but still separate. From his position in the warehouse, Alec deduced he was ranked a little higher than the majority of the coven. He also assumed, from the way this vampire stared at him with a look of shock and distaste when Eiji had called Alec Cronin's fated one, that this strange vampire didn't like the idea.

It was as though he was jealous. So Alec slid in closer to Cronin, keeping a hand on him at all times. It wasn't like him to be possessive like that, but he couldn't help it. He wanted there to be no mistake, human or not, Cronin was spoken for.

Distracting Alec from the unhappy vampire just a few feet away, Jodis put her hand on Cronin's arm, her eyes blue and searching. "Alec is the key? What does this mean?"

"I don't know," Cronin said softly. He turned back to Eleanor. "Eleanor, what have you seen?"

"I've seen Ailig running in dark corridors with walls of stone. There is sand on the floor, and the air is hard to breathe. I've seen—"

Cronin cut her off. "He's in Egypt?"

"Apart from flashes of hieroglyphics, there are no points of reference, but I believe it to be so, yes," she answered.

Cronin turned to look at Alec then, and Alec had never seen such fire in his eyes. Dark and raging, he put his arm around Alec's waist as if needing him to be closer.

"I've seen him fighting," Eleanor continued. "There are many. It is a war indeed, Cronin. The kind that changes everything we know."

Cronin hissed out a breath. "He's *fighting*? Am I with him?"

Her response was short and immediate. "Always."

Alec could feel the relief pour off Cronin. His shoulders even sagged a little, but then he took a deep breath. "Is he..." Cronin's eyes flickered to Alec, then back to Eleanor. "Is he human? When he's fighting. Is he human or vampire?"

"Human," she replied. "I cannot see why, but he needs to be human, Cronin." She shook her head a little. "I don't see the whys or hows, only what is. The key is human."

Eiji spoke next. "And what is the purpose of the key? What is Alec to do?" Eiji looked at Alec, his face concerned. "What becomes of him?"

"That I cannot see," Eleanor said. She moved her head from side to side again, as if trying to urge images to form in her mind. "I see power unlike anything we've seen since the Ancient Egyptians last ruled our kind. It is brewing, it is coming." She shook her head again and her face looked pained. "I can see nothing else. Only that the Key needs heart. Bravery and strength of will to face what comes, I assume."

There was a rush of unsettled murmurs through the back of the warehouse, then a voice called out, "I must see your elders." The man's English was good, though his Arabic accent was very strong.

The crowd of vampires parted to create a path for the man to walk down. Eiji and Jodis both moved to put themselves in front of Alec. It was a nice gesture and all, but it meant Alec had to dodge heads and shoulders just to get a glimpse of the man who came forward.

He was medium height, medium build, a Middle Eastern–looking man. Completely normal, for a vampire, but he was heaving, as if out of breath. And that wasn't normal, was it?

"My name is Bes. I am from the Egyptian Fatimid coven," he said, bowing his head. Vampire or not, he looked scared. "We know nothing of your territory or hierarchy, so please forgive. But I come with news you seek."

"You're from Egypt?" Cronin asked.

The man never lifted his head. "Yes. We've traveled far and fast to be here."

"You said *we*. How many are you?" Cronin pressed.

"There are six of my family, Elder. We sought refuge here, and I risk much by coming here to speak to you."

"Only six?" Jodis asked. "How many answer to your coven?"

"A thousand," Bes answered. He looked up then, for just a moment before his eyes went back to the floor. "But no more. Many left, many were taken, many died. There is much unrest in the lands of my home. The Mamluks, the other Cairo coven—once our enemy—have also fled. Those who left, left together, a banded coven as one."

"You joined covens?" Jodis asked. "From enemies to allies?" From the reaction of those around him, Alec could tell this was not common behavior in vampires.

Bes nodded. "Yes. There is much fear. Not from the Mamluks, but from what lies beneath."

"What is going on?" Cronin asked, clearly out of patience. "You came here with news, so speak it."

The vampire stranger nodded quickly. "There is a new coven, whose name I do not know. It is also a forged alliance, of Egyptian and Illyrian. They're working together."

"Two covens who have feuded for millennia are in alliance?" Jodis asked, her blue eyes wide with disbelief. "Why would the Illyrians join the Egyptians? They were responsible for almost wiping them out!" She looked at Eiji and Cronin. "This is absurd."

"To ensure they are not eradicated this time," Bes answered. "They'll be stronger together. Unstoppable. Maybe they were forced into it, I don't know. Word is, the new Egyptian coven is close, Elders, so maybe the Illyrians believe they'll be spared if they help them. Whether this is foolishness to think such a thing—"

"The new Egyptian coven is close to what?" Eiji asked.

"Close to success. They have acquired a vampire with a particular skill." Bes swallowed hard. "She can resurrect the dead."

A rush of whispers swept through the warehouse, murmurs of disbelief and fear. Cronin raised his hand and silence fell. He stared at Bes, who shifted his weight under Cronin's stare. "Resurrect the dead?"

Bes nodded. "I have seen it. Or rather, I have seen one that was returned." He had the attention of every vampire in the room. "Fully formed, a returned servant. His body... filled out somehow, though still discolored as mummies are, but his hair and nails were not returned, still dirty and black. And the smell" — Bes's mouth formed a watery line — "was exceedingly unpleasant." Bes shook his head, as if to shake off the memory.

"How does she do it?" Cronin asked.

"I know not of the process," Bes answered. "Only the outcome."

"There are thousands of interred dead throughout Egypt," Eiji said. "Still in the sands, in pyramids... Is she making an army?"

Bes shook his head again. "Not just any dead. Egypt's royalty."

"The Ancients?" Eiji whispered, his eyes wide.

Bes swallowed hard. "The rumor is, Elders, that she wants to bring back the worst of them all."

Cronin, Eiji, and Jodis all hissed, and for the first time since this whole thing began, Alec felt fear. Not fear from learning of the existence of vampires, not fear from being in a warehouse with a legion of them, not fear for his life, but fear because if Cronin was afraid, Alec was pretty damn sure whatever was going on wasn't good.

"What does that mean?" Alec asked, his voice quiet.

Eiji looked pale, his usual smile gone. "Osiris," he answered. "She's going to try and resurrect Osiris."

Alec felt the blood drain from his face. "The Egyptian God Osiris?"

Jodis nodded. "The god of the dead."

Bes's voice shook. "She wants to unleash the depths of hell and rule the world in fear."

Oh Jesus. Alec shook his head and asked a question he was pretty sure he already knew the answer to. "How does one bring back a god? One that's been dead for thousands of years?"

Cronin tightened his arm protectively around Alec. "She needs the key, Alec. She needs you."

CHAPTER TEN

The warehouse stood empty, save for Cronin, Eiji, Jodis, Bes, Eleanor, and, of course, Alec.

"You are the Key?" Bes asked, his eyes wide. He stared at Alec.

"We believe so," Alec answered.

"What does that mean?" Bes asked. He looked worried, scared even.

"We don't know," Jodis said.

"There is much we don't know," Cronin said. "We first heard news of covens escaping Egypt last month, with warning that war was coming. We had word from London and Moscow, wondering if the rumors of war were true. So many stories, but little proof."

"I swear to you what I have seen is true," Bes said. His body language screamed of honesty and desperation. It was hard to believe he was lying. "I have seen a returned one. I have smelled it..." He shook his head. "It is rotten flesh and myrrh, cassia, and camphor."

Eiji stepped forward and put his hand on Bes's shoulder. At first Alec thought it was just a reassuring gesture, but then he realized Eiji was using his skill of reading DNA. "We believe you," he said, and Bes was clearly relieved. Eiji gave a small, imperceptible nod to Cronin. Bes didn't see it, but Alec did.

"Tell us what you know of her," Jodis asked. "This woman vampire."

"They called her Keket," Bes whispered. "Queen Keket."

"Queen?" Cronin said.

"She demanded royal status," he said. "No one would dare defy her."

Eleanor swayed. "I see an Egyptian Queen, but there is only darkness around her," the older woman said. "Such anger and rage. But she is well guarded. Not just physically, but mentally as well. I cannot see past her."

"She is young," Bes said. "Only five years young of our kind."

"She's been vampire for just five years?" Eiji asked.

"There is little known of her human life. Some believe she was a doctor, but I cannot prove this," Bes said. "This is all I know. Please, I beg of you. We must stop this." Bes stared at Alec. "I know not what it means for you. I fear…" His eyes darted to Cronin and he didn't finish his line of thought. He looked back to Alec and bowed his head. "I will offer my help, my knowledge, and protection of your life with my own. It is the least I can do so that one day I might return home."

Alec took a step back. Jesus Christ. This man, this vampire, had just offered his life for him. What the hell was he supposed to say to that?

"You honor your coven," Cronin said quietly. "It shall not be forgotten. I hope you may return to your home as well, and if it is within my power, I shall see it done." Then he turned to Eleanor. "Eleanor, take Bes and his family, provide them with the shelter they seek, and acquaint them with territories and laws, so they may feed in peace."

The Egyptian bowed his head again, reverently. "Gratitude."

Cronin nodded just as reverently. "We will talk again soon."

"If visions come to pass," Eleanor said, tilting her head just so, "I will send word."

"Please make sure you do," Eiji said. "No matter how insignificant it may seem. You know where to find us."

"Of course," she said. The older woman put her hand out to Bes, and they took three steps backward before turning and leaving.

Without so much as a word, Cronin put one arm around Alec and touched Eiji with just his hand, who in turn touched Jodis. And the four of them were gone.

* * * *

Alec found himself in Cronin's living room. He immediately took a step back from Cronin so he could shake off the aftershocks of leaping. The pain was no longer there, but the memory of being pulled apart in one location and reappearing in another seemed to linger in his joints and muscles. "Argh," he said, shaking himself. At least he didn't scream.

It was 4:00 a.m. Alec was tired, though not from the lack of sleep, he realized, but from the weight of what he now knew. He ran his hands through his hair. "Well, today was interesting."

Eiji laughed. "Is that what the kids are calling it these days?"

Cronin put his hands to Alec's face. His dark eyes were endless night and swimming with worry. "Are you well?"

Alec nodded. "I need coffee," he said. "And food." Then he shook his head. "Pizza. And scrap the coffee. I want beer." Hell, he'd take shots of bourbon at this rate. "No, not beer. I want liquor. Bourbon, whiskey, I don't care."

"Done," Eiji said, and he walked out of the room with his phone already to his ear.

Cronin frowned, his hands still cupped Alec's face. "You're the key!"

Alec shrugged. "I guess that's kinda important, huh?"

"We have much to discuss," Jodis said, her voice soft but serious.

Cronin nodded and slowly dropped his hands from Alec's face. "Now we know what the Egyptians are planning."

Alec hated that Cronin was clearly upset. It made his chest ache. He put his hand over Cronin's heart, for nothing more than to offer him comfort, even if for just a moment. But he had questions. "I thought you said mummified vampires couldn't be brought back to life?"

"They can't," Cronin answered, then he amended, "Well, until now. This is new to us also."

"And what's up with Eleanor?" Alec asked. "She's blind, yes? But she can see? How the hell does that work?"

"She was blind as a human, what they would now call cataract blindness," Cronin explained. "Normally humans of that age are not turned, though she believes her creator was interrupted. Her blindness came through to this life, but she has mental sight. She is a seer. She can see the future, but not all things. It's a valuable gift, but fallible."

Eiji walked back into the room. "Pizza and liquor is ordered. It will be delivered as soon as possible."

"Delivered?" Alec questioned. "It's four in the morning."

"Money can buy anything," Eiji said with a smile. "Though I was unsure of how much pizza one human could eat." He shrugged. "You are hungry, yes?"

"Starving," he replied.

Cronin flinched. "I should have realized. I apologize."

"It's fine," Alec said. "I didn't realize I was even hungry until now." He turned back to Eiji. "You touched Bes and gave Cronin a nod. What did you read from him?"

Eiji smiled. "You don't miss much, do you?"

"No."

"He has honor. Not just to his country, but to do good. His life has intention, honesty. And he lives a while yet. Many years."

"You can see lifespans?" Alec asked. "What have you seen of mine?"

Eiji smiled, though he looked mostly at Cronin. "I have seen many years for you, my friend. Many years."

Cronin sighed and closed his eyes, as if Eiji's words soothed him. Alec lifted his hand from Cronin's chest to his face. "You asked Eleanor if she saw me human or vampire?"

Cronin nodded. "It's harder to kill a vampire than a human."

Alec understood what he meant. He pulled his hand back. "You would change me?"

Cronin's answer was immediate. "Yes."

"And if I don't want to be changed?" Alec asked. "Were you even going to ask me what I wanted?"

"I thought only of your best interest," Cronin started to say.

Alec pointed his finger at Cronin. "Well, let's discuss your best interest, shall we? If you change me without my consent, you'll spend eternity walking with a fucking limp, understand?"

Cronin had the decency to look rebuked, whereas Eiji laughed long and loud. "Oh, Alec, you are such fun." Even Jodis smiled.

Alec rubbed his temples while Cronin told Eiji and Jodis of their meeting with Kole and how he'd explained the chosen name of Ailig. Then Cronin told them how Kole had relayed the stories of a certain Japanese vampire who'd saved Alec's life many times over the course of his childhood.

Eiji laughed, clearly delighted. He clapped his hands. "Oh, the bike incident was the funniest—"

Cronin's eyes shot to Alec. "What bike incident? You never mentioned a bike incident."

Just as Alec was about to speak, his head began to swim with hunger and fatigue. He was saved by the concierge calling to say a delivery of food had arrived, and Eiji went to collect it. Alec went to the bathroom to wash up, and if he were honest, to avoid making eye contact with Cronin. He was still pissed at him for even considering changing him to a vampire. It was just a few moments later that the aroma of pizza lured him out to the kitchen. Alec hadn't realized just how hungry he was.

He also hadn't realized Eiji had no idea how much pizza one human could eat. "I wasn't sure which you preferred," Eiji said by way of explaining the dozen pizza boxes on the kitchen counter.

Alec stared at the mountain of food. "So you ordered one of each?"

Eiji grinned proudly, then nodded toward the crate on the floor. "And there is also the liquor you requested."

Alec looked at the wooden crate that had twelve different bottles in it: a dozen different types of scotch and bourbon. He opened the first box of pizza, not even caring what kind it was, took out a slice, and bit into it. He scarfed down two pieces and reached for the familiar red bottle cap in the box. Alec wasn't much of a drinker, but his father loved a Johnnie Walker nightcap, so Alec thought it was fitting to choose it.

He didn't bother with a glass. Alec opened the bottle, lifted it to his lips, and drank a mouthful straight. It burned down his throat, liquid fire, and when a rush of breath escaped him, Alec half expected to see flames.

"Jesus," he breathed, shaking his head. "That tickles." And because Cronin looked a mix of concerned and horrified, Alec stared him right in the eye and took another swig from the bottle.

Eiji bit back a laugh and Cronin pressed his lips together, clearly less than amused. "It's not funny," Cronin said. "Inebriation dulls the senses."

"I think he's entitled to have his senses dulled a little," Jodis said. "He was certainly thrown into the deep end today."

Alec bit into another slice of pizza. "Thank you," he said with his mouth half-full.

Cronin looked at Jodis and Eiji then. "Again, Eiji, I am truly sorry for blaming you for withholding information. I should have known better. My reasoning was clouded by fear, and I am sorry. I hope you can forgive me."

Jodis smiled at him. "Your newfound loyalty to Alec is confusing for you, though reasonable, Cronin.

We understand, truly. Don't apologize for something you cannot control."

Eiji snorted out a laugh. "Do you not recall the times when we had not long met that I accused you of harboring affection for Jodis? I was struck with madness."

"You were struck with love and fate," Cronin said with a smile. "And a dash of idiocy."

Eiji raised his eyebrows and gave a pointed nod toward Alec. "Touché, my brother."

Cronin's eyes went wide before he schooled his features, and he quickly turned to face the window. "I, uh…"

Alec raised the bottle of scotch to no one in particular. "I *am* still in the room," he said, annoyed that they talked about him like he wasn't even there. He took another swig of liquor and it burned as much as the first and, as Cronin had said, it dulled his senses. It also dimmed his brain and loosened his tongue. "So, you guys never mentioned you were coven leaders."

Cronin still stared out the window, obviously not going to answer.

"Elders," Jodis corrected Alec gently. "We are the three remaining elders."

Alec was half-tempted to make a joke about their age, but one word stuck out. "Remaining? What happened to the others?"

Jodis answered. "The Yersinians."

"The Black Plague?"

"Yes," Cronin said finally, still staring out across the darkened city. "The elders, as we knew them, were killed."

Alec knew they weren't telling him something by the way Jodis's and Eiji's eyes darted to Cronin. Before Alec could chew his mouthful of pizza and ask what that was about, Cronin sighed and turned to face the other two vampires in the room. "Alec and I need to talk."

Well, that sounded ominous. Alec swallowed his food. "Is this the 'it's not you, it's me' speech?" he joked.

Cronin looked at him, confused. "I don't know what you mean."

"Never mind," Alec said. He took a quick sip of the scotch, his head buzzing. He pretended to speak into a police radio. "This is Detective MacAidan. I request an APB. I repeat, an APB on a sense of humor. Belonging to a Mr. Cronin I-have-no-last-name-like-Cher. Last seen approximately in the year 744. Yes, you heard correctly. 744."

Eiji burst out laughing and Alec joined in with him, swallowing another mouthful of scotch.

Then Alec thought of something. "Hey, when we left the warehouse, you brought these guys home with us," he said to Cronin, pointing his thumb to Jodis and Eiji, "and they didn't have to put their arms around you."

Cronin's lips twisted, and again, Eiji laughed. It only took Alec a drunk-hazed moment to figure it out.

He gasped at Cronin. "I don't need to put my arms around you at all, do I?"

Cronin smiled and looked to the floor. Clearly embarrassed, he shook his head. "No. Touch alone, by a fingertip if need be."

"So you just wanted me to put my arms around you, for no other reason than your own satisfaction?" Alec asked.

Cronin looked him in the eye. "Yes. The very first time, in the police station, I needed to feel you against me. I thought I'd rather die if you didn't." He swallowed hard. "I apologize for misleading you."

Alec snorted. Despite the white lie, Alec preened a little to know Cronin needed to touch him. "I don't know whether to be pissed off or impressed." Then he huffed. "Though don't lie to me again. You know how I talked about you walking with a limp for all of eternity? Well, that's what happens if you lie."

"Duly noted," Cronin said. Eiji and Jodis both laughed.

"And who was the freaky vampire in the warehouse standing to the left who was trying to kill me with his eyeballs?"

"Who what?" Cronin snapped.

"He was about five foot ten, wearing black pants, a blue jacket. Brown hair, dimpled chin." Alec said. He looked straight at Cronin. "Didn't like me standing so close to you."

"That would be Johan," Eiji said.

"Oh," Cronin mumbled. "I ignore him."

Alec bit into a piece of pizza, trying to act nonchalant. "An ex-boyfriend, maybe?"

Jodis, trying not to smile, put her hand on Cronin's arm. "We shall leave you to talk."

"No, we will go," Cronin said. "I want to show him something also."

"Does this involve leaping?" Alec asked, not sure how alcohol would affect his traveling. He also tried not to slur his words. "Because I think I'm drunk, and I don't want to be turning up god-knows-where in a jumbled mess because my brain's too wasted to put me back together again."

This time Cronin smiled. "You won't be affected."

Alec put his head down, suddenly feeling every ounce of alcohol in his blood. "Can it wait?" he mumbled. "This human's had enough for one day."

Cronin was quick to put his hand to Alec's chin and lifted it gently. "Alec?"

"Just tired, is all. And I have so many questions. So many," Alec said, and his eyelids suddenly weighed more than he thought possible. He fought to keep them open, Cronin's handsome face just a few inches away. "I wanna kiss you so bad."

Cronin blinked. "Oh."

"But I'mma go to bed instead." Alec pushed off in the direction of the bedrooms, past the dining table, stumbling over the sofa and almost walking into the hall wall. When he got to his bedroom door, he remembered Sammy and upon finding his own bed empty, he knew where the traitorous cat would be sleeping. Alec opened the door into Cronin's room and found Sammy curled into a ball of purring slumber. Alec considered picking up his cat and taking him back to his own room, but thought he just might lie down next to him on Cronin's bed. It sure did look comfortable, and it smelled so damn good...

* * * *

Alec woke six hours later. It took him a moment to realize where he was. He was sprawled diagonally across Cronin's bed, Sammy was nowhere to be found, and his head felt as though it was in a scotch-induced vise.

He was certain about one thing. He was *really* grateful for the sun-blocking window cover. The darkened room was a godsend, given his watch told him it was almost eleven.

"I trust you slept well," Cronin's voice was soft, coming from somewhere in the room. Too far away to be in the bed beside him, and a pang of disappointment sounded in Alec's chest.

"I must have fallen asleep in here," Alec said. "I was looking for my cat. I think." He sat up in bed and scrubbed his hands over his face and through his hair. "I'm sorry."

"Don't apologize," Cronin answered gruffly. "It would be dishonest of me to admit I don't like the sight of you in my bed."

Alec was still too half-asleep and too hungover, his normally quick-fired wit was nowhere to be found. So he groaned and palmed his dick instead. Apparently social graces were noticeably absent as well. He was also grateful he was still wearing his jeans. At least they would hide his morning wood more than if he'd stripped to his briefs. Though the risqué comment from a normally proper Cronin didn't go unnoticed.

"It's a remarkably great bed," Alec said. "It would be dishonest of me to admit I don't like the idea of you being in it with me."

Cronin cleared his throat, and Alec could hear him swallow hard. "I shall start the coffeemaker for you? Can I order you breakfast?"

"Coffee. I would kill for a cup of coffee."

"Do you always have these homicidal tendencies?"

"Only before coffee." Alec swung his legs over the side of the bed. "Um, were you watching me sleep? Because that's creepy."

Cronin snorted. "No. I came in to set down some clean clothes and fresh towels in this bathroom for you."

Alec stood up and stretched out his back, and then, because his dick was begging for friction, he gave himself a squeeze.

Cronin hissed out a warning. "Alec."

Alec imitated him the best he could with the sexy, gravelly voice, though it was comical at best. "Cronin." He laughed at the scowl the vampire gave

141

him. "Totally not my fault. Your bed smells like it was made just to turn me on."

Now it was Cronin who groaned. "May I suggest you sleep in your own bed?"

Alec nodded toward the bed. "May I suggest next time you join me?"

Cronin took a moment to reply. "May I suggest you take your shower cold?"

Alec snorted as he walked past him into the bathroom. "May I suggest you make my coffee hot?"

Alec stripped off in the bathroom, not caring if Cronin was still watching. In fact, he kind of hoped he was. He was still conflicted about Cronin. Alec wanted to know everything about him, he was intrigued by this age-old vampire, and he wasn't joking about Cronin joining him in bed. He wanted him, Alec couldn't deny it. His attraction to him was confusing, yes. But it was too damn potent to ignore.

Whatever this fated thing was, Alec could no longer doubt it. He felt it in every cell in his body.

That didn't mean he had to just give in or surrender his free will. It didn't matter if the planets aligned for their fates to meet or whatever cosmic, destiny bullshit made it happen. Alec was still a free-thinking human, and this predisposition toward Cronin—a man he'd known for just a few days, and a vampire no less— irritated Alec as much as it amazed him.

Alec didn't want to be told who he *had* to be with. He didn't want to be forced into something he might not otherwise choose. Yet when he thought about Cronin, a warm thrill charged his blood.

It was a heady mix of wanting to throw his arms around him or wanting to wring his freakin' neck.

And thinking about Cronin when in the shower did little for Alec's hard-on. Whether the vampires in the apartment could hear his soft grunts as he jerked his cock or if they could hear how his heart hammered or whatever, Alec didn't care. He stroked himself to mental images of Cronin, on his knees, underneath him, on top of him, inside him, until he came so hard the room spun and his knees gave out. He leaned with his head on his forearm against the tiled shower wall, catching his breath and clearing his mind.

Wow. Alec chuckled to himself. *Intense, and still not enough.* His dick was still hard and a thought ran through his mind that it would never be enough until Cronin took care of it for him. Alec shook his head, startling himself out of the orgasm-haze he'd been in. Alec didn't know whether that was just an errant thought or it was a stark realization.

He turned the hot water off and finished his shower under the cold.

Dressed, showered and shaved, Alec made his way out to the kitchen. Cronin was by himself, leaning against the kitchen counter with a coffee in his hand. He looked so… human.

He handed the cup to Alec. "As you like it."

Alec took the cup, breathing in the aroma as he sipped it. He put the cup on the counter, and leaning against Cronin, he slid his arms around him. Alec wasn't even sure why he did it. He couldn't remember the conscious decision to do it, only that it was a physical decision, not a mental one. Cronin was rigid, obviously shocked at Alec's embrace, but from the way he soon returned the sentiment, it was pretty clear to Alec that he certainly didn't mind.

Alec whispered, "Thank you."

"What for?" Cronin asked, his voice a gentle rumble in Alec's ear.

"The coffee. For letting me sleep in your bed." Alec pulled back. "Did you sleep?"

Cronin gave a small nod. "I took your bed," he said with a shy smile.

Alec wanted to ask if his scent affected Cronin as much as Cronin's scent affected him, but thought better of it. "And you only need a few hours?"

"Two or three."

"Is that where Sammy went?" Alec asked. "He was gone when I woke up."

"He seems to seek me out, yes."

"He's a traitor." Alec sipped his coffee. "I'm considering having him tried for treason. Either that, or I might get a dog."

Cronin smiled. "Did you want breakfast?"

"Yep," Alec said, trading his coffee cup for a pizza box from the fridge.

Cronin looked appalled. "Dinner leftovers?"

"Leftover pizza is the breakfast of champions," Alec said. He put two slices in the microwave and bit into a third piece cold.

Cronin's nose crinkled. "I will have to take your word for it."

"Does the smell bother you?" Alec asked.

"No."

"Did you want to try some?"

"I have as much desire to eat human food as you would to eat furniture. It is simply not a source of nourishment to me."

"So you drink only blood?"

"Yes."

"Is that where Jodis and Eiji are now?"

"Yes."

"Tell me about them," Alec said. "Jodis and Eiji. What's their story?"

Cronin smiled warmly. "Jodis is my dearest friend. A sister, if you will. She was from the village of Tromso, Norway. She was put on the Viking ship as a serf, and when they came ashore in Scotland, she met her end with a careless vampire. Whether he chose to change her or did not care of the outcome, she doesn't know."

Alec was intrigued, and he ate quietly, not interrupting once.

"And yes, she ended my human life and you may find this difficult to believe, but I bear no hard will toward her. It was a difficult time in Scotland, one you can't rightly imagine."

Cronin's lips curled into a small smile. "I was a soldier. We'd fallen in the war of the Picts, our numbers were decimated. I was one of many lying on a battlefield almost dead when Jodis found me. She'd come to the scent of blood — I can still recall the stench of death and peat and piss." Cronin's eyes were unfocused, seeing only memories. His voice was a whisper. "Jodis was young and hungry, scavenging from those clinging to life, feeding while their hearts barely managed to beat. They were going to die anyway, as was I. But by the time she found me, she'd had enough and pulled away before my heart had stopped."

Alec swallowed his mouthful of food. "Is that what does it?" he asked. "Bite, but don't kill?"

Cronin nodded. "Yes."

"And what about Eiji?" Alec pressed. "I mean, in the year two hundred and something... I can't even get my head around that."

"Eiji's story is an interesting one." Cronin smiled. "He was a guard to Queen Himiko. The palace was set upon by three vampires and, though small in number, that is more than enough to do serious damage. He defended his Queen and saved her life, but at the cost of his own. The Queen tried to save him apparently, but when he woke from fever, it was apparent he was no longer human. Even a newborn vampire, he was still devoutly loyal to her. She showed mercy to him for saving her life by sparing him, telling Eiji to leave and not kill any of her people. A true disciple, he did as she asked. He wandered alone for many centuries until he found Jodis."

"And it was fate at first sight?"

Cronin laughed. "Well no, as Eiji said, she scared him. Such beauty and the pull of fate—you've felt it, you know how unsettling it is—and he panicked. He didn't get far, as he told you the other night. He ranted at her in a language we didn't understand. Believe me, we can count our blessings we both speak the same language."

Alec snorted out a laugh. "I guess."

"I left them alone for some months. For my benefit as much as theirs," Cronin said. He blushed a little. "And when I came back, they had learned each other's native tongues."

"I bet they did."

Cronin chuckled. "Language, Alec. Native language."

Alec grinned at him. "How many languages do you speak?"

"Most of them. There are a few dialects from different regions that I don't need to know." Cronin shrugged.

"Just a few dialects, in all the world?" Alec asked, putting his plate in the sink. "Jeez, overachiever, much?"

Cronin fought a smile. "A lot of years, a lot of reading, and a lot of traveling will do that."

"You've done so much," Alec mused. "It's all so fascinating. I can't even imagine…"

"I can take you anywhere you want to go," Cronin said. "When all this is over, I can leap us anywhere you choose. I can give private tours of museums anywhere in the world at three o'clock in the morning, if you so wish. Or take you to the field of Yankee Stadium. Whatever you want."

"That sounds pretty cool," Alec said with a smile. He patted his belly, which was now full of pizza and coffee. Then he thought of something. "When was the last time you fed?"

"Two days ago."

"Is that too long?"

"I will need to feed soon, but it's bearable."

"What is not bearable?" Alec asked. "I'm just curious. I guess I should know these things. I mean, is it uncomfortable for you to be near me right now?"

"Of course not."

"Is it a hunger or a thirst? Does your throat burn until you feed or what?" Alec asked out of pure curiosity.

"It is a hunger," Cronin answered. "Though not like a human hunger. It affects the whole body, not just the stomach. The whole body craves it."

Alec considered this. "I can see that, I guess."

Cronin gave a smile. "You talk of such matter with ease. Does it not bother you?"

"Not as much as I thought it would," Alec said. "I try not to think about the human loss of it, to be honest. Kinda like how I try not to think about the pigs that die to give us the amazing thing that is bacon."

Alec stared out the kitchen window for a while, looking over the city as he thought about what he just said. "I'm not sure when I stopped caring for human life... I'm a cop, I shouldn't..." He shook his head. "I don't know when that changed."

"When you changed," Cronin said softly. "When you met me."

"I changed when I met you?"

Cronin nodded. "As I did when I met you."

Oh. Alec paused. "Is that part of the fated thing? We change?"

"Yes. Fundamental changes to our psyche to adapt to the needs of our significant other."

"But I'm still me," Alec said quietly.

Cronin gave him a small smile. "You will always be you. You just adopt certain tolerances."

"So, normally if something pissed me off with someone, like something they did — like snoring! If they snored — I'd hate it, but if *you* snored, I wouldn't care."

"I don't snore."

"That wasn't my point."

Cronin chuckled. "Your point was correct, yes."

"So what pisses you off in other people but not in me?"

Cronin thought for a moment. "I don't like being interrupted when I'm talking. It is frustrat—"

"Like that?" Alec said with a smile. "Like me interrupting you like that?"

Cronin huffed. "Yes, like that."

Alec snorted. "But it still annoyed you."

"It's a work in progress." Cronin let out a half laugh, half sigh. "It frustrates me far less with you than someone else, believe me."

"Then I shall try my very hardest not to interrupt you ever again," Alec said with a smirk and flick of his eyebrow that meant he shall try his very hardest to interrupt Cronin every chance he got.

Cronin sighed. "I also find sarcasm rather tiresome."

"Excellent." Alec laughed and finished his breakfast and made himself more coffee.

As Alec leaned against the kitchen counter with his second cup of coffee in his hand, it was as though Cronin was waiting for him. He cleared his throat. "So, given the events of yesterday, I wondered whether you wished to continue our date? Considering it was cut short."

Alec hid his slowly spreading smile behind his coffee cup. "I would love to, but I thought research might be in order, given the events of yesterday."

"Research of what?"

Alec was stunned. *Research of what?* "Uh, everything we learned yesterday, none of which makes sense."

"Jodis and Eiji are seeking out information as we speak."

"I thought you said they were eating out?"

Cronin smiled. "They are doing both. They've gone to the Egypt —"

"They've *what*?" Alec cried, interrupting him. "By them*selves*?"

"They're safe," Cronin told him. "They're verifying the information Bes gave us yesterday. Though we've no reason to doubt him, I wanted to be sure."

"You asked them to go?"

"Yes. I took them."

"You *what*?"

"I was only gone for one second. The apartment is well alarmed, and you were sound asleep."

Alec put his cup down and ran his hands through his hair. "And?"

"And they are searching out any other information we might use."

Alec sighed. "And what about me?"

Cronin blinked. "I don't know what you mean. What about you?"

Alec took a deep breath and exhaled slowly. "I'm a detective. Figuring shit out is what I do. I research, I study, I figure shit out."

"Alec, I cannot risk you being out there. Please understand, it's not my wish to see you confined here, but until this risk is over…"

"I don't need to leave here," Alec replied. "As much as I'd like to." He rolled his eyes. "But we have this thing now called the Internet. I mean, it is only recent in your perspective of timelines, and I know you think Shakespeare is still classed as popular culture, but it is the *twenty-first century*."

Cronin glared at him for just a moment. "I take back what I said before. I do believe that I detest sarcasm more than being interrupted."

Alec ignored him and went to his room to get his laptop bag they'd brought back from his apartment. He'd just dumped all his belongings in the room, and everything was just as he'd left it. He didn't really have any intention of unpacking anything—his cheap, everyday things didn't exactly compliment Cronin's expensive furniture and antiques.

Alec tried not to think about what that said about him—about where he stood in comparison to Cronin—and he grabbed his laptop satchel and went back out to the living room. He pulled out the two-year-old laptop and upended the bag, letting the contents of cables and adapters fall onto the sofa. "Have you got Wi-Fi?"

Cronin looked at him for a long second. "I have an office that may suit you better. You know, with that modern Internet technology you speak of."

Alec sighed, long and loud. "You're gonna make me look like an ass for the Shakespeare comment, aren't you?"

Cronin fought a smile. "Come with me. You can make your own conclusion," he said, walking through the kitchen toward the other end of the penthouse where the cinema room was.

Alec followed, and Cronin stopped at a door Alec hadn't paid any attention to. Cronin told him this was the office when they'd gone into the media room the day before, but he didn't think any more of it. "Any other rooms in this place I should know about?"

"No." Cronin said simply. "I have other houses, though."

Alec's eyes widened. "You do?"

"Yes. In Japan, though that's more for Eiji and Jodis. And another in London. I don't really have a need for another house, I can just leap to and from here as I please, but it helps to move around a little."

Alec was flabbergasted. "Right. Of course you do."

Cronin gave him half a smile, then opened the door he stood in front of. It was an office library of some sort, with hundreds of books on the walls, the gilded leather bindings, some hand-stitched, giving Alec a clue to their age. There were some more artifacts that looked very old on one shelf, and all the relics were juxtaposed by a very new-looking dual-screen computer system sitting on the center of the desk.

"Is this the technology you speak of?" Cronin waved his hand at the chair, signaling for Alec to sit in the chair. "I may be old, Alec. But I am not naïve."

"I'm sorry," Alec said quietly. He took Cronin's hand and waited until he looked him in the eye. "I'm sorry."

Cronin finally smiled. "Please, use anything you find in here. What is mine is yours." With a nod, he turned and left Alec alone.

Alec plonked himself in the chair, angry with himself for hurting Cronin's feelings. He thought Alec considered him naïve when the very opposite was true. Cronin knew more of this world and its histories than Alec could even begin to understand. Cronin understood human behavior *and* vampire behavior.

"Cronin?" Alec called out.

Alec half expected him to leap, appearing right before his eyes, but he didn't. He walked slowly at a human pace back through the door. "Yes?"

"Will you stay and help me?"

Cronin smiled, slow and beautiful, and walked into the room.

CHAPTER ELEVEN

Alec smiled, instantly relieved Cronin was going to help him. "I promise not to interrupt or use sarcasm. Or make any reference to your age."

Cronin raised one eyebrow. "Was that sarcasm?"

Alec snorted out a laugh. "No. I mean it. I don't want to hurt your feelings. And I am truly sorry about the whole Shakespeare being popular culture comment."

"Well," Cronin said, leaning against the desk. "He had neither popularity nor culture."

Alec blanched. "No freakin' way. You knew Shakespeare?"

"He was an odd fellow, but open-minded enough to know humans weren't the only creatures who ruled the earth."

Alec couldn't believe it. "You're kidding, right?"

"Yes, totally."

Wait. What? *He was totally kidding.* Alec growled. "I hate you. You really had me going."

Cronin laughed and nodded toward the computer screen. "Research. Where will you start? I have texts on Egyptian hieroglyphics and histories that predate censorship. They may be of use."

Oh right. Research. Alec pointed to the computer. "Well, I thought I'd start with the woman."

"Queen Keket?" Cronin asked. "I don't think she would have her own wiki page just yet."

Alec gaped. "Is that sarcasm? And a sense of a humor? *And* a reference to the twenty-first century?"

Cronin smiled. "Yes. I believe it was."

Alec laughed and shook his head at him, then turned back to the computer screens. "Wiki pages are good for gossip and college students who want to fail, not fact. Let me show you how a detective does it."

And for the next few hours, Alec and Cronin worked side by side. Alec searched the Internet, cross-referencing information, double-checking and filling in gaps on the timelines of missing women in Cairo. The more information he uncovered, the more crosses he put through possible suspects. He was down to three remaining names, so he made phone calls both Cairo University and Cairo police, using his detective credentials and claiming to be working on a related case, and when Alec put the phone down he put lines through two other names, leaving only one. He was certain he knew who it was. He grinned proudly, pleased with himself, loving nothing more than doing the detective work, putting the intel puzzle pieces together.

"Tahani Shafiq," Alec declared. "Twenty-seven years old, parents reported her missing five-and-a-half years ago. She worked at the University of Cairo Medical Research faculty, studies concentrated on stem cell therapy."

"Regeneration," Cronin whispered. "That would explain her ability to regenerate the dead."

"Yes." Alec nodded. "Funny you should mention that. Her colleagues at the university believed her work bordered on unethical. She lost a sister to cancer, and Tahani spent many years devoting her life to—" Alec looked at what he'd written down. "—self-renewal pathways in normal and malignant stem cells. She did lab work outside of 'Board protocol' was what they called it—they wouldn't elaborate any details— just that she was reprimanded twice."

"Hmm." Cronin sighed and closed the book on Egypt mythologies he was reading. "Anything else?"

"Six months before her disappearance, Tahani Shafiq lodged an official complaint to the Faculty board, citing sexual assault by two male colleagues. Her reports to the police were identical, and hospital records support her claims. Charges were never filed. The two men were never even questioned." Alec shook his head. "Those two men, Nader Tulun and Gamal Mahfouz, were found five years ago, bodies drained and mutilated. According to police reports, both men suffered horrendous injuries to genitalia and the anal cavity while still alive."

"She must have been very angry," Cronin said quietly.

Alec nodded. "Eleanor said she saw only anger and rage around her." He threw his notepad onto the desk. "It would also explain her intention to resurrect the god of the dead. I mean, such anger and rage would fuel the desire to see the end of the human race, would it not?"

"I wouldn't dare to guess," Cronin said.

"What did you find?" Alec asked, nodding toward the books Cronin had spread over the desk.

He frowned and his eyebrows almost met. "Accounts of fact vary and much is lost in translation. And of course, what is documented is far from what may have actually happened, even in these early books."

"Okay," Alec said. "Then forget the books. Tell me what you know."

Cronin smiled. "Osiris was a very powerful vampire. He ruled over much of the East around the time of 2400 BC. As lore tells us, he had the power to evade death. He did not just have the immortality of vampirism, but no wooden stake could penetrate his skin and the rays of sunlight did not affect him."

"How is that possible?"

"No one knows. It was his gift, his talent. He is said to have had unusual skin. Impenetrable."

Then Alec remembered the pictures of Osiris he'd seen. "He was always drawn in hieroglyphs to have green skin."

"Yes, that must be why."

"Why do you think Queen Keket wants him?" Alec asked. "Because he was the most powerful vampire to have lived, I guess."

Cronin gave a nod. "It is likely. Her exact reason I can only guess at. Though it has to better her cause, so

I would guess she wants him returned for his powers. Given her skill at regeneration, maybe she can harvest the talent of others? I simply do not know."

"Harvest the talent of others?" Alec repeated in a whisper. He shuddered to think what that could mean.

"Maybe she believes she'd be more powerful with him by her side?" Cronin added. "Maybe she's a megalomaniac who believes all power is victory. Alec, I don't know what her objectives are, other than what we've been told. The rest are merely hypotheticals."

"Well, hypotheticals can sometimes lead to answers," Alec said. "And you're obviously a facts-only kind of guy, you like your information cut and dried, black and white. You don't care too much for the why or how, but that's how I think. If we're to beat this woman, we don't just need to know the what, where, and how. We need to know why. Because it's knowing *why* she's doing this that will bring her undone."

Cronin smiled at him. "To reveal her weakness?"

"Exactly. The psychology behind it is where the answer is. And you know what I fear the most?"

Cronin tilted his head. "What's that?"

"Someone with nothing to lose. And right now, she's all about gaining power, reputation, she's demanding respect with the self-professed title of Queen. Cronin, she has everything to gain and absolutely nothing to lose."

Cronin nodded. "I think you're right."

"How did Osiris die?" Alec asked.

"He was not immune to the powers of others. There was a vampire with the ability to sedate or put in a state of sleep. According to lore, Osiris was overcome by a deep calm and heavy limbs," Cronin said, "and he was embalmed."

"While he was still alive?"

"Yes."

"Oh good. So he'll be pleasant and cheerful when he's brought back to life, won't he?"

Cronin snorted out a laugh. "Yes. He and Queen Keket make a good pair."

"A dangerous pair. Revenge is a frightening motive," Alec said. Then he remembered something. "Hang on a minute. I thought Anubis killed Osiris."

Cronin gave him a small smile. "Anubis embalmed him, yes."

"And who was the sedater? The one who can put vampires to sleep?"

"I don't know," Cronin answered. "I don't believe it was ever said. Probably to protect their identity."

"Is it possible they're still alive?"

Cronin's eyes widened, the question was clearly not one he'd considered. "I don't know. I've not heard of such a vampire in my time."

"Shame," Alec said. "We could use them to help us."

Cronin's phone buzzed in his pocket. He pulled it out and read the text. "Eiji and Jodis need me to collect them."

"Okay."

Cronin looked torn. "I don't want to leave you unattended."

Alec smiled until he saw that Cronin was serious. "I'm sure I'll be fine. You left me before when you took them to... wherever. You said it took a whole second?"

Cronin cringed. "You could come with me?"

"And go through two bouts of unnecessary leaping?" Alec scoffed. "No thanks."

Cronin half turned, but seemed stuck.

"Seriously," Alec said. "In the time it takes for you to get them and come back, I will sit here and have enough time to blink."

"I don't like leaving you," Cronin said softly.

"Then tell Eiji and Jodis to take a plane."

"Air travel is not recommended, especially if the flight has daylight duration."

"I was joking."

"Oh."

"Go. Jeez. You could have been there and back three times by now."

"Are you certain you'll be okay?"

"I'll try not to injure myself blinking in the time you're away."

"I thought you said you'd refrain from the use of sarcasm."

"What can I say?" Alec rolled his eyes. "I must be hungry."

Cronin pulled out his wallet and laid a credit card on the desk. A *black* credit card. Jesus Christ. Alec had heard these existed. Never in his life did he think he'd ever see one.

"Please, order yourself whatever you wish."

Alec reached out slowly and picked up the card from the table. The name on it was James T. Furst, and Alec snorted. When Alec looked up, Cronin wasn't there. He blinked, startled at the sudden disappearance and then almost had a goddamn heart attack when Cronin, Jodis, and Eiji suddenly appeared where Cronin had stood just a moment before.

"Jesus H. Christ!" Alec put his hand to his heart. "Can you ring a fucking bell or something?"

Eiji laughed. "Nice to see you too, my friend."

"Sorry," Alec apologized, though his heart still pounded in his chest. He looked at Jodis. "Sorry for the language."

"Ah, don't apologize," she said with her usual calm smile. "I am used to such customs."

"Did you order yourself something to eat?" Cronin asked him.

"I had exactly enough time to pick the card up off the desk," Alec said, "and blink. Oh, and to have a coronary." Alec ignored the scowl from Cronin and looked at the time. He didn't realize that he and Cronin had been in the study for so long. No wonder he was hungry. It was almost five o'clock.

Alec knew there was a ton of pizza left over, but he'd eaten it for dinner last night and breakfast this morning and he couldn't stomach the idea of eating it again. But before he could think about food, Jodis said, "We have news. And it's not good, I'm afraid."

"What is it?" Cronin asked.

"We found out a little about the woman they call Queen Keket," Jodis said. "She was a research doctor at the Cairo University."

"Yes, her name was Tahani Shafiq," Alec told them. "She worked extensively on stem cell development. She was wronged terribly by two men who assaulted her, then wronged again when she tried to report it and was ignored."

"You know this, how?" Eiji asked. "We've just been to Cairo and couldn't find out that much."

Cronin smiled a little proudly. "Alec is very good at what he does."

Alec snorted. "Yeah, it's called the Internet and being a cop for ten years."

"But there was something else," Eiji said. "We spoke to a small coven of vampires who, like Bes said, were fleeing. They told us Queen Keket had sent out Seekers to search for the key."

Jodis continued. "We told them the Seekers failed. They laughed, Cronin, and said many more had been dispatched. The two who were here in New York earlier were merely scouts. Keket's first division of Seekers are already on their way, the soldiers are to follow. They knew the key was in New York. The scouts or Seekers must have told them."

Cronin hissed through clenched teeth. "How long until they get here?"

"We don't know. We called for you as soon as we heard this," Eiji said. "Possibly a day or two."

"They're coming for me?" Alec asked.

Jodis nodded. "Many."

"Um, quick question," Alec said, his mind swimming. "How did they know I was the Key when we've not long figured it out?"

"A seer, a tracker, or both," Eiji answered quietly. He looked to Cronin. "I wish I'd told you of Alec sooner. He is now threatened, and I am sorry."

Jodis put her hand on Eiji's arm. "You weren't to know."

Right then, with no concept of timing, Alec's stomach growled. He shrugged. "Sorry."

Cronin turned to Eiji. "Can you please order him something to eat?"

"I'm capable of ordering myself something, thanks," Alec said sharply, but Eiji had already nodded and had his phone to his ear. He spoke quickly, a language that was not English, and Alec deduced he was having Japanese for dinner. He threw the credit card he was still holding onto the desk. "Gee. Thanks."

Eiji walked out, his phone still at his ear, a smile on his face.

"We must meet with our coven to discuss options," Jodis said. "We are short on time, Cronin."

Cronin nodded. "Please, see it done. For tonight if we can arrange it."

She nodded and left the room so quickly Alec barely saw her move. He put his hands in his hair and sighed. "So whatever is happening, is happening now. They're coming for me?"

"Yes."

Alec dug the heels of his hands into his eyes, then scrubbed his face. "Even though we still don't technically know what they want me for."

Cronin didn't answer for a long second. "I am sorry I cannot give you more information than that. I wish I knew, because then I would know how to stop it."

"But you have a theory, right?" Alec asked quietly. "You have some kind of idea what Keket actually needs me for? Like what the key truly is?"

Cronin frowned. "I have a theory," he said softly, reluctantly. "Keket wants to resurrect Osiris, we know that. Now, I am not familiar with her abilities, but I am well-versed in Ancient Egyptians. We know Anubis embalmed him and we know in order to do that, he removed the heart of Osiris. There is much speculation about why he removed and weighed the hearts of those he embalmed. I know not why he did it, only that he did."

"You think she needs my heart?" Alec asked. "Is that why I'm the Key? She needs my heart to bring back Osiris?"

"Anubis removed Osiris's heart," Cronin said. "It is one of the only facts that historians got right. It is the one critical component that's missing, so it makes sense that the key is that component."

Alec swallowed thickly. "My heart...?"

"It is only a theory," Cronin said.

Alec looked up at him. "It makes sense." Then Alec remembered something. "And Eleanor said that I'd need my heart to beat her. She presumed it meant courage or something..."

Cronin frowned. "I don't like it, no matter how it's referred to."

Alec took a deep breath. "Well, at least now it makes sense. At least we know what she wants. I guess that's something." He looked up at Cronin. "Why me, though?"

"We don't know," Cronin answered. "As far as memory serves, there's never been a living key. The key has always been an inanimate object: a stone, a scroll, a chalice. Never a person. This is new to us all."

Alec nodded slowly. "My dad said something about my ancestors saying it was in my blood. My name was chosen for me, and those vampires that killed my mother knew I was special, even when I was just a few weeks old."

Cronin sighed. "I would guess they were Seekers in their own right. Eiji killing them both then and there saved them telling of what they'd found and where you were."

"Telling who?"

"Anyone. Seekers usually come with another skill," Cronin explained. "It's what makes them so good at what they do. Some are seers, so they would have seen your future. Some are cloakers."

"What's a cloaker?"

"Someone who can vanish, or disappear."

"Like you?"

Cronin smiled. "No. They don't leap to another place. They become invisible."

"For real?"

Cronin chuckled at Alec. "Yes. For real. Though that kind of talent normally has to be registered within their coven. Such skills can be useful, but they can also be used against the coven, so we keep tabs on them."

"Are there any cloakers in your coven?"

"No. I know of two in the world. One is in China, the other in South America. It is not a common talent."

Alec leaned back in the chair and sighed. He needed to know everything he could, to at least try and understand what he was up against. "Talents or skills from human lives develop into vampire talents, yes?"

"Sometimes, yes."

Alec spoke his theories out loud. "And Jodis's ability to turn objects into ice, I can assume is from her Nordic heritage. She was a Viking; they came from icy lands. I get that. And if Tahani Shafiq was some expert in stem cell development when she was human, that made her talent as a vampire to regenerate the dead."

"It would seem so, yes."

"But sometimes talents are random, like Eiji, right? He sees DNA coding? Well, I can assure you, when he was human there was no such knowledge of any of that. So sometimes it's just random."

"Yes. And not all vampires have a talent or gift. Though all vampires have speed and agility, very quick thought processes, and we can concentrate on many things at the one time."

"And your ability to leap? That was random, yeah?"

"I've given this a lot of thought," Cronin said. He leaned against the desk, such a human thing to do. "Many of my friends, my brothers, were all married with families by the time they turned eighteen years, some were sixteen. I was twenty-four when I died, and I was not married. That is many years past what was the norm for my time.

"I did not fancy any girl in my village or that of any neighboring village. I didn't fancy any girl at all. A boy or two had caught my eye, but I was not free to act on such urges. So I busied myself with the war," Cronin said softly. "I spent a lot of time wishing I was someplace else, Alec. That's the only reason I can think of that my talent in this life would be leaping. I wanted to be anywhere else." He shrugged. "Now with just a thought, I can be."

Alec got to his feet and stood in front of Cronin. The sadness in his story, in his voice, hurt Alec in a way he couldn't vocalize. He slid his hand along Cronin's face and pulled him against his chest. The intimacy of it surprised Alec and he expected Cronin to pull away, but he didn't.

Then a soft rumble vibrated in Cronin's chest, and Alec gasped when he realized Cronin was purring. He pulled back and lifted Cronin's chin upward. They were so close, their faces just inches apart, and Alec wanted so badly to kiss him. He licked his lips and leaned down. Cronin's lips parted, his eyes closed slowly, and his fanged teeth glinted behind soft-looking lips. Alec could taste the sweetness of Cronin's breath, their lips just about to touch...

And there was a knock at the door.

Cronin growled and Alec took a step back, shaking his head of the lust-infused haze, just as Jodis opened the door.

"Apologies," she said, looking between the two men, a small smile playing at her lips as though she knew damn well what she was interrupting. Alec was pretty sure she wasn't sorry at all. "Cronin, a word?"

Cronin snarled. "Whatever is so important, just say it."

Jodis looked from Alec back to Cronin, her back straight and her smile gone. "You need to feed. It's been too long, and I don't suggest getting that close to Alec without being well-fed. His safety is my only concern."

"I would never hurt him," Cronin whispered. It was eerily quiet, yet somehow threatening.

"Cronin," she said calmly with an almost-smile. "I am not saying you would. I'm saying it's not worth the risk. May I suggest you take the time to feed before we have to deal with whatever comes our way? Your strength will depend on it, as does Alec's life."

Cronin grumbled something Alec couldn't quite make out.

Jodis gave a nod. "Until this is over, I think it would be safer if we fed separately, leaving two of us with Alec at all times, and it would probably be best if you went first, Cronin. I can't imagine you wanting to leave Alec the closer we get to any possible confrontation."

They were talking like Alec wasn't even there — again — and it really pissed him off. "I don't need a babysitter," Alec said.

Both Jodis and Cronin stared at him for a heartbeat, then back to each other like he hadn't spoken a word.

"What?" Alec said. "I can look after myself for a freakin' hour. Or did you forget that you locked me away in your ivory tower?"

"Alec, you are the key," Cronin said.

"So what?" Alec replied. "I can be here for an hour by myself, surely."

"You are also wanted by not one ancient coven, Alec," Jodis said, "but two. The Egyptians *and* the Illyrians want you. You will not be left alone."

Alec hated being spoken to like a child. "I beg your pardon?"

"I don't like it either," Cronin said. "But Alec, have you not understood any of what's gone on? Do you not know how important you are?"

Alec spoke through clenched teeth. "I'm not made of glass."

Cronin picked up the glass paperweight off the desk and crushed it in one hand. "You may as well be."

"Ugh," Alec groaned in frustration. He'd gone from compassionate to aroused to angry in the space of five minutes. "I know how important I am. Important enough to be held fucking hostage!" Alec stalked out of the room, pulling the door behind him, glad that it slammed shut.

He could hear a muffled argument between Jodis and Cronin as he stormed out to the living room. Eiji was standing near the sofa and gave him a sad smile. "Alec," he started to say.

Alec ignored him and pushed the door handle that lead out onto the patio. "He's the most infuriating fucking man I've ever met," Alec said, not caring if Cronin heard it. He kind of hoped he did.

The sun was almost set behind the city, though a few strands of sunlight still shone over the patio. Alec realized the height of the penthouse, bathed in the most sunlight, had its advantages.

No vampire could get him there.

He smiled as he felt the warmth on his face and the satisfaction that the three vampires inside were helpless to come out after him. Then a creeping feeling of apprehension crawled over him because... because Cronin was helpless to come out after him.

After a minute or two, he turned to face the glass wall. He could see nothing inside, only himself and the city mirrored back at him. He knew they were watching, though. He could feel Cronin's eyes on him and as much as it annoyed him, as much as it infuriated him that Cronin was watching him, it was oddly reassuring.

Nevertheless, he turned around to allow the sun to wash over him. The warmth of it on his skin after days of hiding felt heavenly, and he stayed that way until the sun had almost disappeared.

Alec knew the moment Cronin left, because he was barreled by a sudden wave of unease; restlessness and agitation sat heavy in his chest. He spun to face the wall, and the door opened.

No one came out, but Eiji spoke. "He's gone to feed. Your dinner is here also," he said.

With a sigh, Alec crossed the patio and stepped inside. "Thank you," he whispered.

Eiji smiled at him. "Please don't be mad at him. The conflict you feel, how your mind and heart push and pull, is the same for him. He has been alone a very long time, and he only wants you to be happy. You will have to adjust together."

"I know." Alec winced. "Has he gone for long?"

Eiji shook his head. "No. Even if you weren't being hunted by Seekers right now, that unease and fear you feel will keep him from being gone long."

"He feels it too?" Alec asked, pushing the heel of his hand against his heart.

"Yes."

Alec frowned and pulled the takeout container and chopsticks out of the bag, not sure he could eat, despite how hungry he was.

"Alec," Eiji said softly. "Don't disregard his concern for you. I don't think you grasp the severity of what could happen. His concern is not only for you because of what you mean to him, but for what you mean to all vampires, and humans for that matter."

Alec swallowed hard. He was embarrassed that he'd acted so childishly. "It's just all been talk so far. I get told I'm the key, I'm important, but it doesn't mean anything because it's just fables and stories, you know what I mean?"

Eiji blinked. "Not really, no."

"And Cronin," Alec continued. "God help me, that man does my head in."

Jodis walked into the kitchen and smiled. "Cronin is…" She seemed to search for the right word.

"Stubborn," Alec prompted. "Sexy as hell, frustrating, he smells so damn good, he's funny and so serious, and he completely does. My. Head. In."

Eiji laughed, his eyes crinkling at the corners. "That's funny," he said. "Cronin said something similar about you."

"He did?" Alec asked, probably a little too quickly. "I mean, not that I care."

"Mmmhmm," Eiji hummed. "Of course not."

Jodis put her hand on Alec's arm. "Cronin is very smitten with you. He falls deeper every day. It's confusing for him, but it's equally wonderful. Be patient with him. He's worth it."

Alec's head lolled back and he let out a deep breath. He didn't dare admit that he'd passed smitten like it was standing still. Instead, he collected his takeout and chopsticks and walked back to the door. "I might eat out here. The sun is almost gone."

Alec was distracted: his mind in a dozen different places, he was so hungry but had no appetite, and Cronin's absence twisted in his gut. He'd barely crossed half the patio and wondered briefly how much sunlight, or lack thereof, was required for vampires to walk around in the day when two vampires suddenly appeared in front of him.

Dark, hulking, and menacing, their sneers did little to conceal their fangs, and they both took another step toward Alec. "There will be no war if there is no Key," one of them said, his Russian English jagged and sharp.

Everything happened so quickly yet in slow motion at the same time. Eiji and Jodis were in front of him in an instant, defending him, protecting him. Like it was happening at half speed, Eiji snatched the chopsticks Alec had on top of his takeout and spun around at the vampires in front of him. Jodis turned too, her long white hair twirling around her like ribbons. Her hand went out and both vampires were still, frozen. Eiji used the chopstick like a stake, spearing one vampire in the chest, then the second vampire turned to dust as well. Alec was picked up and removed back into the safety of Cronin's apartment, all before his takeout dinner could hit the patio floor.

CHAPTER TWELVE

Alec was pressed up against the living room wall, his heart beating so damn hard it felt as though it would stop. He was safe, he knew he was, because it was Cronin who pressed against him. His scent was like a balm, soothing and warm. Cronin's hands pressed to Alec's face. "*Rug mi ort, rug mi ort,*" he whispered over and over. It was Gaelic, though Alec had no clue what it meant. Cronin pressed his cheek to Alec's. His eyes were closed. "*Sàbhailtcachd, m'cridhe.*"

All Alec could do was breathe, and even that wasn't easy. "What the… what the hell was that?"

Jodis and Eiji were back inside now in a flurry of checking doors, and some kind of metal walls were slowly rising to the ceiling where the glass wall used to be. "They were Russian," Eiji said.

Cronin pulled back, still cupping Alec's face. "Are you hurt?"

Alec shook his head. "No. Scared the crap outta me, though." He held up his hand and it was shaking.

Cronin was quick to take his hand and gave his fingers a gentle squeeze. He closed his eyes again and took a deep breath. "That was too close."

"Yes, it was," Jodis said. She still had her calm demeanor, though there was a fire in her eyes. "Alec, please tell me you are okay."

"I'm fine," he said. "Thank you. For saving me."

Eiji stood beside Cronin, but he spoke to Alec. "Do you understand now?" Eiji said. "Can you see the danger now?"

Alec nodded.

"They know where we are," Jodis said. "Cronin, you must take him. Just for an hour or so. It will be safer if he's not here right now."

Cronin nodded and looked at Alec. "It is not my intention to remove your free-will, but you must understand—"

"I'll go," Alec said. And he would. He'd go anywhere with Cronin. "I'll go with you."

"Grab a coat," Cronin said.

Still in shock, Alec took the first coat he could find in Cronin's closet, and with shaking hands, he put it on. When he went back out to the living room, Cronin was talking quietly with Eiji, and Jodis had a phone to her ear. Cronin was quickly by Alec's side. "Are you ready?"

No, I'm really fucking not. But he nodded anyway, slid his arms around Cronin and held him as tight as he could as they leapt.

* * * *

Whatever place they'd 'landed' in was dark, windy, misty, and cold. Alec shook off the aftermath of leaping, and although he didn't want to let go of Cronin, he did.

"Are you okay?" Cronin asked.

"Yeah."

"You're still shaking," he whispered.

"It's been a helluva day," Alec said. "And it's freezing."

Cronin did the buttons up on Alec's jacket. "I should have suggested gloves as well, sorry."

"'S'okay," Alec said. "Just a bit of a shock coming from a climate-controlled apartment to being outside in the cold in half a second. I'll get used to it." Looking around, he tried to take in his surroundings, but it was too misty and his eyes had not yet adjusted to the dark. "Where are we exactly?"

"Scotland."

"Really?"

"Yes. Can you not smell it?"

"Can I smell Scotland? Uh, no."

Cronin snorted. "The moors and damp heather. It is wood and peat, yet there is an underlying sweetness."

"You just described how you smell," Alec said quietly. "Though I would have just called it an earthy smell."

"I smell of earth?"

"You smell of moors and damp heather, apparently," Alec said. He didn't have time to be embarrassed for noticing such a thing. He looked around again, and this time could make out large stone walls, mossy and wet, and Alec had the distinct feeling he was outside. Was it an open corridor? "Are we safe here?"

"Yes. For now." Cronin took a step back from Alec, putting a foot of distance between them. "I wanted to bring you here the night before, though you were tired."

"Your accent seems a little thicker here," Alec noted. "I like it."

Alec's eyes had adjusted enough to see Cronin smile. He could also see that they actually were in some kind of open corridor, stone walls but grass underfoot. "Where are we in Scotland *exactly*?"

"This is Dunadd Hillfort, or Dún Ad as it was known, in the Kilmartin Valley, Argyll," Cronin said in thick Scottish brogue. "It is an open fort, long abandoned. We are completely secluded. No one will find us here."

"Why did you want to bring me here?" Alec asked. He leaned back against the stone wall to keep out of the wind and folded his arms for warmth.

"To keep you safe. Are you okay?" Cronin asked. "You had quite a fright."

"I, uh, yeah. I really wasn't ready for that," Alec admitted. "I was just talking to Eiji and Jodis about how none of the so-called danger felt real because it had just all been talk." Alec let out a laugh that sounded a little tight-strung. "Well, it's fucking real now."

Cronin took Alec's hands in his. "You're safe here with me."

Alec knew he was. He felt nothing but safe with him. "Can we stay here forever?"

Cronin laughed. "Ah, no."

Alec felt better already. The cold air, the closeness of Cronin almost made him forget two vampires had just tried to kill him. "You wanted to bring me here last night..." Alec prompted.

"Well, yes... I wanted to discuss a private matter. The other night when you asked about the elders," Cronin said. "The elder vampires who came before Eiji, Jodis, and I, who were slain by the Yersinians in 1346."

"The time of the Black Plague."

"Yes."

"You weren't telling me something then," Alec remembered. "Eiji and Jodis both looked to you but you stayed silent. Why was that?"

"I wanted to tell you about someone I was... *intimate* with," Cronin said quietly. "I didn't want you to hear it from someone else, and I don't want secrets between us."

"What was his name?"

"Willem."

An irrational acid burned in Alec's stomach at the thought of Cronin being with someone else. "Was he... did you... were you fated to him?"

Cronin smiled sadly. "No. I am fated to only you."

Alec tried to let out a breath of relief slowly. "But you loved him?"

"No." Cronin shook his head adamantly. "Not love. Though I respected him."

And somehow that hurt Alec more than if he'd loved him. "Oh."

"He was an elder. He was four hundred years older than I."

"Cradle robber."

Cronin chuckled. "He was an intellect and he was kind, but what we had was nothing more than physical. A convenience." Cronin looked at Alec and waited a moment before speaking again. "He took me to his bed chambers no more than eight times in all those years. I don't mean to hurt you by telling you this, but I wanted to be the one to tell you. I didn't want you to hear this from someone else. I'm not naïve to Johan's affection to me, although I've never entertained the notion of taking advantage—"

"It's okay, Cronin."

"I didn't want him to tell you with vain hope that you'd grow angry with me."

"I'm not angry," Alec said softly. "How could I be? I can't expect that you wouldn't have been with other people in all those years. I mean, really? One other guy in seven hundred years is... actually that's pretty lame. You've lived a helluva lot longer than me, and I've certainly had my share—"

Alec's words were cut short by a low growl in Cronin's chest.

"Are you growling?"

"I can't help it," Cronin said. "It's an involuntary reaction. I thank you for being honest with me, but I'd rather not hear of your... physicality with other men.

It might not be reasonable of me to expect you to hear of Willem yet I am not able to hear of yours. It makes me…"

"Growl?"

"Irrationally angry. Those who have touched you in such ways are still living, and I—"

"You can't kill them."

Cronin pouted and seemed thoughtful for a moment. "Well, I could."

"Yes, but you won't," Alec said. "I thought I'd imagined it before, you know, when I heard you make that noise. I mean, it sounded like a growl, but I didn't know it was an actual growl. You sound like a lion." He slowly put his hand to Cronin's chest, over his breastbone. "Do it again."

It took a moment, but Alec could feel a faint vibration under his hand before he could hear the sound. Even in the darkness, Alec could see Cronin's face—the intensity in his eyes. As they stared at each other, the rumble got louder. Though it wasn't a growl at all. "You're purring."

Something flashed in Cronin's eyes. Vulnerability? Alec wasn't sure. "I can't help it," he whispered.

"I love it," Alec murmured. He inched forward, sliding his hand up to Cronin's neck, then his face, and Alec slowly, slowly leaned in, and for the briefest moment, their lips touched.

And Cronin was gone.

Alec fell forward a step before he caught himself, blinking at where Cronin was, or rather, where there was now only misty air.

"Sorry," Cronin whispered behind him.

Alec spun around, startled. "Jesus!" He put his hand to his heart. "Two heart failures in twenty minutes probably isn't good for my mortality." He took some deep breaths. "And you know, if you don't want to kiss me…"

Cronin scoffed out a laugh. "Quite the opposite," he said. "I want it too much. Maybe Jodis is right. Maybe my desire to have you overrules my other faculties."

Alec's heart tripped in his chest. "Your desire to have me?"

"She fears if we are… intimate… my urge to bite you will be too strong."

"Oh."

Cronin chuckled, obviously embarrassed. "You see my dilemma?"

Alec was beginning to, yes. "So, when we have sex you'll bite me?"

Cronin's eyes went wide. "You are not shy to just say that out loud, are you?"

"I'm a man of my times," Alec said with a shrug. "But that's what you mean, isn't it? That when we do end up in bed together, you'll inevitably change me into a vampire."

Cronin swallowed hard. "Yes. It is in our nature to bite when… coupled."

"Oh." Alec paused for a moment. "Is that why she keeps interrupting us?"

"I believe so, yes," Cronin said with a smile. "Also that Eleanor said she saw you as human when we are in Egypt."

"When will we go to Egypt?" Alec asked. He knew it was now only a matter of when, not if.

"I would think soon," Cronin said softly. "I would rather see you there on our terms than have them take you."

Alec swallowed. "Me too."

"I won't let them touch you, Alec," Cronin whispered.

"Tonight, with those two attackers, that was really close, wasn't it?"

Cronin nodded. "Yes."

"Eiji and Jodis saved my life."

"Yes."

"I don't think I really took it all too seriously," Alec admitted. "Until now."

"Is that what Eiji meant?" Cronin asked. "When he asked if you understood now."

"Yeah. I'd told him none of it felt real. All the talk of crazy Egyptian vampires and ancient pharaohs. I mean, it's all a little out there, even for me. And I'm pretty good with weird." Alec looked at the stone wall before he reached out and touched it. It was wet and cold, and it made him shiver. "I believe it now, though. Those two vampires would have killed me if Eiji and Jodis weren't there."

"I shouldn't have left you." Cronin reached out and touched the wall too. "It is not a mistake I will make again."

"You need to feed, Cronin," Alec said. The old stone seemed to crumble a little under his touch. "Did you... you know, feed tonight when you left?"

"Yes."

"Well, good," Alec said. "I'm glad."

Cronin raised an eyebrow.

"I can't bear the thought of you being hungry," Alec answered honestly. "I didn't eat. I dropped my food on the patio floor when Eiji stabbed some vampires with my chopsticks."

Cronin smiled at that. "Probably not something you'd ever thought you'd say."

"Ah, no." Alec scoffed.

"We will need to get you some more food," Cronin said.

Alec nodded. "What did you say to me when you took me inside?" he asked. "When Eiji was fighting those guys, you picked me up and carried me inside. You put your hands to my face and said something in Gaelic. What was that?"

"Oh," Cronin said, ducking his head. "You bring out my native tongue."

Alec put his hand under Cronin's chin, lifting it. "Don't be embarrassed," he said. "It was something about a rug?"

"I said *rug mi ort*," Cronin said with a smile. "It translates roughly to 'It's okay, I have you, I have you.'"

"And the rest of it? Shab something, then Mac something?"

"*Sàbhailtcachd, m'cridhe*," Cronin whispered. "You don't miss anything, do you?"

"No."

Cronin's eyes looked impossibly black compared to his pale skin in the dark. "It doesn't translate well, but it means, 'You are safe, my heart.'"

"Oh." Alec was grinning now. "I think it translates just fine." His heart was beating triple time, which he had no doubt Cronin could hear. "You might want to teach me your native tongue sometime."

Alec was going for all the puns and sexual innuendos, but it was ruined by his chattering teeth.

"You are cold," Cronin said.

"No, I'm freezing," Alec said. "Are you not cold at all?"

"No. Our bodies acclimatize to our surroundings."

"Of course they do," Alec grumbled.

"Come." Cronin held out his hand out. "This way."

Alec wasn't sure if he was offering his hand to hold on to or if he was showing him the way, but Alec didn't hesitate. He took Cronin's hand in his, and from the way Cronin hesitated, it was pretty clear his proffered hand was for direction, not for holding. But he didn't let it go. Alec smiled at him. "What? No leaping this time?"

"It is within walking distance, though I could leap us if you want."

"Ah, no thanks. Walking is fine." Alec let Cronin lead the way, thankful he did so at a human pace. It was dark, downhill, and the grass was slippery with dew. "You can see where you're going, right?"

"Very clearly," Cronin replied, still holding Alec's hand.

"You can see everything in the dark?" Alec asked as they walked along a grassy path. "All vampires have super-sight, right?"

"Night or day is the same, just a different color," Cronin explained.

The night looked dark and misty to Alec, nothing more. If it weren't for the cold, Alec wouldn't have believed he was in a different country. The smell, though, the scent of damp heather, as Cronin had identified it, was very distinct. It was very Cronin.

Alec really couldn't see where he was, though as their walk became more even-footed and less downhill, Alec thought he was in what looked like a field. The grass was long and heavy with dew, making Alec's jeans damp to above his knees. The wet added to the cold, but Alec never complained or stopped walking. Wherever Cronin was taking him must have been important, and even if it weren't, just being outdoors, walking and holding hands despite the cold, felt wonderful.

Then Alec realized why Cronin had brought him here. He gave his hand a squeeze. "This is where you're from?"

"Yes," Cronin said. "I grew up not far from here. The village to the north, but it was not exactly where it is now." Cronin laughed a little. "My brothers and I would go to the River Add and fish for eel. Oh, I'd not recalled that for a long time," he said. "I'd not given thought to that in so long! My mother would be so cross. We were supposed to toil fields or collect reeds to be dried, but when the weather was warm, we'd make off, hunting rabbit in the glen."

Alec could listen to him tell stories all night long. "How many brothers did you have?"

"Two. I was the youngest. They were both bigger than I, strong with black hair. Then there was me, just a wee lad with my mother's fair skin and red hair."

Alec grinned at his use of such Scottish dialect. It rolled so beautifully off his tongue. "Hence the name Cronin, I take it. It means red, doesn't it?"

Alec could see Cronin's smile, even in the darkened night. "Yes. I don't recall a great many things from my human years. I do remember my mother would weave baskets. And I remember a town feast, I was very young, but I remember the music and dancing, people drinking and eating, laughing. I don't recall the cause of such celebration, but I remember that."

"I can't even imagine it," Alec said. "What did you wear? I mean, what was the fashion of the eighth-century Scotland?"

"What did I wear?"

"Yes!"

"Fabrics were coarse, woven wool or hemp, some were dyed, some were not," Cronin said. "We were not wealthy enough to have finery."

"And your shoes?"

"Leather boots," Cronin said. "Just a very basic form of what you wear today, bound with leather strapping."

"I am intrigued by it all," Alec said, squeezing Cronin's hand again. "It helps me see who you are."

"I have not told anyone these stories," Cronin said quietly. "Of my brothers, of my mother."

Cronin stopped walking and let go of Alec's hand. He was quiet, seemingly lost in his memories. He turned in a circle, letting the tall grass skim his fingertips. "I've not been here for a very long time."

The mist seemed to float above them, and as Cronin had said it would be, the air was a fraction warmer than it was on the hill. Alec's eyes had adjusted a little and he could see that yes, they were in a field. There was a dark line about a hundred yards to the west that Alec presumed were trees. There was absolutely nothing there, yet Cronin had stopped in this particular spot for a reason.

"Why did you really bring me here?"

Cronin looked at Alec then, and he swallowed hard. "Because this is where I died."

Alec blinked.

Because this is where I died...

Alec blinked again and shook his head. What the hell could he possibly say to that? "Oh my God."

"I haven't been here for a long time," Cronin said, his voice a distracted whisper as he looked around the field. "This was a battlefield. There were hundreds of men who died here... boys, really. I was twenty-four. Much older than most. Some were fathers, grandfathers, though most were just boys. My brothers died here, my father died here. I don't know what became of my mother..."

Alec couldn't help himself. He had to touch him. He put his hand to Cronin's face. "I can't even imagine."

"It was a very long time ago."

Time had passed, yes. Almost thirteen hundred years, to be exact. But it was obvious to Alec that there were wounds time would never heal.

Cronin leaned his face into Alec's hand, and Alec found himself leaning in toward him. He lifted his other hand to cup Cronin's face, which made him finally look up at Alec. His dark eyes were vulnerable, searching, and Alec was overcome with an unprecedented urge to comfort him.

He pulled Cronin against him and held him. It wasn't like an embrace when they leapt, this was different. This was comfort and consoling, a need to protect and reassure.

And the vampire allowed himself to be held.

Alec couldn't fathom how long Cronin had gone without the comfort of touch and without allowing himself the human need of being held. He pulled away but didn't let Cronin get too far. He gently touched Cronin's face one more time. "Thank you for bringing me here. Thank you for showing me this part of who you are."

The corner of Cronin's lips pulled up in a small half smile, but his eyes were still cast down. "Alec, since we met everything has been so crazy. You must feel like your head is spinning. I wanted to show you this, to take just a moment in all the mayhem, so you may see there is more to this than just your purpose. I am now inexplicably linked to you, and this fated thing is as new to me as it is to you. I know you don't exactly like being drawn to me. I don't blame you for that. You feel as though your choice has been removed, and that is not easy."

Alec pulled Cronin's face upward and with his eyes open—looking for any signs of fear or hesitation—he slowly, so slowly, pressed his lips to Cronin's.

It was soft, warm, and very sweet.

Cronin's eyes fluttered closed, and every cell in Alec's body tinged with bliss, but he pulled his lips away before he could deepen the kiss.

"That wasn't fate," Alec whispered, "me kissing you right now. That was my will, my decision."

Cronin ducked his head and smiled, and Alec thought he saw fangs. He put his hand to Cronin's mouth, swiping his thumb across the bottom lip. It was a little hard to see with only moonlight, but yes, there were definitely fangs.

"I'm sorry," Cronin whispered, embarrassed. "I can't help it. It's an involuntary reaction to you."

Alec moaned softly. Knowing Cronin was affected by him was a heady feeling. Intoxicating. "Don't apologize," he whispered. "I'd like to kiss you again."

Cronin stared at him, his dark eyes like onyx. "You are very forthright."

"I can't help it," Alec admitted. He repeated Cronin's own words back to him. "It's an involuntary reaction to you."

It made Cronin laugh, and Alec's heart soared at the sound, and he kissed him again. Alec opened his mouth just a little, enough to taste the sweetness of Cronin's breath. He pulled Cronin's bottom lip between his for just a moment, and the rumbly noise coming from Cronin sounded a mix of purr and growl.

Alec smiled as he ended the kiss. He ran the pad of his thumb across Cronin's jaw before letting his hand fall away. "While we're talking forthright, can I ask you something?"

Cronin looked a little kiss-drunk, but he answered anyway. "Yes."

"Your teeth... how dangerous is it for me to kiss you?"

"You mean, is it dangerous for a human to kiss a vampire?"

Alec chuckled. "Well, when you put it like that. But seriously, if my tongue were to touch your teeth, your fangs, and it cut me —"

Cronin took a small step back, but he was smiling. "Making me think of your blood in my mouth probably isn't very wise."

"I take it that it wouldn't be good for me," Alec prompted. "Would it... change me?"

Something flickered across Cronin's face that Alec couldn't quite catch. "I would need to pierce your skin with both teeth."

"So you can't just taste for fun. It's either to kill or to change?"

"Yes."

"Have you ever changed anyone?"

"No."

Alec smiled. It pleased him to know this. "Will you change me? Is that what happens?"

Cronin took a moment to answer, and looked out across the field. "Eiji has said so. Though he also once told me the one I was fated to was a warrior with a shield, so his 'readings' aren't exact."

"A shield? You mean my police badge?"

Cronin chuckled now. "It would seem so, yes. Though in my time, I would have believed it to be a literal representation."

Alec snorted. "You must have been disappointed when I was not some brave warrior on horseback with a dirk and taber."

Cronin laughed loudly at that and shook his head. "Oh, I am far from disappointed."

Alec found himself smiling, his chest warmed through at the compliment. He reached out and took

Cronin's hand, and they stared at each other. "Thank you for being honest with me, and thank you for bringing me here. We'll come back here, yes? I'd love to see it in spring, just before the sunrise."

Cronin nodded. His voice was just a whisper. "I would like that. Very much."

By Cronin's reaction to his offer of returning here, Alex realized that must have meant a lot to him. "I'd like that too."

"As much as I wish it otherwise, we should be going back now," Cronin said.

Alec wished he could stay there as well, in the long grass of the field, despite the cold. He saw a side to Cronin that was profound and wonderful and... human. Alec wanted to stay in that moment forever, but he knew they couldn't. "Where will we go?"

"My apartment," Cronin answered. "Jodis and Eiji will have secured it by now."

Alec nodded. "Okay, I guess we have a lot to organize. If this is all happening sooner than we thought, we're running out of time."

Cronin squeezed his hand. "Are you ready?"

"Yes. And don't think I've forgotten your little fib about having to put my arm around you to leap."

Cronin chuckled. "It was not fair of me, but I just could not help myself. Again, I apologize."

Alec faked a grumble and slid his arm around Cronin. "Well, it's not all bad." Then he ran his nose along Cronin's jaw to his ear. "I wouldn't get to do this if I just held your hand."

194

Cronin shuddered. "You might not want to distract me when we leap, or there's no saying where we'll end up."

Alec laughed at that and when Cronin put his arm around him, he held him a little tighter. And they were gone.

Cronin's apartment was well-lit and a lot warmer than where they'd just left. It was also a lot busier. Eiji and Jodis were there having some kind of confab, phones pressed to their ears, laptops on the coffee table, and screens filled with tabs. But there were others too. Eleanor was there, as were two other Egyptian-looking vampires who were with Bes showing some other vampire something onscreen. Johan was there too, staring at Alec, trying not to look too hurt by the way Cronin kept him close.

"Are you all right?" Cronin asked Alec quietly.

Alec shook off the splintered feeling from leaping. "Yeah."

"What do you need?" Cronin looked worried for him. "Anything, and I will get it for you."

After being attacked and almost killed, after Cronin taking him to the open fields of Scotland and sharing his past—and sharing their first kiss—Alec had a renewed sense of purpose. He was ready now to focus on the war, as they'd called it, focus on the psycho-sociopathic vampire who was hell bent on using him to resurrect Osiris, the god of the dead.

The vampires in the room, all busy quietly gathering intel and strategizing plans, reminded him of his time as a cop. No, Alec didn't have their vampire abilities, he wasn't as fast as them, and he didn't have their mental capabilities.

A vampire he was not. But Alec was two things: he was a good detective, and he was good with weird.

Alec looked at Cronin and smiled. "What I need is food, a few untraceable cell phones, and a shitload of cash."

CHAPTER THIRTEEN

Cronin understood why Eiji and Jodis had organized the meeting at his place. It was secure, impenetrable—unless another leaper appeared—and Cronin knew it was the safest place for Alec to be. He just wished for privacy.

And suddenly, after more than twelve hundred years of wishing time would move faster—of wishing his fated one would hurry and arrive—he now wished for time to stop. He wanted to spend precious minutes with Alec untroubled by pending battles. He wanted to tell him more stories of the years he waited, he wanted to explore his body, he wanted to change him—as selfish as it was—so he would have him forever.

Yet when he watched him, he marveled at the humanness of him: how his blood would heat, how his heartbeat spiked and calmed, how he would absentmindedly scratch an itch, bite his lip when in thought, or run his hand through his hair. It was a truly beautiful thing.

Alec read up on some websites on Osiris as he ate, while Cronin answered questions from the others, discussing strategies, tactics and options. He never took his eyes off Alec, though, and had an unquenchable desire to be near him, to touch him. Their brief kisses in the fields at Dún Ad had been Cronin's first kiss in a very long time, and had been perfect. And it most certainly sealed what he already knew: he wasn't just fated to Alec. He was falling in love with him.

"What have you learned?" Cronin asked Alec. He sat beside him at the table, their chairs close together, their thighs touching.

"That from six different 'expert' documents, all facts—if that's what you'd call them—vary. Which leads me to believe they're all wrong."

Cronin smiled. "There are the books in my study."

"I might start on them next," Alec said. "Did you get the phones? And the cash?" Alec cringed a little. "I hate asking for money like that."

Cronin chuckled and nudged his knee to Alec's. "Please, think nothing of it. I have more than enough and"—he smiled as he spoke—"what's mine is yours."

Alec smiled as well and it seemed only then did he realize how close their faces were. His pupils dilated, his breathing hitched a little, and his heart rate soared. He leaned in closer, and his tongue swept along his bottom lip. Cronin knew Alec was going to kiss him again, and he wanted it like nothing else on the planet.

Jodis cleared her throat, making the two of them pull back. "Uh, Cronin, my dear," she said sweetly. "We talked about trying to tamp down the sexual tension, yes?"

Eiji shook his head and groaned. "You're killing us over here."

Alec blanched. "They can feel that?"

"You give off certain pheromones," Cronin answered softly. "Apparently."

Cronin thought Alec might recoil from embarrassment, but instead he laughed. He looked around the room at all the vampires watching him. "You're welcome."

Eiji and Eleanor laughed, and Jodis smiled and shook her head. Bes and his family smiled also, but Johan wasn't too impressed.

Cronin knew that Johan wasn't strictly pleased that he'd finally found Alec. Johan had long held hopes that, as two vampires with similar inclinations, they would find convenience and pleasure in each other's company. Cronin had politely refused the offer, and Johan had never pushed the matter, though his affection for Cronin remained.

It also appeared Johan now harbored a distaste for Alec, which offended Cronin greatly. But with a well-placed hand on Alec's back and a brief but well-aimed glare at Johan, Cronin didn't need to say a word.

He put the cell phones Alec had requested on the table, and six bundles of hundred-dollar bills in ten-thousand-dollar lots. "Is this enough? There's plenty more."

Alec stared wide-eyed at the neat and crisp bankrolls. "Um, shit. I didn't mean that much."

"You didn't specify amounts," Cronin said. "I don't know how much a *shitload of cash* is in quantifiable figures."

Alec smiled at him. Their faces were close again, and he whispered, "I like it when you talk all middle ages."

Cronin blushed and ducked his chin, and Eiji laughed. "Please, would you two stop that already?"

Alec laughed again and took out his own cell. "I can't use mine," he said. "They'll be tracing it, no doubt. But I need some contacts out of it." He scrolled through some numbers until he found the one he was after and entered it into one of the phones off the table. Then he called it. Cronin could hear the whole conversation.

"Campbell, it's Detective MacAidan."

The voice sounded muffled, tired and still-asleep. *"It's three o'clock in the fucking morning. What the fuck do you want? I told you the other day I don't know nothing."*

Alec smiled. "No, no, no. It's not about that. I need you to do something for me. Are you at home right now?"

Silence. *"It's three o'clock in the fucking morning. Where else would I be, asshole?"*

Cronin gritted his teeth. He didn't like this Campbell fellow at all.

"Then put some fucking pants on, and walk out into your living room," Alec said, seemingly unfazed at the language used against him.

"The fuck?"

"Do it!" Alec snapped. "Get your ass out of bed. I have a deal for you."

Cronin heard mumbling and what sounded like the ruffling of blankets through the phone. *"This got anything to do with your little disappearance the other night?"* Campbell asked. *"Don't think we ain't heard about it."*

"Just do as I say, asshole." Alec clicked off the call, stood up, and pocketed the other phone and two bundles of cash. Then he walked over to the table and picked up the small wooden bullet he'd found in Mikka's ashes.

Cronin was quick to be beside him. "Alec?"

"You just need an address to be able to leap?" he asked Cronin.

"Yes." Cronin was concerned. "Alec, where do you propose we go?"

"I want to pay a visit to an old friend of mine."

"A friend?"

"Well, someone I busted a time or two."

"You want me to take you to see a felon?"

Alec rolled his eyes. "I'm pretty sure vampire trumps felon." Then Alec showed Cronin the address on his phone. "Trust me."

Cronin gave a little growl and pulled Alec against him, making him moan and smile. And with Alec firmly against him and the address in his mind, Cronin leapt.

* * * *

The room was small, dark, and stank of stale beer and old food. A man, who Cronin assumed was this Campbell, was sitting on the sofa. He was African American, possibly thirty years old, and screamed like a child when Cronin and Alec magically appeared in his living room. His legs lifted, and it appeared he tried to climb up the back of the sofa.

Alec gave a shudder—he was growing more tolerant of leaping every time—and he put his hand out, palm forward, to Campbell. "It's me, MacAidan."

Campbell blinked and gaped, his heart stuttering dangerously in his chest, and Cronin wondered if it would actually stop. It didn't. "What the actual living fuck was that?" he cried, his eyes bulging.

"New mode of transport," Alec said.

Campbell stood up, visibly shaking, though his adrenaline now surfacing as anger. He went to grab Alec, and Cronin was in front of him in the blink of an eye. "Do not touch him."

Campbell fell back into the sofa. "Who the fuck are you? How'd you move so damn fast?"

"Who I am is not your concern," Cronin sneered. He showed his fangs.

Campbell blanched. His eyes shot between Cronin and Alec. "What the fuck?"

"Calm down," Alec said. "He won't hurt you unless you try to hurt me, or if you run."

Campbell swallowed hard and fidgeted. Cronin could tell the human was warring between his fight and flight instincts, and apparently Alec could tell this too. "Don't even think about it, Campbell," Alec said, completely at ease. He pulled out one bundle of the bills and let it drop heavily onto the coffee table.

Campbell straightened up immediately. Clearly money was the motivating factor for this man. Cronin realized now why Alec wanted it.

"Ten G to start," Alec said. His street-cop talk sounded so natural to Cronin, who had never heard him speak in such a fashion.

Campbell shook his head. "Wh-wh-whaddya want? Why me?"

"I want bullets," Alec said, sitting in a chair across from Campbell. "Special bullets."

"You a cop, man!" Campbell said. "Ain't no way I'll admit to knowin' nothin'."

Cronin refrained from correcting his poor use of the English language. Instead he hissed at him. "You will help him if he so asks."

Campbell shrunk back into the sofa. "How do I know you not tryin' to punk me?"

"I *was* a cop," Alec said. "You said yourself that you heard about my disappearing act that kinda put me on their now-wanted list. I wouldn't be here if I didn't need your help."

"Why me?"

"Because I know you've been manufacturing this shit for years," Alec said. "And I know your product is good."

Campbell still looked unsure, so Cronin stepped a little closer. He might have shown his teeth when he spoke. "Bullets?"

"Okay, okay," Campbell said quickly. "Hollow point, open tip, soft tip, frangible, exploding, armor piercing?"

Alec didn't answer. He reached into his jeans pocket and pulled out the small wooden bullet. "I want hardwood."

Campbell blinked, then shook his head and laughed. "Is that some kinda joke?"

Alec didn't laugh.

Campbell's smile died. "You kiddin' me, man?"

"I want lead casing, hardwood tip and core." Alec thought for a moment, then looked at Cronin. "What kind of wood would be best?"

Cronin gave him a smile. "There is a certain type of hardwood that was common in Ancient Egypt and would be perfect. It is called Christ's Thorn."

"Christ's Thorn it is, then," Alec said simply.

"In *Ancient* Egypt?" Campbell asked. "You got a time machine I don't know about because where else am I gonna get that shit from?"

"That timber is still found in parts of Northern Africa," Cronin told him. "You can source it."

Campbell looked as though he was about to object when Alec pulled out the other bank of ten thousand dollars and threw it onto the coffee table. "Make some phone calls," he said. "Don't tell me you're not connected."

Campbell blinked a few times in quick succession. "How th' hellami gonna make wooden bullets? Why would you even need wooden bullets? You gonna fight a bunch of vamp..." His question trailed off when he looked up at Cronin. His mouth opened and shut a few times like a gaping fish. "Oh."

Alec put the second cell phone on the table. "I will use this phone to contact you. Keep it charged and if it rings, you will answer it. If the police ask you questions, you will tell them nothing. Believe me, these are not enemies you wish you make." Alec nodded toward the money. "I will double the payment on collection."

"How many you need?"

"As many as you can make. Hundreds if you can do it."

Campbell made a face as though he was working things out in his head. "When you need 'em by?"

"Two days."

"Two days?" he cried. "You fuckin' crazy?"

Cronin let a growl rip through the air, and Campbell cried out in fear. His eyes went wide, his hands up. "Okay, okay. Right, got it." He grabbed his crotch and Cronin caught a brief whiff of urine. The man had almost pissed himself.

Alec stood up. "Forty grand, all said and done. It buys me what I want, and it buys me silence. You speak of this to no one, ya hear?"

Campbell never took his eyes off Cronin, but he nodded.

Alec grinned. "Good." He put one arm around Cronin's waist and held up his other hand showing two fingers. "Two days," he said to Campbell, and probably scaring the religion out of him, they leapt.

* * * *

Cronin leapt them back to his apartment, and more specifically, his bedroom. Alec groaned through gritted teeth and shook his body out, only to then try and look around. Cronin realized Alec couldn't see in the darkened room. "We are in my bedroom."

Alec's heart calmed immediately. "Oh. Thank you. It's so dark in here," he said, keeping his arm around Cronin. "Everything okay out there?" he asked, nodding toward the door.

"Yes," Cronin answered. He listened for a moment, knowing Alec could hear nothing, and told him, "They're making maps."

"Just wondered why we're in here?" Alec whispered, and Cronin could feel Alec's lips move as he spoke.

"I just wanted a moment with you," Cronin said. "It's been a long night."

"It's been an incredible night," Alec said, moving his hand up Cronin's back. "Going to Scotland with you was... well, it was the best thing ever."

"You were great with that criminal," Cronin said. "I must admit I liked seeing you in your element. You must have been a remarkable police officer. The bullet idea is genius."

Alec snorted out a laugh. "That *criminal*, as you call him, has a name. Campbell's a street thug with a penchant for guns and ammunition. He's been on our list for years. And the bullet idea wasn't mine." Alec pulled out the small wooden bullet from his pocket. "Do you think it will work?"

"I can't see why it wouldn't," Cronin said. "And even if it doesn't, it has to be worth trying." Cronin took the small wooden bullet from Alec and held it between his fingers to inspect it. "Is it not crazy that such a small insignificant object can kill a creature such as myself?"

Alec's brow furrowed. "It can kill bad vampires, not you."

"A wooden stake, a wooden bullet, or sunlight does not discriminate between good and bad, Alec."

Alec frowned and shook his head as though it didn't bear thinking about. "And you're not a creature, thank you very much."

Cronin smiled. "Well, I am not human."

Alec lifted Cronin's chin and whispered against his lips, "You are vampire."

A warm shiver ran down Cronin's spine. "And you are remarkably tolerant of such things."

Alec drew his nose along Cronin's jaw. "I am remarkably smitten with such things," he whispered, then froze apparently realizing he'd said it out loud.

"Smitten?"

"Shut up," Alec said with a smile. He pulled back a little. "And you did that growling thing again. I think you scared the shit outta him."

"Urine, actually," Cronin corrected.

Alec laughed louder at that. "Well, at least he took me seriously." He took Cronin's hand. "As much as I'd like to stay in here with you—and lock that door so Jodis can't interrupt," he said louder, knowing she'd hear him, "we should probably go out there and tell them what I did."

Still holding Cronin's hand, Alec led the way out to the living room, where the vampire intelligence confab was still in full swing. There had been progress: the dining table was now covered in maps, a row of laptops were on a shelf, all displaying what Cronin recognized as pyramidal tunnels in three dimension.

"I wasn't going to interrupt you," Jodis said, smiling at Alec. When she saw that Alec and Cronin were holding hands, her smile turned to Cronin. "Things went well?"

"Very," Cronin said. "And here?"

"Productive," Eiji said. "Did you get what you were after?"

"Ordered, not acquired," Alec said. "As many wooden bullets as he can make."

"Wooden bullets?" Jodis asked. "Like the one that killed Mikka?"

"Similar," Alec explained. "I can only assume that bullet came from a blow dart or some such thing and that you'd need vampire strength to fire it to be effective on a vampire; a human would not have the lung capacity. These will have a half-jacket of lead, so I can fire them from a gun, but with a hardwood tip and core."

All the other vampires stared at Alec, a little wide-eyed, though mostly impressed, even Johan. Eiji grinned and said, "I knew I liked you."

Alec shrugged. "I don't have superhuman strength like you guys, so I figured I should up my ante."

Cronin, still holding Alec's hand, pulled him a little closer. "I thought it was creative and effective. Though we should try it here before we leave for Egypt."

"I'm not shooting anyone here," Alec said, alarmed. "Remember? Bad vampires, not the good guys." Then he said, "Oh, maybe I should source some crossbows too."

Eiji clapped Alec on the shoulder, with his usual grin. "I can order those! They'll be here overnight if you like."

Alec nodded. "It can't hurt. We'll need to look at special arrows."

"Leave that to me," Eiji said. "When will your bullets arrive?"

"I gave him two days," Alec answered, then looked around the room at the laptops, the maps, the books. "Is that too long? Things look like they're moving quickly."

"You have four days," Eleanor said. "I see you moving on the fourth day. It is a new development, Cronin," she said. "I would believe that Queen Keket has implemented a course of action, and so my vision changed to reflect this."

Alec looked at Cronin. "Four days," he whispered.

Cronin squeezed his hand and swallowed hard. Almost thirteen long and lonely centuries had come down to just a matter of minutes. "It is too soon."

Alec dropped Cronin's hand and went to stand by the table. "We have to learn everything. What are these maps for?"

Cronin was quickly by his side and reclaimed his hand. "Stop."

"We don't have time to waste," Alec started to say.

"Stop," Cronin said again, a little more adamantly. Alec turned to face him. His voice was softer now. "I have learned many things in all my years on this earth. And, Alec, there have been many years, days, hours, but none so important as these. Not for learning, not for preparing for war, but to be selfish. We will learn tomorrow, I promise. But for now, in these few hours, please give me us."

Alec's expression was stunned, apparently so moved by Cronin's words and the haunted sincerity in his eyes that all he could do was nod.

Cronin sighed; Alec's agreement was a balm to his aching heart. Without another word to anyone else in the room, Cronin squeezed Alec's hand and led him to his bedroom.

CHAPTER FOURTEEN

Cronin's room was pitch black and it took a moment for Alec's eyes to adjust. He knew he stood near the bed, though he couldn't see it. He could feel Cronin's hand in his, and he could barely make out the pale silhouette of his face in front of him. "Please don't think it bold of me," Cronin whispered, "to ask for time alone with you and to lead you to my room."

Alec smiled at the nervous, formal tone to his voice. "I don't mind."

"Four days," Cronin whispered. "To think I have had all this time. I have had nothing *but* time, centuries of wasted years. And now when I wish to cling to it, it is taken from me."

Alec thought his heart might burst from Cronin's words alone. "Nothing will be taken from you," Alec whispered in return. "Eiji said we have many years. He said that. So whatever we face in four days, we will win."

Cronin frowned. "I fear for your life. They will stop at nothing to retrieve the key, Alec. Your heart…"

Alec lifted Cronin's chin. "My heart is not theirs to take," Alec whispered. "It belongs to someone else."

Cronin's eyes closed slowly as he smiled. "As mine belongs to you."

Alec pinched Cronin's chin between his finger and thumb, and his mouth fell open slightly. White fangs glinted in the darkness, and Alec slowly, slowly, covered Cronin's mouth with his own, kissing him.

The kiss started soft and sweet, with open mouths and closed eyes. But Alec needed more. He slid his tongue into Cronin's mouth and slid his fingers into his hair, pulling their faces together, hard.

Cronin's reaction was instant: a growly purr filled the room, and Alec found himself on his back on the bed, his thighs apart, with Cronin between them, leaning over him. Their mouths, their bodies not quite touching, but there was a fire in Cronin's eyes.

"I don't dare harm you," he whispered, his voice a husky rumble.

"You won't," Alec replied, his voice barely a breath. He lifted his hips off the bed, needing, craving contact, friction, anything. Alec ran his hands down Cronin's sides, over the small of his back to his ass, and he pulled their hips together.

Cronin hissed, but Alec was lost in a desire he'd never felt before. He hooked one of his legs around Cronin's thigh, one arm around his back and the other hand around Cronin's jaw and neck, bringing their mouths back together.

Alec was so turned-on, he was so hard and needy he was writhing and grinding his hips into Cronin's. He could feel Cronin's erection pressing against his own, the denim between them doing little to hide their desire.

Alec raked his hands over Cronin's back, his shoulders and into his hair as they kissed, tongues tasting and teasing. Yet Alec still wanted more. He slid his hands between them, ripping the button-fly of his jeans apart, and when he popped the button on Cronin's jeans, the vampire froze.

Alec expected him to pull away, but he didn't.

Cronin held himself above Alec, their faces just inches apart, and Alec slowly pulled down Cronin's zipper. Alec expected him to tell him to stop, but he didn't.

Alec slid his hand inside Cronin's pants, wrapping his fingers around his silky steel-hard cock, and he expected Cronin to tell him no.

But he didn't.

Instead, Cronin leaned up on his hands and slowly thrust his hips into Alec's fist. His head lolled back a little, his mouth open and his fangs out.

Alec had never seen anything so beautiful.

So powerful, yet completely at his mercy.

Alec gave Cronin's cock a squeeze and started to pump him. "Look at me," he whispered.

Cronin let his head fall forward, and his eyes were black fire. Alec's blood boiled in his veins; he could feel it—like mercury—rolling toward Cronin, wanting him to bite him, to have him, claim him, and fuck him. Alec was just about to beg him to please, please have him, when Cronin bared his teeth and bucked his hips, a growl ripping from his chest as he came.

Alec was transfixed, hypnotized by the sight of Cronin, so turned-on he only had to grip his own cock before he came.

When the room had stopped spinning and the blood stopped pumping in his ears, Alec opened his eyes to find Cronin still above him. He was staring at him with a look akin to wonder.

"Am I still alive?" Alec mumbled.

Cronin surprised him by barking out a husky laugh. "Ah, it would appear so."

"Fuck, that was so hot," Alec said, still a little lightheaded. When Cronin ducked his face, Alec lifted his heavy hand to stop him. "*You* were so hot."

"I am long out of practice," Cronin whispered.

Alec smiled at him and waggled his eyebrows. "Well, now we know you don't bite when we fool around, we can remedy the practice part."

"I may never want to stop," Cronin murmured.

Alec's smile became a grin. "Even better."

Cronin's eyes intensified in the dark. "Alec, I wanted to bite you. It took a great deal of self-control not to."

Alec put his hands to Cronin's face and ran his fingers through his hair. He studied him for a long moment before looking into his eyes. "I wanted you to," he answered. "Every cell in my body wanted you to."

Cronin closed his eyes slowly and swallowed hard. He pulled away from Alec, but stayed on the bed. "It's probably best not to say such things to me."

Alec could see Cronin needed a little physical distance, so he didn't push the issue. Instead, he looked down at the sticky mess that covered them both. "Um, quick question. Vampire jizz. Harmful to humans?"

"Jizz?" Cronin repeated.

"You know," Alec said, running his finger through the cooling puddles on his stomach. "Come."

"Oh," Cronin said quickly, and Alec swore he heard Eiji laughing. Cronin smiled. "No, not harmful to humans."

"They heard everything we just did?" Alec asked, turning his head toward the door.

Cronin nodded. "Yes. Vampires have exceptional hearing. I'm sorry, I should have told you beforehand..."

Alec felt no shame at all. In fact, he laughed. "Hope you enjoyed the show, guys, and the brief intermission. We're now up for round two, also known as the shower scene," he said, knowing the others would hear every word. Alec climbed off the bed and took Cronin's hand, leading him into the bathroom.

* * * *

Alec stripped naked and walked into the long, marble-tiled open shower. He turned the water on and stood under the hot spray, knowing Cronin was watching. Alec never turned around, though, wanting to give him a little show. "You need to be in here with me," he said, soaping up his body. He gripped his hard-again cock and gave himself a few hard tugs as he finally turned around.

And stopped.

Cronin stood naked before him. His body was lean and strong, pale. His cock was uncut, hanging heavy and long, and his pubic hair matched the rusty color of hair on his head.

But that wasn't what stopped Alec's breath.

For on Cronin's chest, right across the sternum, on an angle to the left, was a silver scar. Two inches wide, seven inches long, with jagged lines. Not raised or indented like a normal scar, but as part of his skin.

Alec didn't have to ask. He knew what it was.

Cronin had told him his human life had ended on a battlefield with an axe to the chest. Left to die on a muddy, blood-filled field, before Jodis had found him…

Cronin stepped before him, and Alec reached out and ran his finger softly down the silver scar.

"I bear the mark of my death," Cronin whispered. He looked so vulnerable, so exposed.

Alec lifted his right knee, showing the bullet wound on his thigh. He thumbed the divot in his skin. "We each have scars to bear." Then Alec flattened his hand so his palm was over Cronin's skin. He could feel the beat of his vampire heart. "You are perfect," Alec replied.

Cronin almost smiled. "As are you."

Alec cupped Cronin's face in both his hands, and tilted Cronin's face upward and kissed him. Alec suddenly found himself under the hot water, still kissing Cronin, but both of them now under the steaming, sluicing water.

Alec smiled into the kiss. "Either I lose track of time and place when I kiss you, or you move me."

Cronin laughed, putting his head back into the water. "I have vampire speed, remember?" he said. Then he whispered, "And I had a sudden urge to taste you wet."

Alec bit his bottom lip and slowly pushed Cronin against the tiled wall. "That's a really good idea," he said. He kissed Cronin's lips, his chin, then dropped deliberately and Cronin gasped when Alec kissed the silver scar on his chest.

Alec went lower still, kissing down Cronin's stomach, his navel, licking and drinking the water as it ran over his skin. He pushed Cronin's hips against the tiles, his straining cock near his lips, and Alec looked up to see lust-black eyes and the hint of fangs behind kissed-red lips.

"Alec," Cronin said, his voice a mix of plead and warning.

Smiling, Alec flattened his tongue, not taking his eyes from Cronin's as he licked the head of Cronin's beautiful cock.

Cronin groaned and his eyes closed, as if trying to rein in the sensation. Or savor it. And when Alec opened his mouth and took in the tip, slowly sinking his lips over the crown of his cock, Cronin's head fell back against the tiles and his hands went to Alec's hair.

The room filled with steam and a low keening growl, and Alec knew Cronin was close. He wanted to taste him, and he wanted to take his lover's seed. He would take anything he gave him. He wanted to give Cronin this pleasure, and he knew then, on his knees in front of Cronin, Alec finally, finally, realized what fated meant.

He wanted to be everything to Cronin. And he would be. Everything he needed, everything he wanted, Alec was it.

As Cronin was to him.

And Alec had never wanted anything more. He pulled off Cronin's cock, kissed his hips, his thighs, nuzzled his balls, and licked the length of his shaft. "Let me drink you," Alec whispered before taking him deep one more time.

And Cronin did.

Alec drank every drop.

When Alec got up from his knees, he chuckled at Cronin. His eyes were dark, heavy-lidded yet somehow still wide, a smile played at his lips, and he was leaning back against the tiles as though he couldn't stand on his own.

"I have never..." Cronin started to say. He shook his head.

"Well, now you have," Alec said before he kissed him, pressing against him, feeling the warmth of his body and the water.

"You still have need," Cronin said, rolling his hips into Alec's erection. "Will you allow me to touch you?"

Alec answered with a fevered kiss and a moan, and Cronin responded in kind. He slid his hand between them and took Alec, gently wrapping his fingers around him. Deft fingers, skillful and precise, heated kisses and the scent of Cronin, wet and steaming, filled every sense.

The coil of pleasure wound tighter and tighter until Alec couldn't contain it anymore and it burst free, firing blinding stars behind his eyes as his orgasm rocketed through him.

Alec slumped against the wall and Cronin caught him, concerned. Alec laughed and pulled Cronin against him. "I think it's sleep time for me," Alec said, feeling as though his bones had turned to sponge. He could barely keep his eyes open.

When they'd dried off, Alec crawled into Cronin's bed and held the blanket up in invitation.

Cronin smiled shyly and he tentatively lay down beside him. Alec flung himself over half of Cronin, his thigh, his arm, and rested his head on Cronin's shoulder. He traced his fingers over the scar on Cronin's chest.

Cronin seemed to freeze at first, but Alec soon felt Cronin relax, and he put his arm around his shoulder. A soft purr rumbled in Alec's ear, soothing him to sleep. Alec knew that tomorrow was when everything would change. Tomorrow would be all about tactics and intel, gathering armies and warfare, about numbers: how many they'd fight, how many they'd lose. It would be about mystical things, vampires, the undead, and the returned, horrors Alec couldn't even fathom.

Yet in Cronin's arms, he was safe and untouched by it all. He smiled as he closed his eyes, and slept like the dead.

* * * *

Alec woke slowly, the world around him coming in like cognizant waves. First, the scent of Cronin all around him, then his absence. He wasn't far away, Alec knew, he could feel Cronin's presence just a few rooms away. He didn't know *how* he knew. He just knew. Alec stretched out, naked and smiling, remembering what they'd done the night before.

Before he let his mind wander too far with images, memories of tastes and pleasure, Alec rolled out of bed with a groan. He had a lot to do today, a lot to learn, and a lot to take in, and although he started with a shower, what he really wanted was coffee and Cronin. In no particularly order.

Dressed in jeans and one of Cronin's T-shirts, he padded barefoot out into the living room. He had no clue what to expect, who would be out there, or what the developments would have been in the few hours he'd slept.

He didn't care, though. Because standing in the kitchen, leaning against the counter was Cronin, holding his freshly made coffee for him. He wore black jeans and a black long-sleeved shirt with the sleeves pulled up to his elbows. The dark clothes matched his eyes perfectly and gave stark contrast to his pale skin and rust-colored hair. His pink lips smiled just for Alec.

Alec took the cup from him and set it down on the counter so he could lift Cronin's face and kiss him. He leaned against him, pushed against his body with his own, and kissed him again.

Someone cleared their throat, and Cronin smiled into the kiss. Alec slowly pulled his lips away and turned to face whomever had interrupted. Only it wasn't just one person. There were six vampires watching them. Alec assumed it was Eiji who'd interrupted, not because he was grinning, but because he spoke first. "I trust you slept well."

Alec didn't move or pull back from leaning against Cronin. "Good morning," Alec said.

"It's almost six at night," Jodis said.

Alec shrugged. Yes, he'd worked nights as a cop, but in the days since he'd kept company with vampires, his nights truly *were* becoming his days. Still not moving from Cronin, Alec stretched his arm out to collect his coffee and sipped it over Cronin's shoulder. "So, what did I miss?"

"Cronin, apparently," Jodis said with a smile.

Cronin chuckled against Alec's shoulder, but he slid his arm around Alec's back to keep him right where he was.

Bes and his two coven members took their leave from the kitchen, and Johan followed them out. Alec pulled back a little so he could see Cronin's face. "Are we still making them… uncomfortable?" he asked. "I thought my pheromone levels would have dropped a little bit after last night."

Cronin laughed into Alec's chest and ducked his head, clearly embarrassed. Eiji snorted. "Or they're worse," he said with his usual smile.

Jodis laughed quietly, but she shook her head. "They've not fed for a few days," she explained. "It's not your pheromones they find distracting. It's your blood."

Oh. "Are they, um… should I go somewhere else…?"

Cronin looked up at Alec, still smiling. "They're fine. They'll go out when the sun has set."

Alec stared into his dark, dark eyes. "You look so good today."

Cronin laughed again, his eyes crinkling at the corners, his fangless teeth perfectly white. The sound of him laughing filled Alec's chest, as if he could feel Cronin's happiness. "I could say the same about you," Cronin said, leaning up so he could kiss him.

Alec grinned into the kiss, but before it could get too serious, Eiji tapped them both on the shoulder. Cronin growled and Eiji rolled his eyes. "Oh, calm down," Eiji said. "I know you two are just getting acquainted and I know how all-encompassing that is, believe me. And when this whole mess in Egypt is over, we will leave you alone so you can maul each other twenty-four hours a day for months on end—and you will—but right now we have more important things to deal with."

Alec finally pried himself away from Cronin. He put his coffee to his lips to hide his smile. "Twenty-four hours a day for months on end, huh?"

Cronin fought a smile. "It's okay, Alec. We can clear your schedule."

Alec raised his eyebrows and snorted out a laugh. He looked disbelievingly at Eiji. "Did you hear that? I believe that was a budding sense of humor!"

Jodis chuckled, a light melodic sound. She put her hand on Alec's arm. "I don't think he was joking, Alec."

Alec looked at Cronin with challenge in his eyes. "Even better." All jokes aside, Alec knew there were serious matters to tend to. He drained his coffee cup and put it in the sink. "I guess we should get started, huh?"

"I said *after* the mess in Egypt," Eiji cried. "Not now. We don't have time for you two to start anything."

Cronin chuckled. "I believe Alec meant we should get started on the plans for Egypt."

"Oh," Eiji said flatly. "Sorry."

Alec clapped Eiji on the shoulder. "No need to apologize. I happen to like the way you think." He smiled at the smaller Japanese vampire. "So, Egypt? You guys have a plan, right?"

CHAPTER FIFTEEN

Alec sat on the sofa as the others recounted what they'd come up with, and the plan really was very simple.

Create a diversion for the legions of *returned* vampires, enter the hive — preferably undetected — and take out the Queen.

Simple? Well, in theory.

In reality, it was filled with unknowns, improbables, and un-fucking-likelies, but Alec knew they had little choice.

Many vampires from around the world were prepared to join forces to take Queen Keket down. There had been video conference calls with coven leaders in London, Italy, Buenos Aires, and India, and a thousand vampires with tactical experience were ready to deploy at a moment's notice.

The plan was to send in platoons of *good* vampires to take out the *bad* ones, SWAT-style as Alec described it, before Cronin would even consider leaping Alec onto Egyptian sands.

Cronin didn't like the idea at all and was rather vocal about it, but Alec's role as the Key — however unclear it seemed — would be to end the Queen herself.

Johan showed Alec the maps of the Great Pyramids he'd drawn with Bes's help, and, more specifically, the underground tunnels. "It is these tunnels that permit transport and movement," Johan said. "There are many, they intercross and dissect. It is important that you know where to go. If you get lost or trapped..."

Alec studied them, taking in each tunnel, the direction they ran, which ones were a dead ends, which ones lead somewhere, and the chambers that joined them. "I will remember them," he said. He tilted his head as if confused.

"What is it?" Cronin said, standing beside him.

Alec shook his head. "Nothing." He'd always known there were tunnels through the pyramids and underneath them—he'd seen countless documentaries on such things—but he'd always wondered about their significance.

"And we think she's taken over the King's Chamber in the Great Pyramid, the largest in Giza?" Alec questioned.

"It would appear so," Bes answered.

"Do we know, or do we assume?" Alec questioned. "Forgive my doubt, but working with fact is far less likely to see us killed."

Bes nodded once. "Talk was, yes, she has claimed the Great Pyramid as her own. But only rumor. I have no physical proof."

"Osiris is buried at the Great Pyramid," Cronin added. "It would make sense."

"And the three main pyramids of Giza are not linked by these underground tunnels?" Alec questioned, looking again at the maps Johan had drawn.

"Not to each other, no," Bes said. "At least as far as has been documented by vampire or man."

Alec thought for another moment. "It would make better sense if they were."

"Better sense for what?" Johan questioned. There wasn't contempt in his tone, only curiosity.

"For movement, transport, like you said," Alec said. "If these three locations"—he pointed to the three large pyramids on the map—"were joined underground, the way we have roads and highways aboveground. If these have been critical components for vampires over thousands of years, surely it makes sense that they can get from one to the other without encountering daylight."

Bes shook his head. "Forgive me, Alec, but joining those tombs would be the last objective any vampire would want. These were tombs of evil creatures. Not to be kept safe, but to be kept buried forever. No one wanted them found, let alone joined. Creating underground roads for these evil ones to make easy travel was not ever planned."

Alec smiled at him. "*We* wouldn't want them joined, no. But I'm pretty sure Queen Keket would. She'd have herself an underground city full of all her *returned* servants."

Cronin considered this. He looked at Alec. "Do you think it possible there are new tunnels that join the pyramids?"

Alec shrugged. "I don't just think it's possible. I think it's likely."

"It's not *im*possible," Bes allowed. "Why do you think this?"

Alec's answer was simple. "Because it's what I'd do."

Bes studied the map, and his brow furrowed as if he was going through hundreds of mental catalogues. "If it is true, the connecting tunnels must run from the subterranean chambers, obviously. How deep they go and how many sub-branches there are, I cannot say and we cannot map."

"We'd be going in blind," Alec said, not taking his eyes from the map. "But hypothetically speaking, if she's been making vampire drones for four or five years, could she have them digging out tunnels? Like the old pharaohs who'd force slaves to build pyramids, she's making them build tunnels."

Bes swallowed hard and concentrated on the maps. "It would explain the numbers that are claimed to be underground. They don't come to surface of a night, as in the ancient days; they are her slaves. We have only seen a few that managed to escape."

"If there are new tunnels that we don't know about," Cronin said, "then she has the advantage."

"She'll not be expecting us, and that gives us the advantage," Alec said. "She's sending out Seekers to bring me to her. She won't be expecting me to turn up unannounced."

Cronin growled. "Because it is not a sane plan."

Alec smiled at him. "Which is why it's the best plan we've got. It will be the last thing she expects."

"I don't like it," Cronin said.

"Neither do I," Alec admitted. He took Cronin's hand. "None of us chose this. None of us wished for this, but we're facing it anyway, and we need to deal with it. We need to be as educated and prepared as possible."

Cronin grumbled but he didn't argue, which Alec took as a win. He squeezed Cronin's hand. "Will you read through those textbooks with me?"

Cronin nodded and spoke quietly. "Of course."

"Hey," Alec said softly. He lifted Cronin's chin and kissed him, reassuring him. It was such a private moment, despite the audience. Alec didn't miss that Johan smiled sadly before looking away.

* * * *

Alec sat on the sofa, burying himself in texts and talking to Bes and the other Egyptian vampires, trying to find out everything he could. What he determined was not all pharaohs were gods, not all gods were vampires. The most notorious vampires of Ancient Egypt, however, were Osiris, Anubis, Isis, Ra, and Ammit, a vampire "goddess" who apparently decimated many thousands of humans in her time.

All of these ancient vampires were mummified and entombed within the various burial chambers of the Great Pyramids.

Cronin sat with Alec, studying and profiling, answering questions, and forming as much intel as possible, not on Queen Keket, but on the vampires she wanted to resurrect. As Alec had said before, it would tell him more about Keket in figuring out why she wanted the vampires she did than the study of her would discover.

Osiris was the first. Known as the god of the dead for very good reason, he was the most notorious Egyptian vampire of them all, and Alec had no doubt Keket wanted him for his power. If she could master him, she'd be unstoppable.

Anubis was the vampire who removed Osiris's heart, embalmed him, and sent him to the afterlife. Would she resurrect the only vampire who could kill Osiris? If he became too powerful, a threat to her rule, would she end him for a second time?

Isis made more sense for Keket to return, Alec thought. For one, she was female, and not a sexual threat. Isis, it was claimed by some, was responsible in part for the death of Osiris, along with Anubis. She was often depicted with wings, and Alec wondered if her vampiric talent was the ability to fly. Lord knows, nothing was impossible at this stage.

There was also Ra. He was the god of the sun, which was odd, because as a vampire, he never saw the light of it. In most all hieroglyphs, he was shown to have a round dinner-plate-sized disk on his head, and he also held an ankh. There was little else known about him, including where exactly he was buried.

Ammit was a particularly nasty vampire, who was known as a devourer of millions and for her divine retribution. Alec shuddered at the thought of that combination. If Keket hadn't resurrected this particular vampire already, she'd no doubt be on the short list.

There was so much to take in, so many what-ifs, and still, so many questions. "Why didn't the Ancient Egyptians just stake these guys in the heart? Seriously, then none of this would be happening."

Cronin shrugged. "We don't know. It was a long time ago. Maybe they thought embalming was the right thing to do, and in all honesty, who would have thought we'd encounter someone who wanted to resurrect them?" He smiled at Alec. "And who knows what we'll be doing in three thousand years."

Alec snorted. "Probably thinking those twenty-first-century people were a bunch of idiots."

Cronin laughed. "Probably."

After a while, Alec needed to stretch out, his body aching from sitting still too long. He lifted Cronin's arm and leaned against him, tucking himself into his side, stretching his legs out on the sofa. He simply brought Cronin's arm back down over his chest and kept on reading, only looking up at Cronin when he chuckled.

"Comfortable?" Cronin asked, a smile in his voice.

"Very," Alec said.

Alec was pretty sure Cronin didn't do a great deal of reading, more transfixed with the feel of Alec against him and the smell of his hair, and the occasional kiss to his temple. He didn't mind, though, he didn't mind one bit. Alec couldn't describe just how good it felt to be lying with his back against Cronin, but also how right it was.

As much as the whole fated idea grated on his sense of independence, he certainly couldn't deny its power.

Alec had to force himself to concentrate on the books he was supposed to be reading. He carefully picked up another book. The pages were thick; they felt like papyrus, the writing on them hand scribed in cursive ink. The cover and binding were frail. Alec remembered Cronin saying these books predated censorship, so he guessed it was dated before the twelfth century. He held it as gently as he could. "I'm taking it this is a first edition?"

Cronin laughed. "Something like that." Cronin took the book and turned it in his hand. "This one I got from a library in Bohemia. There was a funny little librarian man who kept it guarded in a vault. He was well-read in the paranormal. I had no doubt he knew what I was."

"Did you kill him?"

"Of course," Cronin said. "Uh, I, um, well... It was a civic duty to my kind. Couldn't have him telling anyone that vampires were real, could I?"

Alec snorted out a laugh. "Of course not." It was a little hard to feel sympathy for a man that died a thousand years ago. Alec felt a soft rumbly purr come from Cronin's chest, and Alec sighed deeply. He took the book from Cronin, their hands brushing, touching, and neither of them moved as Alec turned page after page, reading all he could. He was sure Cronin could read each page in just a few seconds, but he never complained as Alec went at a human pace.

After the third book, Alec sat up and opened all three books on the coffee table to certain pages showing hieroglyphics. He pointed to one in particular. "This is the ankh, yes?" Alec asked.

Cronin gave a nod. "Yes."

Alec studied the ankh. It looked like a religious cross with a looped head or handle. It was all through Egyptian drawings and mythology, held by gods and pharaohs alike.

"What does it mean?" Alec asked. "I know the Egyptian historians say it's a symbol of eternal life, but what do you make of it?"

Cronin leaned forward, scanning the three open books. "Ancient Egyptians, vampire and man, had symbols for most everything," Cronin said. He turned his face to Alec. "What do you think it is?"

"I think it's a key."

Suddenly there were six vampires in the room, looking at him, waiting for him to explain further.

"It's in hieroglyphs that span thousands of years. Many symbols changed and morphed over that amount of time or from one pharaoh or god to the next, but not this," Alec said, tapping a picture of an ankh. "I mean, it *looks* like a key! Well, sort of, in an Ancient Egyptian–kinda way. I don't know how, or what it symbolizes, whether it's a warning symbol like all the cats, or if it's trying to tell us what we need to do with the key… I don't know." Alec looked at Cronin. "I just think it's significant. Too significant."

Cronin picked up the first book and flipped through the pages, then the second and then the third. Alec had grossly underestimated the speed with which Cronin could read. "It could be," he said quietly. "Nothing proves it otherwise. It does resemble what we now call a key. Is this where the term originated? I don't know. But if it is, if it does relate to the key we are referring to, what does it mean?"

Bes picked up the first book, and not quite as quickly as Cronin had, he read through it. "This is a remarkable text," he said. "A rarity indeed." He read the second book, then the third, and each book got passed to the next vampire.

Jodis nodded grimly. "It doesn't appear to be a warning. These images of pharaohs and gods show them happy to hold the ankh, they offer it to gods, they use it as a weapon…" She looked at Cronin first, then at Alec. "Alec, I think you're right."

"A symbol to show what, though?" Alec wondered out loud. "Do we have pictures of where Osiris is buried? It might give us some clue."

"Osiris is buried in a shaft under the Sphinx," Cronin said.

Alec blinked. "Of course he is," he mumbled. "The largest statue of a cat in the world."

"There are shafts along the tunnel that lead from the pyramid to the Sphinx," Bes said, pointing to the map he'd helped Johan with, more specifically, to the deep shaft with a small tomb at the bottom. "There are no markings, no hieroglyphs, nothing to say who is buried there. But the sarcophagus is most definitely his."

Alec considered that. "Well, I doubt his casket is still there. Those rooms would be too small, and there's only one way in and out. I doubt Queen Keket would risk such a position. She would have moved him to a bigger area, where she can have a bigger audience."

"The King's Chamber," Eiji said.

Alec sighed. "Well, I was hoping some hieroglyphs might have told us what to do, but obviously not." Alec went back to the maps. He looked at both Bes and Johan. "What other shafts are there? Can we add as much as possible?"

He spent the next little while scouring Internet sites and using Bes's knowledge to add a capillary of smaller shafts. Then Alec asked Johan to mark where Bes thought the other known vampire mummies were buried.

In no time at all, the map of the three main pyramids of Giza were littered with lines of shafts and tunnels and asterisks where the other burial tombs were or were rumored to be. It resembled an ant farm, a sectional picture of chambers, tunnels and, nests.

The map looked a little different now from when they'd started, and Alec was happier with it. He clapped Johan on the shoulder. He had dutifully done everything as instructed and even seemed pleased with the end result. Cronin was right; Johan was a skilled cartographer. "You're very good at that," Alec told him, nodding toward the map in front of them. Alec doubted Google Maps or Google Earth with satellite imagery could have done such a good job.

Johan nodded in gratitude. "Thank you."

"Can I ask you something?" Alec said. He was still looking at the map and didn't wait for Johan to reply. "As a cartographer, a maker of maps with an eye for architecture, if you were to add tunnels like we think Keket has, where would you put them?"

Johan was clearly surprised by Alec's question, obviously not expecting him to value his opinion. Johan indicated on the map with his finger. "Given she hasn't had much time, the quickest route from A to B is logical."

Alec nodded. "Agreed."

"But see here?" he said, running his finger along an imaginary line. "For me, it would make sense that there was large chambers in this space. Not just tunnels, but rooms to house her army. Barracks, if you will." Johan gave another nod and Alec realized it was more submissive than of gratitude. "So if you need to get from here" — he pointed to the first pyramid, then to the second — "to here? I would not expect an easy road."

Alec smiled. He hadn't thought of that. "You think there are chambers of returned vampires in there?"

Johan nodded again, though it was more of a bow of his head. "She would need to house her army."

"I think you're right," Alec said, clapping his hand on the vampire's shoulder. "Can you draw them in?"

Johan's eyes widened just a fraction. "Of course."

Alec gave him a warm smile. "Thank you."

Johan drew in an educated guess of possible new tunnels that Keket might have ordered to be dug and possible chambers, or barracks, as he called them. It was an apt description, Alec conceded. Barracks to house her army. It made perfect sense.

Cronin soon stood beside Alec and put his hand on the small of his back. He seemed pleased that Alec had made an effort to include Johan, making him feel equal instead of left out.

When the map was done, it looked more complex than Alec cared for. Their simple plan really wasn't simple at all. Alec sighed deeply and ran his fingers over the drawn map, taking in every corridor, every turn, every chamber, angles and distances. "There are so many unknowns," he said. "I don't like dealing with unknowns."

"So what do we know as truth?" Cronin asked.

"Not much," Alec answered. He sighed again. "All the intel we have is secondhand, rumors, guesswork, and visions. If I were to take this to my division captain in the force, he'd laugh. For a week."

"Do you not believe it to be true?" Cronin asked, his eyes more concerned than inquisitive.

"I do believe it," Alec said quietly. "And I think that's what scares me. Knowing about vampires and the way history has been modified so humans remain blissfully ignorant, I have no choice *but* to believe. I believe what Bes says—how the covens have fled—and I've read your books on the Ancient Egyptian vampires. And the fact two vampires tried to kill me the other day so Keket would have no key kinda pushed it home as well."

Cronin frowned, but he didn't say anything.

"What we *do* know so far," Alec said, "is that the Egyptian covens have moved out, the self-appointed Queen Keket is building an army, and she wants to bring back the most evil of vampires, Osiris. And if Eleanor's visions are correct, I am to be human to fight her. So if she does need my heart to bring back Osiris, it needs to be *beating*?"

Cronin growled. "She'll not touch you. I swear my life upon it."

The heat in Cronin's voice surprised Alec, the fierceness was breathtaking. Alec felt lightheaded, drunk almost, and very turned-on. Eiji cleared his throat behind them.

Alec quickly shook his head and laughed it off. "Eleanor? What else have you seen?" he asked. "You said she needs me to be human, yes?"

The old woman vampire shook her head slowly. "No. I said *you* need to be human. She needs your heart, yes, but if it needs to be human, I do not know. I can't see past her. And the reasons for you needing to be human?" she said, her voice small in the huge apartment. "What for, I cannot see. I believe it is not clear to me because it is not clear to you, Alec. I think you will know why when you see it, then so will I. But until then…"

Well, that was really un-fucking-helpful.

"Okay," Alec relented. He sat back down on the sofa and Cronin sat beside him. "So we need to work with some assumptions, given what information we have to work with is limited. We need to turn up, with the element of surprise on our side, and somehow I need to be the one to take out the Queen before she… well, before she takes me out."

Alec felt the rumble in Cronin's chest before he heard it.

Alec sat up straighter and took Cronin's hand. "It is a possibility," Alec said quietly. "Despite what Eiji has seen."

"How can you talk of such things?"

"Because I'm a cop—or at least, I was," Alec said. "It's how I operate. Strategic, informed, and prepared, Cronin. It's the only way."

Cronin frowned, his dark eyes piercing. "I cannot consider a reality in which you do not exist," he said quietly.

Alec squeezed his hand. "But we need to discuss this rationally," he countered. "We need to discuss options, and have plans A through to Z worked out. We need to have fallback plans. But first and foremost, we need to be clear on objectives." Alec looked around the room at all the vampires. "Our only goal is to ensure this Queen Keket doesn't get what she needs. And that's me. Not just *me* me, but me alive."

"What are you saying?" Cronin asked quietly.

"That if a choice has to be made," Alec said simply, "between saving the world and saving me, then—"

"No!" Cronin barked.

"We need to be reasonable about this," Alec pressed. "I'm not keen on the idea either, I have to say. I'd prefer I live a little longer than three days from now too. But if Keket needs me alive and we're losing on every front, if she has me hostage and we've all but lost, Cronin, then take me out of the equation."

"Do me a favor," Cronin said, his mouth a flat line. His eyes were an angry black. "Leave nobility to fools and kings."

Alec put his hand on Cronin's arm. "Please try and understand why I'm saying this—"

Cronin flew off the sofa; his anger was abrupt and startling. "Don't tell me that I should tolerate your death or, like I could even fathom the notion, be the one to kill you myself! Have you lost your mind? Are you aware of what fated means, Alec? Do you not know? The death of one fated partner is the death of the other."

Alec blinked. "No," he said softly. "I didn't know."

Cronin threw his hands up and, frustrated, ran them through his hair. His voice was quieter, his anger gone. "I guess you weren't to know if you weren't told."

"I kind of haven't been told anything," Alec said. "Except for the fact that vampires are real, a whole legion of them wants me dead, vampires from all around the world want me dead too in some kind of attempt to put an end to this whole fucking mess, and oh, yes, there's a crazy bitch in Egypt who wants to rip my heart from my chest to bring back a vampire whose special talent is death itself. And let's not forget that my entire existence is now inextricably linked to someone I just met four days ago."

Cronin walked at a slow human pace back to Alec, and knelt in front of him. He tentatively took Alec's hands and brought them to his face, sighing and leaning into the palms. "I wish things were different. I wish you were not involved in this in any way. I wish only to keep you safe."

"Do you wish you'd not met me?" Alec asked.

Cronin's gaze shot to his, his black eyes wild and honest. "It burns in my heart to hear you say such a thing. Please, Alec, don't ever doubt what you are to me."

Alec's heart tripped in his chest. "What am I to you?"

Cronin's reply was short and immediate. "Everything."

A slow smile spread across Alec's face, matching the sweep of warmth that filled his chest. He leaned forward and kissed Cronin, and the spark of contact stole his breath.

"So, please," Cronin said quietly. "No such talk of self-sacrifice. I cannot bear it."

"Okay," Alec agreed.

Cronin narrowed his eyes at him. "And not just talk of it. There can be no plans of it either. No errant thought, no resignation in the back of your mind. Please, Alec."

Alec smiled at him. "Okay, okay." He leaned back on the sofa and patted the seat beside him. "Sit with me again," Alec said. He didn't admit to not liking it when Cronin was mad at him, and when Cronin did sit back down, Alec swung his leg behind him and pulled the vampire against his chest. "Your turn to lean against me."

Cronin was a bit stilted and tense, clearly unsure of being in such an intimate position. Alec put his arm around him and nuzzled his nose into his hair, doing what Cronin had done to him. Alec put his lips to Cronin's ear. "I like having you between my legs," he whispered. "Then again, I rather liked being between yours too."

Cronin started to growl, soft but firm.

Alec chuckled and nudged his nose to Cronin's ear. "I'm nothing if not versatile."

In the blink of an eye, Cronin turned and pressed him into the sofa, bringing Alec's legs up and himself between them. Their noses touching, Cronin's fangs were showing and there was a feral black desire in his eyes. "It's probably best not to talk of such things to me."

Alec chuckled again. "You like the sound of it, though?"

"Aye."

That made Alec laugh. "Aye? How very Scottish of you."

Cronin grinned wickedly, his eyes glinted with mischief and his fangs looked even better with a smile. "Would you like to see how very Scottish I can be?"

Alec could barely breathe, every nerve was strung tight. "Very much."

"Okay, lovebirds," Eiji cried. He let a book fall flat onto the table with a loud smack. "Enough. Please. We could carve the testosterone and pheromones in here with a knife. You're killing us!"

Alec turned his face to look at Eiji but kept his hands on Cronin's ass, keeping him firmly between his thighs. "He was helping me read."

Eiji snorted at him. "I can see that."

There was a less than happy growl rattling from Cronin's chest when he slowly peeled himself off Alec, but he was smiling salaciously. Missing the feel of Cronin against him, Alec slid his hand over his crotch and gave his own dick a squeeze.

Cronin turned to Eiji, but waved his hand at Alec. "See? It's not my fault. He does *that* and I can't help it."

Eiji laughed at Cronin's facial expression, and Alec laughed too. He swung his leg back over so both feet were on the floor and picked up the forgotten book. "I'm hardly to blame," he said, giving Cronin a fake glare. "*You're* the reason I have to do that. Just sitting there, all Scottish and sexy as hell."

Eiji looked up at the ceiling and groaned. "The others are heading out now to feed—and to get some fresh air away from you two, if you know what I mean. That leaves just me and Jodis here with you, and it is too difficult to protect you, Alec, when we are so distracted."

"Maybe Cronin and I could go check out how Campbell is doing with my bullet order," Alec suggested. "That'll leave you and Jodis here *alone,* if you know what I mean." Alec waggled his eyebrows. "You can be distracted all you like."

Cronin stood and held out his hand to Alec, which he took quickly and stood beside him. Cronin was fighting a smile. "Should you call him first?"

Before Alec could answer, Eiji spoke. "Jodis and I will go with you also. I think Alec should have full protection wherever he goes. Cronin, I make no judgment on your ability to protect him. I know you're capable." The smaller Japanese vampire looked to Alec, his usual smile gone. "I know you don't like it, but, Alec, it's not worth the risk of being caught unprepared."

Alec thought Cronin might object, but after a long second, he gave a nod. "Thank you."

Eiji left, Alec assumed he went to get Jodis, and Alec pulled out the cell phone he used to call Campbell on. He hit Call, and while he waited for

Campbell to answer, he whispered to Cronin, "What was that about?"

Cronin gave him a sad smile. "Eiji's doing it for both our sakes. If you were to die, it would mean certain death for me also, and that is something he'd rather not suffer through."

Oh.

The cell phone in Alec's hand clicked when Campbell answered the call. "Hello?"

Alec blinked a few times and slowly put the phone to his ear. "Campbell? It's MacAidan. You alone?"

"Yeah."

"Up for a visit?"

"Have I got a choice?"

"No."

CHAPTER SIXTEEN

Campbell's reaction to having people suddenly appear in front of him the second time was no better than it was the first time. Maybe it was worse because four people unexpectedly materialized in his small living room. Maybe it was because, as was clear from the dark circles under his eyes, he hadn't slept. Maybe it was the way both Jodis and Eiji spread out in a tactical formation to maximize coverage and minimize their collective target mass; Alec had seen SWAT teams do similar moves.

Campbell dropped a box of bullet casings, sending them clinking and scattering to the floor. "Jesus!" he cried. His eyes were wide as he looked between the four intruders, his eyes finally stopping on Alec. Then he clutched his heart with shaking hands. "Fuck. Can you not knock on the fucking door like a normal person?"

Alec smiled at him, and not even bothering with introductions, he said, "How're my bullets coming along?"

Campbell's hands were still shaking, and he closed and opened his fists a few times, warily looking at Eiji and then Jodis. "Yeah, they're good... I mean, I'm on track... I think." He looked at Cronin and slinked back into himself, very obviously afraid of him. He swallowed hard. "W-would... you wanna see 'em?"

Alec smiled at him, trying to make him relax a bit. At this rate Campbell was gonna have a heart attack before he finished the job. "Sure."

Campbell led them through the small house, the kitchen and hall just as grimy and dirty as the living room, and he stopped in the laundry room. Clearly agitated and looking over his shoulder nervously, he rolled back the linoleum to reveal a door in the floor. He lifted the trapdoor and stood back, waving his hand at the dark space.

Jodis shook her head. "You first."

Campbell nodded quickly and scampered to get down through the hole. The only stairs were a ladder that descended straight down. When he'd disappeared into the darkness, Cronin grinned and disappeared also. Lights flickered to life in the underground room, and then Campbell screamed out like a small child. "Stop doing that!"

Cronin laughed. "The room is clear."

Alec rolled his eyes and started to climb down the ladder. "You're gonna give him a coronary," he said.

"Yeah," Campbell quickly agreed.

When Alec was at the bottom, he found himself in what looked like an old bomb shelter. There was a shelf along one wall filled with all kinds of metal-pressing tools, vises, and trays of different hand tools and metals. *Weapon-making tools*, Alec corrected himself. It was quite the setup.

Jodis and Eiji were suddenly beside Alec, though he was used to vampires and their sudden, fluid movements. Campbell obviously wasn't. He shivered violently and Alec thought for a moment that Campbell was going to be sick.

In the center of the room was a workbench where Alec saw a tray of neatly arranged wooden and brass bullets. He picked up one and inspected it. It was exactly what he'd asked for. A half jacket, wooden tip, perfectly carved and smoothed.

Campbell spoke quickly. "I've only done about fifty so far, but it was hard in the beginnin' with the wood and all. I know what I'm doing now, so it's easier. I should have the rest done no problem."

Alec was still looking at the bullet he was holding. "Beautiful work," he said softly, marveling at the darker wood against the bright brass of the casing. Alec finally smiled at Campbell. "You're very good at this. I never really appreciated your ballistics skills as a craft before."

"'Cause you was always tryin' to bust my ass," he mumbled, obviously without really thinking about it, because his eyes flashed to Cronin and his hands went up. "Not that there's anything wrong with that. Ya know, bein' a cop and all."

Cronin hadn't even moved, but he fought a smile at Campbell's reaction. Alec sighed. "Well, I'm not a cop anymore," he said, putting the bullet back in its place on the tray. "You've tested them, I assume? I'd like to see for myself."

Campbell hesitated, eyeing Cronin first, then Eiji and Jodis. "Well, I had to see if they was gonna get out of the chamber before I went an' made a few hundred of 'em, didn't I?"

"Exactly," Alec agreed. Then he held out his hand. "So? Your 9mm?"

Campbell reluctantly reached to his back and pulled his pistol from his waistband. He handed over the Glock, which Alec took. Then Alec extended his other hand. "And the silencer."

Campbell huffed but obviously knew arguing was not a wise thing to do. He pulled the very illegal sound suppressor from his jeans pocket and handed it over too. With a familiar ease, Alec screwed on the silencer, pulled the slide on the handgun back, and fed one bullet directly into the chamber.

Now he just needed something to fire the bullet into. He looked around the room.

"Jesus!" Campbell cried. "You're not gonna fire that in here, are ya?" Then his eyes went wider still. "You're not gonna shoot *me* in here, are ya?"

Alec snorted out a laugh. "Campbell, I thought we were friends. I don't shoot my friends." The truth was, Alec hadn't shot anybody before. He'd raised his weapon plenty of times but never fired it with intent to maim or hinder.

"Shoot at the wall," Eiji said, nodding his head toward the wall he stood next to.

"You can't just be shootin' up my momma's house, man." Campbell said.

Alec ignored Campbell and raised the gun to shoot the wall. He felt the cool resistance against his trigger finger and squeezed.

Campbell fell back a step, the three vampires didn't appear to move, but the bullet never hit the wall.

"What the...?" Campbell whispered. He looked at the wall, then at the three non-humans in the room. He finally looked at Alec, more scared than before. "What th' hell, man? Bullets don't just disappear!"

Eiji held up his fist and turned his hand, palm facing upward, to reveal the bullet.

Knowing he must have caught it, much like when he'd bent the bullet's trajectory years ago from hitting him in the head, Alec grinned at him. "Show-off."

"It fired well," Eiji said, putting the wooden slug, still in perfect condition, back on the table.

Campbell was stunned into silence, his jaw slack, his eyes wide. Alec smiled at him. "Perfect," he said, clapping the man on the back. "Good job."

All the poor guy could do was nod.

"Another twenty-four hours, yeah?" Alec reminded him.

He nodded again.

"Take a breath for me," Alec said. Campbell finally inhaled and took a few quick breaths. "You good?"

Campbell looked at Alec and nodded quickly. "Yeah, I'm good."

Alec gave him a full-on grin. "Good. We'll be back tomorrow."

"I, uh..." Campbell started to say. "I, um, I could just leave the bullets here—" He swallowed hard. "—when I'm done making all I can. I'll message you. You come get 'em, leave the cash here. Message me when you're done. I ain't bullshittin' ya, man. But I don't think I'm up for another visit."

He truthfully didn't look too well. "Fine," Alec agreed. "Send me a text when you're done, twenty-four hours from now, with a total number of bullets. We'll... drop in... and leave payment. I'll message you when we're gone."

Campbell looked relieved; he nodded enthusiastically. "Yeah, man. Yeah, let's do that."

"You won't tell anyone what you've seen tonight, will you," Cronin said quietly. It wasn't a question.

Campbell paled again and shook his head vehemently. "No. No, man, I swear."

"Good boy," Jodis said. "I'd hate to have to come back." She ran her finger down Campbell's arm, leaving a trail of cold gooseflesh in her wake.

Campbell recoiled immediately, walking back into the shelf along the wall, and Alec knew it was time to give the poor guy a break. He turned to Cronin. "You ready?"

Cronin gave a nod and moved at vampire speed to Alec's side, where he fit just right, his arm around Alec's waist. He simply held his other hand out to Eiji, who in turn held his hand out to Jodis, and they leapt.

* * * *

The apartment was empty when they arrived except for Sammy, who was curled up asleep on the sofa. Eiji and Jodis disappeared quickly enough, and Cronin nudged Alec's jaw with his nose. "You don't feel the effects of leaping so much anymore," he said softly.

"Guess I'm used to it. I'm getting used to this too," he said, sliding his hand down Cronin's back and over the swell of his ass.

"We do have some alone time, it would seem," Cronin whispered, his breath warm on the skin under Alec's ear. It made him shiver.

Alec suddenly found himself leaping again, this time landing on his back in the middle of Cronin's soft bed, his thighs spread wide with Cronin lying between them. The bathroom light was on, leaving a diffused light across the otherwise darkened room.

Alec shivered again, not from leaping but from the onslaught of desire. "We could have walked in here."

Cronin's eyes were impossibly black, his fangs glinted in the soft light. "Why waste precious seconds walking when I could have you in here like this already?"

Alec laughed, a throaty sound. He raised his hips off the bed, seeking Cronin's. "I'm beginning to see your point."

Cronin was apparently done talking. He lay his full weight on Alec, his hips squarely lined up with Alec's, their hardness pressing against each other. Cronin covered Alec's mouth with his own, running his hands the length of Alec's arms to his hands, which he held and slowly lifted them above Alec's head, pinning them to the mattress.

The groan Alec made would have been embarrassing if he cared. He was totally caught by desire, his need to submit to Cronin like nothing he'd ever felt. His thighs fell open, his pelvis tilted and even completely dressed, he offered himself to Cronin.

Cronin growled as he kissed him, a purring rumble sounding deep within his chest, spurring on Alec's want and need. And he'd wanted nothing more. He wanted to touch him, to feel him, to pull him close and grind against him—he needed it—yet Cronin held his hands fast to the bed.

Alec made a whining noise that was half frustration, half begging. He pulled his mouth from Cronin's and ground out a warning. "Cronin."

The vampire pulled back just enough so Alec could see his face. His eyes were blazing black, his lips swollen, and his tongue swept across his fanged teeth; he truly was sex personified. Alec was so turned-on, frustrated to the point of tears. "I need to touch you, please."

Cronin slowly released Alec's hands, only to touch the side of Alec's face. His look of lust and heat quickly became one of concern. "Are you hurt?"

Alec shook his head, bringing his hands first to Cronin's hair, then his face, his jaw. Down to his chest, then to his back and his ass, touching everywhere he could reach. He pulled Cronin's hips harder against his. "I need you," he whispered. "Like nothing else."

Then Alec forced his hands between them to undo Cronin's jeans, fumbling, failing, his frustration growing into desperation.

"Slow down," Cronin whispered in his ear.

"No," Alec said, pulling Cronin's shirt over his head instead.

"You'll bring my self-control undone," Cronin growled. "I can barely contain it as it is."

"I want you to let go," Alec said. "Show me the real you."

Cronin pulled away then to sit on the side of the bed, his eyes downcast, his smile not a happy one. "Alec, I cannot. I've told you, it would result in the end of your human life."

Alec scampered to his knees on the bed. "We've fooled around before and look!" He thumped his chest. "Still human! We did just fine before. We did better than fine before. It was hot as hell."

"You want more…"

"Of course I do!" Alec said.

"I cannot give you what you desire."

Alec whispered, "I want you to be yourself. I want the vampire in you to be, well, vampire."

Cronin smiled at that. "Vampires bite, Alec."

"You won't bite me," Alec said adamantly. "You don't have my permission."

"Your permission?"

"Yes." Alec slid off the bed and pulled his jeans off, then his shirt. And in only his underwear, he sidled over to where Cronin still sat on the bed and swung his leg over to straddle his hips. Alec deliberately ground down hard on him and tilted his head back so he could kiss him.

"I want more with you. I will always want more with you," Alec whispered. Cronin's pale skin looked silver in the light, and Alec traced his fingers over the silver scar on Cronin's chest. "I want the human you." Then he slid his thumb across Cronin's bottom lip to reveal his fangs. "I want the vampire you."

"We cannot…" Cronin cringed, not willing to say the words.

"Have penetrative sex," Alec finished for him, grinding down on him once more. "Because sex means biting."

Cronin barked out an embarrassed laugh, which Alec silenced with a kiss. "For what it's worth, Cronin," Alec murmured. "I look forward to it. The fucking, the biting…"

Cronin hissed out another growl. "Alec. You shouldn't say such things to me."

"Make me come, Cronin." He mouthed the words against his lips, and Cronin reacted with a sharp growl and demanding hands. He gripped Alec in all the right places, holding him tightly while Alec slid his arms around Cronin and slid his tongue into Cronin's mouth.

They ground their hips, seeking friction and touch. This time when Alec moved his hands to the button on Cronin's jeans, he wasn't stopped. And when Alec slid his hand around Cronin's hard cock, he bucked upward, his whole body taut.

Then Alec flexed against him, the friction all he needed to send his orgasm spinning through him. Cronin wrapped his fingers around Alec's shaft, and as he spilled between them, Alec arched his back and gave a silent scream. Cronin followed soon after, and for the longest, most perfect moment, they barely moved. They just rocked back and forth a little, collecting their breaths and semblance of thoughts, Alec still straddling Cronin with no intention of ever moving.

"Shower?" Cronin asked eventually.

All Alec could do was nod against Cronin's shoulder. He'd almost fallen asleep.

Cronin stood up, holding Alec right where he was, and walked into the bathroom and into the shower. Cronin turned the water on with one hand, still holding Alec with such ease, slowly leaning him back into the streams of hot water. And slowly, slowly, Alec slid down until his feet hit the tiles. Still sleepy, he kind of slumped against Cronin, his face buried in his neck, while Cronin soaped them both with slow and languid hands.

"You need to sleep," Cronin murmured.

Alec nodded again. "You need to come to bed with me."

When Cronin spoke next, there was a smile in his voice. "You tempt me, *m'cridhe*."

Alec stood to his full height then, resting his forehead on Cronin's, making the vampire have to look up. The look in his eyes took Alec's breath away. "*Am* I your heart?"

Cronin's eyes slowly closed and he whispered, "Aye."

Alec smiled at that. "I love it when you speak Gaelic to me."

Cronin ducked his head, pressing his forehead against Alec's jaw down to his neck. "You bring it out in me. It is not a tongue I've used in many years."

Alec lifted Cronin's chin, making eye contact between them. "You'll not use your tongue for anyone else," he said gruffly. He knew Cronin meant tongue as in language, but he couldn't resist. "It is for me, and me alone."

Cronin flushed at Alec's words. His eyes darkened and when he licked his lips, Alec saw his fangs. Alec was laying claim to him, and Cronin's reaction told him he more than liked it.

"Now take me to bed," Alec demanded. "I haven't finished with you yet."

Alec immediately found himself lying in Cronin's bed, the vampire over him once more, both of them dripping wet. "You leave my will power in ruins," Cronin murmured.

The power Alec held over Cronin was heady, a heat expanding through his body, resonating in his chest. "Good. Now get on your back."

Cronin bared his vampiric teeth just a little, but did as Alec asked. Alec rolled over him, nestling himself between Cronin's thighs. They were both hard again, and Alec rolled his hips, rutting against him.

Alec kissed him then, resting on his elbows, still sliding their cocks together, frotting and grinding. "Grip us together," Alec told him.

Cronin wrapped one hand around both their cocks, and Alec fucked his fist. Cronin was growling, a steady rumble, and the sound buzzed straight to Alec's cock. He groaned into Cronin's mouth and rolled his hips harder. "This is how I will fuck you," he rasped out.

Cronin flexed underneath him, arching his back as he came. The sight, the feel of Cronin's cock pulsing against his own, ripped Alec's orgasm from his very toes.

When they'd collapsed, Alec could barely open his eyes. He felt Cronin move, then felt a cloth wiping him clean before the bed dipped one last time and Cronin lay back down. Alec was on his side, so he lifted his arm, implying that Cronin needed to put himself in the vacant space.

He did just that, of course, and once Cronin was settled, Alec snuggled against him, half lying on top of him. Still with his eyes closed, he reached blindly for Cronin's hand and threaded their fingers. Alec smiled when he felt a gentle purr vibrate from Cronin's chest, and he fell into sleep.

* * * *

When Alec woke up, Cronin was still there. Still lying there with his arm around him, still nudging his nose along Alec's hair. "Hmm." Alec stretched out. "You're still here."

Cronin kissed the side of Alec's head and whispered, "Given we're three days from going to war, there is no place I'd rather be."

Alec sighed and let his still-sleepy brain catch up. "I don't even know what day it is." He lifted his arm to look at his watch. "What's the time?"

"It's one in the afternoon."

"I've lost track of day and night," Alec mumbled. "Being here with the windows all blacked out, it's disorienting."

Cronin kissed his temple. "Are you hungry? I can fix you some coffee if you wish."

"Sounds good." Alec didn't move, though. "Are you hungry?"

Cronin hesitated a moment. "What do you mean?"

"I mean, hungry, thirsty, whatever. Do you need to feed? It's been two days."

"I will have to soon," he said quietly. "I might leave when the others get back."

Alec leaned up so he could see Cronin's face. "Are they not back yet?"

"Not yet," Cronin said simply. He certainly didn't look concerned. "They're not children."

"But it's daylight!"

"They'll be somewhere safe. They've lived hundreds of years, Alec. They know what they're doing."

"Hmm." Alec frowned. "I guess." He sat up and rubbed his eyes, trying to wake himself up. "Are Eiji and Jodis still here?"

"Yes. Eiji took a delivery of his crossbows. He's very excited." Cronin smiled fondly.

"Oh, cool," Alec said, getting off the bed. "I wanna check them out." He started to walk to the door, then stopped and looked down at his naked self. "Might need some clothes first, huh?"

"I'd rather you didn't," Cronin said with a sly smirk, "but the others might not share my sentiment."

Alec heard Jodis mumble something from the living room, and Cronin laughed. He got out of bed and pulled on his jeans with a vampire speed so fast Alec barely registered the movements. When he stopped being a blur, he stood, fully dressed, looking all kinds of fucking gorgeous, and still smiling. "You like to shower upon waking," he mused. "I will have your coffee ready by the time you are done."

Alec couldn't help himself. He walked slowly, still buck naked, his cock hanging thick and heavy, and stood in front of Cronin. Alec put his hands to Cronin's face to angle his head upward a little and planted a kiss on his lips. Then without a word, he simply turned and walked into the bathroom.

* * * *

Showered, shaved, dressed, and now fully awake, Alec followed the scent of coffee to the living room, where Cronin had his steaming cup waiting for him. Eiji had boxes opened on the floor and dining table. There were six crossbows in total, and a grinning Eiji. "These were the best idea," he said excitedly. "Care to try one?"

"Uh…" Alec was unsure. He looked at his coffee, then around the room. Jodis smiled warmly at him. "I might have my coffee first, but thanks for the offer."

Eiji didn't seem bothered. Still excited, he held up a long black wooden arrow. There was no metal tip, the fletches were so small they looked almost like a groove in the wood, and there was a simple plastic nock where the string of the bow would fit.

Alec looked back to the streamlined feathers at the end of the arrow. "What's with the fletching?"

"Well, I asked for these specifically," Eiji said. "I calculated that with the pressure with which a vampire can fire a bow, and what is sure to be close proximity to our targets, the less drag on the arrow, the better."

"They'll be like sleek wooden missiles," Alec furthered.

"Exactly!" Eiji was still grinning.

Cronin stood in close to Alec and gently slipped his fingers around Alec's free hand. "I told you he was excited."

"He's like a child waking to gifts on his birthday," Jodis said, looking at Eiji with such warmth and love that Alec found himself blushing. He quickly turned away and Cronin pulled him into his side with a laugh.

Cronin was smiling his eye-crinkling smile. He waved his hand at a brown paper bag on the table. "I took the liberty of ordering you some toasted sandwiches from a delicatessen. I asked for a popular selection. I hope they're to your liking."

"Thank you," Alec said quietly. He loved that Cronin was thoughtful to his needs. He opened the bag and took out the first. It was roast beef and vegetables with melted cheese on Turkish bread. Alec moaned as he tasted it. "Oh my god, it's really good." He finished the first one and downed his coffee in record time, not realizing how hungry he was. "You know, I never thought I'd say this, but I can't wait to go grocery shopping so I don't have to have someone order me food all the time."

"You can order more groceries online and have them delivered," Eiji said. He was now holding a crossbow, and yes, still grinning. "Isn't it pretty?"

Alec snorted. "Not sure if pretty is the word I'd use." He looked at Cronin. "But I'd really like to do the online grocery thing, if that's okay?" Alec wasn't sure why he didn't think of it before.

"Of course!" Cronin said quickly. His dark eyes were wide and he frowned. "I'm so sorry I didn't think to suggest you order your own things earlier."

Cronin looked so sorry, it squeezed Alec's heart. He kissed him hard and quick. "It's no big deal. Eiji got me some before, and I didn't think of it either. We'll do it now."

"Oh!" Eiji cried. "I will need some melons."

Alec blinked in surprise. "What on earth for?"

Eiji held up the crossbow and grinned. "So I can shoot them!"

Cronin obviously wasn't waiting for anything else, he pulled Alec's hand and led him through the doors to the office. Alec was still chuckling when he sat at the desk. "Does he get this excited all the time?"

"Not always," Cronin said, amused. He leaned against the desk and put the credit card in front of the laptop. "He gets excited about many things. Each new development in technology is a marvel given from the eras we are from. But there was this time at the turn of the 1900s. It was New Year's Eve, we were in Paris, and they were showcasing a phonograph. It played the sweetest music, and Eiji thought it was fantastic. We had to acquire one, for sure."

"Because it was amazing," Eiji called out, still in the living room, but no doubt hearing every word spoken. "Nothing like CD players or iPods these days, but oh, how we danced."

Alec tried to listen but heard nothing. He nodded toward the door. "Are they dancing right now?"

"He won't put the crossbow down," Jodis answered.

Alec laughed, and Cronin smiled fondly. He turned and spoke to the door, presumably to Eiji and Jodis. "Do you remember that time in 1862, we took accommodations in that townhouse with internal plumbing?"

Jodis's musical laughter carried through the apartment. "He turned the tap on and off, on and off."

Eiji appeared at the door, looking solely at Alec. "I once carried pails of water from streams or dug wells for it, and there it was coming freely from a faucet in the comfort of the house, as needed. They mock me, but I remember harder, simpler times. You'd think these two were born in the twentieth century."

Cronin threw his head back and laughed. "I appreciate running water, my friend. I just didn't play with the tap for two days straight like a simpleton."

Eiji's mouth fell open. "I seem to recall you being impressed with the airplane and motorcar" — he turned to face the living room — "and you my dear, the wonders of bottled shampoo, because washing your white hair with charcoal was so much fun."

Alec burst out laughing. He didn't hear what it was Jodis said back to Eiji, but he grinned wickedly before disappearing at a vampire speed followed by a loud peal of Jodis's laughter.

Cronin was smiling widely, the kind that creased the corners of his eyes. It spread warmth through Alec just to see him so happy, and Eiji and Jodis as well. It was as if, for just a moment, the seriousness of the whole Egyptian-Queen-trying-to-steal-his-heart mess was forgotten.

"Airplanes and automobiles?" Alec asked Cronin.

"They were exciting times," Cronin said, still smiling.

"I guess you don't need either of them with the whole leaping thing, do you?"

Cronin's mouth twisted into an almost pout. "I've never driven a car."

Alec couldn't believe it. "You what?"

Cronin chuckled. "As you said, I've never had a need. If I need to be somewhere, I leap there."

"But you'd like to?"

"One day."

"Then I will teach you."

Eiji was suddenly at the door. "And me?"

Alec laughed. "Of course!" he said. Eiji smiled so hard, Alec wondered how it didn't split his face. "When all this mess is over, I will take you all driving."

Eiji was gone again, speaking so fast Alec couldn't understand him, and Jodis laughed soon after. Cronin leaned down, and doing what Alec had done to him a few times, he put his finger under Alec's chin and tilted his head up so he could kiss him. "Thank you," he said.

Alec wasn't sure if Cronin was thanking him for the promise of driving lessons or for making his friends laugh. He guessed it didn't matter which. "You're welcome."

Alec ordered his groceries, and given the standard vampire kitchen was lacking pots and pans and a sandwich press, he added those to his list as well.

"I feel terrible for depriving you of such basic things," Cronin said. He hadn't moved from where he was leaning against the desk at Alec's side.

Alec stood up and leaned against Cronin. He put his forehead to Cronin's so he would see the sincerity in his eyes. "You know, when I first got here, when I first learned that I was kinda stuck here, I was pissed off. I felt like I'd been taken hostage."

Cronin pulled his face back, with a look of horror and shame. Alec quickly took his face in both hands.

"But now I know it's not like that at all. Cronin, you've not *deprived* me of anything. In fact, you've given me more than I dreamed possible. And I don't mean material things, I mean in here." He took Cronin's hand and put it over his chest. "No, it's not an ideal way to meet, but I'm still grateful we did."

Cronin smiled so shyly, a faint blush tinting his pale cheeks. "I am grateful too."

Alec took Cronin's hands and held them in his. He leaned in and kissed him sweetly. "We have a few hours to fill in, yes?"

"What do you have in mind?" Cronin asked, his tone dripping with suggestion.

Alec laughed. "You still owe me that first date."

* * * *

"This is disturbing," Cronin said quietly.

Alec had thrown himself onto the plush corner sofa in the theater room and Cronin joined him as the little spoon. They were lying on the sofa like a normal couple, arms and legs entwined, watching their second movie.

"Disturbingly good? Or disturbingly bad?" Alec said with a laugh.

"Disturbingly accurate."

"Oh."

The film *Interview with a Vampire* was halfway through, but Alec hadn't thought of actual credibility when he chose it. He just wanted Cronin to see some vampire movies, given he hadn't seen any.

"You lived like that?"

Cronin nodded. "It's not far wrong."

Alec tightened his hold on him and started watching the movie with a new appreciation. "Will you tell me all about it one day?" he whispered.

Cronin sighed. "It's nothing glorified. Some of it was brutal and unforgiving. You may think differently of me if you knew some of the things I've done."

Alec kissed the back of Cronin's head. "No I won't. You are who you are, no excuses, no regrets. I don't have any pretenses about what vampires do. I just want to know more about you, the man. What you lived through, what you've seen."

"You've mentioned that a few times now," Cronin mused.

"It fascinates me," Alec said. "I can't even imagine it."

"Can you imagine the things you will have seen a thousand years from now?"

Cronin said it so casually, like it was a given that Alec would see a thousand years. An assumption that he would be turned vampire, to live a millennium with Cronin by his side.

Just a week ago that would have enraged Alec. He would have bristled, pissed off that someone dare assume the course of his life. But now it felt right, and better yet, Alec couldn't wait for it to start.

He breathed in deeply and, with smiling lips, kissed the back of Cronin's head once more.

* * * *

It had been such a perfect evening and just what Alec needed. Quiet conversations, quiet kisses, hand holding. Alec had almost forgotten about the pending war with a certain Egyptian Queen, despite the maps of pyramids strewn over the living room. It wasn't until his cell phone beeped with a message from Campbell that he remembered.

His order of vampire-killing wooden bullets was ready for collection.

It was two in the morning—his body clock now completely warped—and he read the message out loud. "Order ready for collection. Leave payment on table."

Cronin held out his hand. "Are you ready to go?"

Alec went to the kitchen drawer he'd put the other bundles of cash the other day and took three. "I only owe him twenty grand, but I'll give him thirty." He looked at Cronin, and considering it was his money, Alec asked, "Is that all right?"

Cronin nodded. "Of course. Pay him what you like."

"He's had a pretty rough couple of days," Alec said with a shrug.

"Why did you agree to not meeting with him again," Cronin asked, "but prefer to just collect in his absence?"

"The guy was about to drop dead of shock and fear," Alec said. "And I figured if we ever needed some arsenal again at some point, he might be a good contact to have."

Cronin nodded. "Fair enough."

"Would you like us to come with you?" Jodis asked.

"No thanks," Alec said with a smirk. "I think you scared him the most with the little icy touch at the end of your last visit."

Jodis grinned at the compliment. "Thank you."

Cronin laughed quietly, put his arm around Alec, and they were gone.

The pickup was simple. The small bunker room was empty, save boxes of wooden-tipped bullets on the middle of the table. "There are two hundred," Cronin said simply.

"Are you like Rain Man or something?"

"Who?"

"Never mind."

Cronin picked the boxes of bullets up; Alec exchanged them for the three separate bundles of ten thousand dollars. He put his arm around Cronin's waist and they leapt back to Cronin's apartment.

Cronin put the bullets on the table, and Alec quickly sent Campbell a message, telling him there was extra payment for his trouble and not to forget to destroy the phone. He wasn't going to, but in the end, he added that if they needed anything he could help with, they'd be in touch.

He didn't need to add the fact they could find him wherever he was hiding. Alec was pretty sure Campbell knew that already.

But the exchange of bullets made Alec think of something else. Cronin was quick to notice. "What's wrong?"

"Nothing really," he said, distracted.

"The line of your brow tells me otherwise," Cronin said with a smile. "As does the way you worry your lip when you think."

Alec smiled at him. "Well, I think we need to visit the police headquarters."

Cronin stared at him, as did Eiji and Jodis. The room was deathly quiet. "What for?" Cronin asked coolly. "You know you can't go back there. You've seen the papers and reports. They're still looking for you, Alec."

"Not to my old department," Alec corrected. "There's a large storage room in the fourth level basement. It's where they keep the recovered weapons and bulletproof vests."

"Bulletproof vests?" Eiji asked, somewhat intrigued, somewhat amused.

"Not for me," Alec said. "But for you guys."

This time the three vampires looked at him like he'd lost his mind. Alec picked up a bullet. "If we have these, what's to say they don't? I mean, they killed Mikka with a wooden bullet to the heart, didn't they?" Alec shrugged. "I don't want that to happen to any of you."

"Okay," Cronin whispered. Alec wasn't sure if he agreed out of fear for his own life or because Alec was worried, but he was just happy he agreed. He gave him the address, and with a promise to return quickly, Alec and Cronin leapt to the NYPD headquarters.

CHAPTER SEVENTEEN

The storage room was deserted and lit only with emergency lighting. There were rows of shelves filled with boxes, all with case file numbers, every type of gun ever made that the police had confiscated from the streets, and the bullets to go with. There were knives, swords, shivs, bats. You name it, it was shelved, catalogued, and stored right here.

Alec had been to the Property Clerk Division, or the storage vault as they called it, a few times over his years as a cop. He knew it was locked to the whole force, manned only by officers at the front of the cage-like front wall who required approved paperwork before retrieving the specifically numbered item to the requesting officer.

No one else could get in here.

Unless you could just magically appear by way of quantum leaping.

"This place isn't manned from 10:00 p.m. 'til 6:00 a.m., but it's locked tight. We shouldn't be interrupted," Alec explained. "Most of this stuff is for criminal cases—evidence, confiscated weapons, that kind of thing."

"Good lord," Cronin whispered, taking in the height and length of shelves full of weaponry. "I'm glad Eiji didn't come with us. He'd never want to leave."

Alec snorted out a laugh. He was officially on the run from the police, he'd hacked into an online streaming account, and he was now stealing police property. There was no doubt on which side of the cop/felon line he now stood. He didn't even try to justify his reasons in his head. He looked at Cronin and had every reason he'd ever need.

He searched the shelves until he found a military style backpack and started to collect what he wanted. He took a few Glock 9mm pistols, a dozen empty magazine cartridges. He found the holsters next, thigh, shoulder and ankle, and put them into the backpack. He saw some flares and on second thought, added them to his collection as well.

Next he found the cache of crossbows. "Remind me to come back here at Christmastime for Eiji," Alec said.

Cronin laughed. "What can I get for you?"

"The vests?" Alec said. He scanned the shelves. "I don't know where they are."

Cronin left him to it, and Alec collected a few crossbow arrow quivers, knowing Eiji would *love* them. The sleek quivers strapped onto the back like a holster and held arrows at the ready. Alec smiled as he added them to his cache in the backpack.

"Stop!"

Alec froze.

"Put your hands where I can see 'em!" the voice barked. The voice was a few shelves over and Alec realized it wasn't being said to him, but to Cronin.

And that just pissed Alec off.

He stalked toward the offending voice, with no concern for his own safety, snatched a pistol from the shelf, and clicked a magazine into it. The sound was deafening in the silence. He pointed the handgun out, ready to fire, and found a middle-aged, pudgy uniformed officer holding a gun at a smirking Cronin.

"Stop pointing your gun at him," Alec demanded, his voice booming in the otherwise quiet room.

The man spun and then had his gun pointed at Alec. "How did you get in here?" the man asked. Then he narrowed his eyes, recognition flashed in them. "Hey, you're MacAidan! The cop who disappeared." He turned back to Cronin, his voice was shaking. "I saw you in the footage too."

In the time it took to blink, Cronin stood in front of the officer and had the standard issue handgun pulled into four misshapen and bent parts of metal. He held them on the palm of his hand. "Your gun fell apart. You really should be more careful."

The officer, now wide-eyed and three shades of white, took the deformed pieces of what was his gun in his shaking hands. "What the... how'd you... what the hell are you?"

Now that the cop was unarmed, Alec put the gun on the shelf beside him. He made a point of reading the man's name badge. "Officer Bryant, we're not going to hurt you. And yes, I am Detective MacAidan. So now that we're acquainted, you're going to help us. I need bulletproof vests and night vision goggles. Where would I find those?"

The older man shook his head. "I can't…"

Cronin snapped out a growl. "You will do everything Alec asks of you."

Bryant took a reflexive step back, clearly his instincts screamed at him that Cronin was dangerous, a realization that Alec found amusing. His wide and frightened eyes met with Alec's and he nodded. "Third aisle, at the back."

Alec gave him a warm smile. "See? We can all get along."

Cronin herded Bryant along with Alec until he found what he was after. "Excellent," he said, putting one pair of NVG in his almost-full backpack. Then he found the vests. There were six. "We'll take all of them."

Cronin picked them up easily. "Is there anything else you'd like?" he asked Alec.

"Yeah," Alec said, looking at the corner security camera and then to Bryant. "I want you to give De Angelo and all the boys in my division a message for me. For all the times they laughed and called me crazy, tell them this: they don't know the half of it. They're clueless to a whole other world." Then Alec looked back up to the camera. "And De Angelo, consider this my resignation. I'm not missing, I wasn't abducted, you're an asshole, and I fucking quit." Alec punctuated his little speech with a salute.

Cronin laughed. "Have you everything you need?"

"Yep," Alec said simply. Then, considering Cronin was holding an armful of armored vests, Alec walked behind him and slid his free arm around his waist, holding on possessively. He rested his chin on Cronin's shoulder and smiled at Officer Bryant. "Wanna see something special?" he asked him. The pale-looking policeman shook his head. Alec laughed, and they leapt.

* * * *

Alec was still laughing as they arrived back at the apartment, though the effects of leaping made it sound more of an amused groan. But as soon as they arrived, they noticed a panicked movement to their right. Cronin quickly threw the vests onto the floor, stood in front of Alec, and gnashed his teeth.

Alec hadn't even blinked.

Cronin realized before Alec that it wasn't a threat, but reason for concern nonetheless. Johan, Bes, and Eleanor were there, talking so fast Alec could barely understand them, but he recognized the look on their faces.

Something was wrong.

"They were attacked," Eiji explained. He looked just as worried.

"What happened?" Cronin asked, only then moving from in front Alec.

"We were coming back last night," Johan said, "long before sunrise, when Eleanor saw us being ambushed. We had the advantage of foresight, but their numbers were many."

"What did they want?"

Johan's gaze slid quickly to Alec. "They wanted the key."

Cronin started to growl, and Alec put a reassuring hand on his lower back.

Bes spoke next. "They were from Northern India, Cronin. I know this from their dialect. We heard them say they would get rid of the key so the war is over."

Cronin's growl got louder.

"And they attacked you?" Cronin asked. "Why?"

"To get near Alec," Bes said. "For us to lead them to him. That is why we stayed away. We have covered many miles and my other family members split off to create a diversion." His eyes were wide and honest. "We would not risk Alec's life by them following us."

Johan bowed his head at Cronin. "I am sorry to speak such words so harshly, Cronin. But they want Alec dead so Queen Keket is at a stalemate. She cannot succeed if he is not alive."

Alec looked at Cronin. "I know. I said something similar."

Cronin's jaw bulged. "No."

"Cronin, there was another coven," Johan said, his head still bowed.

"They were Egyptian," Bes said. "They were like an army, military precision. In the alleys like a checkpoint, asking for the Key's whereabouts to take back to their Queen."

"These are the vampires we were warned of," Jodis said softly. "When the Seekers had located Alec, they said she sent forth battalions."

Bes nodded. "Yes. I fear this also."

"How did you get away?" Eiji asked Bes. "Did they not recognize you as Egyptian?"

Eleanor answered, "I saw the Indian coven approaching. I knew they'd argue with the Egyptian guards and serve as a distraction for us, so I talked until they arrived. As soon as the Indian coven arrived, the Egyptians were more interested in them. We fled. From what I could see, they had no tracker with them, though he could have been cloaked, hidden from my view. The best trackers have both abilities."

"We are sure we were not followed here," Johan said.

"I worry for my family," Bes said. "They are not familiar with these lands."

"We will find them," Eiji said, putting his hand on Bes's arm. "They served us well and that won't be forgotten."

Bes gave a hard nod. "Gratitude."

"The gratitude is ours," Cronin said. "Thank you, all of you, for what you have done to keep Alec safe."

Then Eleanor tilted her head, clearly seeing something no one else could. Her milky eyes flickered and everyone waited for her to speak. "They know Alec is the key. Whether from trackers or seers or even from the news that showed him disappear with you.

They know he is in New York, but the trail is cold. They now wish to harm those closest to Alec, to bring him out, to expose him." She faced Cronin directly. "They're moving in, seeking out anyone who knows anything about him."

"So these vampires are trying to take out anyone I care about?" Alec asked. Cold fear ran down his spine, a thousand tiny needles of realization. He looked at Cronin, his voice was just a whisper. "What if they go after my dad?"

Cronin pulled out his phone and put it to his ear. "Jacques? … Yes, yes, we thought as much. Where is he now? … I need you to present yourself to Alec's father … Right now. Wake him up. Tell him I sent you, tell him who you are, and tell him we'll be there shortly."

Cronin ended the call, looking squarely at Alec. "We'll bring him here."

Alec nodded quickly. "Thank you." Then Alec turned to Johan, Eleanor, and Bes. "Thank you, all of you, for what you did." He didn't know what else to say. What could he say that would adequately convey his gratitude?

Cronin spoke to Eiji. "Get in touch with as many coven members as you can. Tell them to be on guard, warn them. Tell them if they find Bes's family, to take them in as their own."

Eiji gave a nod and was quickly texting someone on his phone when Cronin put his arm around Alec and leapt him to his father's house.

The living room was dark, though the moonlight cast enough light for Alec to see. There were voices in the kitchen. "Dad?"

Kole came out, dressed in his pajamas and looking a little pale, followed by Jacques. "Alec?"

"Oh, thank God you're all right." Alec's relief was immediate.

"What the hell's going on?" his father asked. "This guy" — Kole pointed his thumb at Jacques — "woke me up and told me you were coming. I gotta say, I was thinkin' my number was up, being woken by a vampire and all." Kole shrugged at Jacques. "No offense."

Jacques gave a nod. "None taken." Then Jacques looked at Cronin. "I was just explaining who I was."

Alec guessed Jacques didn't want Cronin to think he wasn't doing his job. "Dad, can you pack a bag?" Alec asked. "We'll explain later, but you're not safe here."

"What?" Kole asked again. "Course I am."

Just then, a shadow moved past the front window. Kole's eyes went wide and then a keening, scratching noise came from the back of the house. Both Cronin and Jacques crinkled their noses as though they could smell something the humans couldn't.

"There is no time," Cronin said. He touched Alec with one hand, Jacques with his other. Just as Alec put his arm around his father, a vampire came through the kitchen door, and they leapt.

* * * *

Alec's father's reaction to leaping was much like Alec's had been that first time. As soon as they appeared in Cronin's living room, the older man sucked back a breath, groaned out a scream, and his whole body trembled.

Alec put his hand on Kole's shoulder. "You're all right, Dad. It doesn't hurt anymore."

Kole straightened himself out and shook his arms and legs. "What the hell was that?"

"It's called leaping," Alec explained.

"Like quantum leaping?" he asked, still looking a little pale.

"Yes," Cronin answered. "I apologize."

"Who was the vampire in my house?" Kole asked.

"From his clothes and the color of his skin, I would assume he was Egyptian, possibly Illyrian," Jacques answered. "I didn't hear him speak."

By this time, Eiji, Jodis, and the others were all standing there, alarmed. "What vampire?" Eiji said.

Cronin was more specific. "He wore a *shendyt*. His skin was very dark, like a mummified corpse, his face somewhat distorted, and there was a foul smell."

Bes nodded. "The stench of a returned vampire is unmistakable."

Cronin nodded. "Yes. He was definitely one of Keket's men. He broke into Kole's house when we were there or because we were there, I don't know." Then Cronin looked at Alec. "Are you well?"

Alec gave him a relieved smile. "I am, thank you. That was close."

"Too close," Cronin agreed.

Kole was looking at Eiji, recognizing him, and the small Japanese vampire smiled at him. "Nice to finally meet you," Eiji said, holding out his hand.

Kole shook Eiji's hand. "Thought you looked familiar."

Alec interrupted to do introductions of everyone in the room, and Kole took in his surroundings. The older human was clearly overwhelmed. "How about a drink?" Alec suggested. Not waiting for an answer, he came back out with the bottle of Johnnie Walker scotch and one tumbler. He poured his dad a healthy nip and Kole, taking the glass gratefully, threw the liquor back without flinching. Alec poured him another.

Kole sat slowly on the sofa, and Alec was reminded of his reaction the first night he got there. "Dad, you're safe here. All doors, windows, and exits are blocked, the elevator is blocked, and the shaft is monitored. This place is like Fort Knox."

Kole nodded. "What happened?"

Alec sat beside his father, and having explained the basic vampire histories and lore to his dad beforehand, he only had to fill him in on the latest. "Queen Keket, an Egyptian vampire, has sent out swarms of vampires to bring me to her," Alec said. "And there are other covens from around the world who are also trying to get me. They figure if they get me first, then the Queen can't wage her war. We realized tonight that because they couldn't get me, they'd go after those closest to me."

Kole was silent for a long time, his wide hazel eyes scanning his son's face. "Because you're the key."

Alec nodded. "Apparently."

"What does that mean?" Kole asked. "What does the key mean to her, this Queen Keket?"

Alec thought a little omission about having his heart ripped out was in order for the sake of his father's health. "She needs me to bring back a dead pharaoh."

"Right," Kole said flatly. "Of course she does."

Alec shrugged. "Weird, huh?"

Kole was quiet for a minute, then his brow furrowed. "And how are you supposed to do that?"

"I'm not going to do it," Alec said. "We're gonna take her out before it gets to that."

Kole raised one questioning eyebrow. "And how are you gonna do *that*?"

"Well, we're gonna turn up at her place and stake her in the heart," Alec said, simplifying a very not-simple plan.

Kole laughed. "You can't lie for shit." So he turned to Cronin instead. "How are you gonna take her out?"

Cronin's eyes darted to Alec first, then back to Kole. For a second, Alec thought he was about to divulge everything about their plans and Queen Keket's plan to take Alec's heart, but he didn't. He lifted his chin a little and said, "We're gonna turn up at her place and stake her in the heart."

Eiji laughed and even Alec chuckled. "Here, Dad," he said, pouring another nip of scotch into his glass. "Dad, you're gonna have to stay here for the next few days, until this is all over. Then you can go home. The kitchen's through there" — Alec pointed in that direction, then in the opposite direction—"bathroom's through there. There's a home theater with a screen as big as your living room wall through there. We'll set you up in the spare bedroom." Alec waved his hand at the metal wall. "That's normally a window and, Dad, the view is... well, it's something else. But we've got the security wall up for the time being, but you wait 'til you see it, Dad. The views over New York City are like nothing you've ever seen."

Kole nodded slowly and swallowed the rest of his scotch.

"I know it's a lot to take in," Alec said quietly. "But I'm glad you're safe." He looked at his watch. It was almost 5:00 a.m. "You okay?"

Kole nodded, but he looked every one of his fifty-eight years. He looked around the penthouse living room, though it looked more like a tactical response room at the moment. He looked at the maps, the crossbows, the bullets. "So this is it, huh? What you were born to do?"

Alec nodded. "I think so, Dad."

"I wish it were me," he said quietly. "I wish I could take your place, Ailig, and you could just live out your days in peace."

Alec petted his dad's knee. "It'll be fine. I'll be fine. I've got these guys to help me." Alec waved his hand around the room, but he looked at Cronin. "We'll be fine."

Cronin gave a hard nod. "Mr. MacAidan, I will do everything within my power to bring him home safely. You have my word."

Kole nodded, and the overwhelmed look on his face gave way to exhaustion. Alec stood up. "Come on, Dad. You can rest a bit while we go through some details."

Kole didn't argue, and Alec led him to the spare room. When he left his dad and closed the door, Cronin met him in the hall. "Is he well?"

Alec nodded slowly. "Shocked, I think. I'm sure he'll be fine."

"He is worried for his son," Cronin whispered. He put his hand to Alec's face and searched his eyes for a moment. "As am I."

Alec threw his arms around Cronin, and the two stood in the hall in a long, silent embrace. Alec relished the warmth, the feel of Cronin against him, a scent made just for him, and he felt his worries falling away.

"Cronin," Eleanor said from another room. "Cronin!"

Cronin flew to the living room, and by the time Alec reached him, Eleanor had come in from the kitchen. "It's changed. Everything's changed," Eleanor said quietly. Her milky eyes were scanning for something. "You don't have three days."

"What?" Jodis asked. Everyone in the room was now on their feet, staring at the blind vampire woman. "What do you see?"

Eleanor swayed her head back and forth. "Queen Keket has decided she won't wait. If Alec isn't brought to her by tomorrow, she'll come for him herself," Eleanor said quietly. She swayed some more and shook her head. "She will kill anyone and everyone who gets in her way."

CHAPTER EIGHTEEN

The room became a flurry of motion. "Get London on screen," Eiji said. His smile was long gone, a fierce determination in its place.

Johan had a laptop open, and in no time, the screen flashed with a face Alec recognized from before.

"Elders," the English voice said.

Eiji nodded and replied with an equal respect. "Elder."

"Have you news?" the English vampire asked. "Our seer has seen plans change."

"Yes, so has ours," Eiji replied. "Just now. Our deadline has moved to tonight. Are you ready?"

The English vampire nodded. Alec could see people—vampires—moving in the background. Their headquarters was a blur of movement. Alec interrupted Eiji. "May I?"

"Yes, of course," Eiji said, making room for Alec to sit in front of the screen. Cronin stood beside him. Eiji made the introductions. "Kennard, this is Alec. Alec, Kennard heads the London coven."

Alec looked at the screen. Kennard had dainty features, pale skin, and pink, boyish lips. Alec's first impression was that Kennard should be wearing a Tudor-era prince's clothing. He looked no more than sixteen, and yet Alec was sure it was the leader's innocent looks that made an underlying almighty and ferocious nature all the more frightening.

He held rank over London, and Alec knew without doubt that it was for good reason.

"It's an honor," Alec said.

"The honor is mine," Kennard said. "You are Ailig, yes?"

Alec nodded. "I am."

"The key," Kennard mused. "And human."

"Guilty."

"And you belong to Cronin," Kennard said, his eyes full of delight.

A week ago, Alec would have bristled at the suggestion that he *belonged* to anyone. Now he smiled. "I would not assume to correct an Elder, but you are mistaken," Alec said with a smile. "It is Cronin who belongs to me."

Cronin quickly took Alec's hand and gave it a squeeze. When Alec looked at him, he was fighting a smile but his eyes gave him away.

Kennard laughed, looking younger still. "Hearts lay broken around the world at such news."

Cronin leaned in so Kennard could see him. "There will be time for flattery and acquaintances later, my friend. Though for now we should concentrate on impending news."

Alec nodded and looked at the young Elder. "I don't know what precautions you've taken, and I don't presume to tell you how to defend your coven. What I offer is merely a suggestion," Alec said. He needed to be diplomatic, and he'd spent enough years in the police department kissing political asses to know how to phrase recommendations. "We believe the Illyrians could be armed with a type of wooden bullet. I have seen a vampire die from such wounds. If you are able, Kennard, have as many of your coven wearing any type of armor to protect their hearts."

Kennard frowned at first, then he appeared distracted by something off-screen. When he looked again at Alec, he nodded. "To be forewarned is to be forearmed, I guess."

Alec nodded. "Thank you, for doing this. I am sure when this is all over, I will meet with you and get to shake your hand in person."

Kennard bowed his head. "I would be honored to meet not only the key to save our kind, but also to meet the one who collared the lone wolf that is Cronin."

Cronin rolled his eyes, making Alec laugh. But he looked back at Kennard, his smile fading quickly. "Good luck tonight."

Kennard nodded once, a silent thanks. "I know not of what your future holds, Ailig. Though we wish you success in whatever it is you need to do tonight."

Cronin interrupted and directed the conversation away from Alec's fate. "You have all plans in place, Kennard?" he asked, with a no-nonsense set to his jaw.

"Of course."

"You will take the second pyramid, the Pyramid of Khafre."

"Yes. We have leapers to take us. There are twenty of us ready to go." Alec knew twenty was a strong front; after all, it took only nine vampires to take out the Ancient Illyrians.

"I will not leave Alec's side," Cronin said. "Eiji and Jodis will be with us also. The three of us will guard him and get him in and out as neatly as possible. I will notify the Eastern and Western American covens that the time of attack has moved to tonight."

"I will notify the Italians," Kennard said.

"Thank you." Cronin sighed.

Kennard took a deep breath. "*Tha am blàr teann, seana-charaid*. Battle is at hand, my old friend."

Cronin finally smiled. "*Cuir cath cruaidh, Na Saighdearan Dearga*. Fight bravely, Redcoat soldier."

Kennard laughed. "Oh, Cronin. You bloody Scots are all the same." He was still smiling. "We shall talk again before we leave." The screen went black.

Alec sighed deeply. "They're really doing this, aren't they?"

"Doing what?" Cronin asked quietly. He squeezed Alec's hand again and put his other hand over the top of Alec's.

"Going to fight."

"Of course."

Alec frowned. "What if I don't know what to do?" He swallowed hard and looked into Cronin's dark eyes. "What if I get there and have no clue what to do? How many of us will die if I fail?"

"Alec, you won't fail," Cronin answered softly. "You'll know what to do. You will feel it. And we'll be there to protect you."

Alec nodded, but said nothing more.

"Uh, Alec?" Eiji said. He'd upturned the backpack on the sofa and was grinning again with wide, excited eyes. "What is all this?"

Alec smiled, despite his sullen mood. "Cronin and I went shopping in the NYPD stores division." He walked over and picked up a quiver. "I got you and Jodis both back and thigh quivers."

Eiji grinned so damn big. He gave Alec a quick, somewhat-careful hug, then got busy strapping the arrow holsters onto his body.

Alec collected all his shopping efforts into a pile and put them in Cronin's bedroom. When he came back out, Eiji had on one back quiver filled with arrows, a thigh holster, and he was holding his crossbow, and of course, he was grinning.

His long black hair was out, hanging long and silky past his shoulders, his dark clothes giving him a ninja look. Alec laughed. "I don't know if you look more like Katniss or Legolas."

Eiji's grin impossibly widened. "I don't know what that means."

Alec snorted out a laugh. "I swear, starting tomorrow after this is all over, I'm making you all watch some freakin' movies."

Eiji laughed, but he looked at Cronin, then back to Alec. "I'm pretty sure you won't be watching movies, my friend."

Before Alec could blush at what Eiji was implying, Cronin was at Alec's side. He took Alec's hand once more and kissed his shoulder.

Eiji ignored them. He picked up one of the bulletproof vests. "And these?"

"For each of you," Alec said.

Eiji was still amused. "Have you ever heard of vampires needing armor?"

Alec's response was short. "Ever seen a vampire die from being shot in the heart with a wooden bullet?" Eiji's eyes shot to his and Alec sighed. "Eiji, humor me. Wear it, please. All of you," Alec said, looking around the room. "Please. We don't know what weapons they'll have, if any at all. But it's not worth the risk."

Eleanor spoke up. "Cronin? I don't advise that."

Cronin turned to look at the seer. "It was an errant thought."

"What was?" Alec asked.

Cronin looked at him, with troubled eyes. "I was just thinking that maybe I could leap there. Before we all go."

"What?" Alec whispered.

"I could leap there. I'd be in and out in less than a second, but I could see into these chambers," Cronin said, walking over to Johan's map and pointing at the different rooms in the pyramids. "You said yourself, Alec, you hate going in blind. You hate not knowing all the variables. It's dangerous. For you, and for all of us."

Alec shook his head. "No."

"They wouldn't even know I was there, and even if they did, I'd be gone so quick they wouldn't be able to catch me." Cronin looked back at the pyramid. "We would know then how many numbers we're talking. If she has dozens or thousands."

"No." Alec's solitary word cut the air. He walked up to Cronin and took his chin between his thumb and forefinger. "Do you think, for one second, I would let you do that?"

Cronin went to say something, but Alec wasn't done. "Do you not understand? It's not just you anymore. It's you and me. You tell me that I cannot offer my life for others because it would mean your death as well." Alec let go of Cronin's chin and pointed him in the chest. "Well, the same goes for you."

"My only thought was that it would be safer for you in the long run," Cronin said.

"Then send someone else," Alec said. "But not you. It can't be." His voice died to a whisper. "It would kill me to even think you went in by yourself."

Cronin's eyes softened. "It was just a thought."

Jodis turned to Eleanor. "If another leaper was to go?"

"Multiple leapers," Johan suggested. "To confuse, maybe?"

Eleanor tilted her head. "It could work."

"How many leapers are there?" Alec asked.

"There are nine in America," Cronin said. "Myself included."

"There are two in the UK," Eiji said. "And as many as fourteen across Europe and Russia."

Jodis put a cell phone to her ear and singlehandedly organized a group of four leapers from around the world to simultaneously leap into different parts of the pyramids. It was scheduled to happen at one p.m. New York time, and they would report their findings. While she was talking on the phone, Eiji undid the strap of his back quiver and pulled it off, then he picked up a bulletproof vest, and without a word of protest, he simply put it on and refastened the straps, making it fit snugly. Then he put the quiver back on.

Alec smiled at him. "Thank you. And for what it's worth, you look more like Hawkeye from the now."

Cronin put his arm around Alec's waist. "Are you hungry? Tired?"

Alec had to think about it. "Um, yeah, I guess I am. Both." Then Alec asked him, "How about you?"

Cronin sighed. "I should feed, but I don't want to leave you." Then he looked at Eiji and Jodis. "And you should feed as well."

"It's not safe for you to be out right now," Bes said. The scared look on his face told Alec the threat was real. "Too dangerous."

Alec gave Cronin a smile. "Take Eiji and Jodis out for dinner."

Cronin shook his head. "I won't leave you."

Alec picked up a handgun magazine and loaded wooden bullets into it before clipping it into place. "I will get myself something to eat in the kitchen and have this with me at all times. Bes and Johan will be here. Eleanor, do you foresee any trouble?"

She scanned her mind's eye. "No, no trouble."

Alec slid the pistol into the waistband of his jeans and kissed Cronin on the lips before walking into the kitchen. "Just don't take too long."

Alec heard Jodis say, "Get rid of the arrows, Eiji," then Eiji replied, "But I like them," and when Alec turned around, he saw Cronin smile before they were gone.

Bes stood next to Alec like a bodyguard, his back turned as though on protection detail and a wooden stake in his hand, while Alec made himself something to eat.

"You okay, Bes?" Alec asked him.

He looked at Alec only briefly. "I wish this trouble to be over. I would like to go home."

"Me too," Alec said. "I wish it was over too." Alec took a deep breath and exhaled slowly through the uncomfortable twinge in his chest at Cronin's absence.

"Alec, are you okay?" Bes asked, wide-eyed.

Johan was suddenly in the kitchen beside him, obviously alarmed by Bes's tone. "What is it?"

"Yeah," Alec said, grimacing through the heavy ache that was spreading under his ribs. "It's just when Cronin and I are apart…"

"Ah," Johan said with a nod. "It causes physical discomfort."

Alec nodded quickly and breathed through it. He looked at Johan, knowing he was once or possibly still was infatuated with Cronin. He pressed the heel of his hand against his chest to ease the ache. "How long have you known him?"

Johan smiled a little and bowed his head again. "I met Cronin in Luxemburg, where I am from, in 1932."

"Oh." Jesus. Did everyone know Cronin for centuries longer than Alec had? Alec barked out a sharp breath. "I have to admit, I'm kind of jealous that everyone knows him better than me."

Johan shook his head. "Oh, Alec. To the contrary. You are the closest he's been to anyone."

"Apart from Eiji and Jodis," Alec amended.

Johan conceded a nod. "They are his closest friends and confidants. They've been a trio of immeasurable force for many years. But Alec, it is you who he looks upon like—" Johan seemed to search for the right words. "—as I would imagine the warmth of spring sun after a long winter feels upon your skin."

"Oh." Alec blushed, but he smiled at that.

Johan lifted his face a little and closed his eyes. "I remember the feel of it, from my human years. Bitter winters followed by warm and spreading sun on my face."

Alec found himself smiling at Johan. "It feels nice."

Johan opened his eyes and smiled at Alec. "How that feels, that remarkable affirmation of life, is how Cronin looks at you." Alec felt his cheeks heat, and Johan laughed. "Don't be embarrassed, Alec. You look at him the same."

"Do I?" Alec asked, though he was sure he already knew the answer.

Johan smiled, more sadly this time. It was clear he was still disappointed that Cronin would never be his. "You are well-suited for each other. Fate is an undeniable thing, is it not?"

"It is," Alec agreed. He really wasn't sure if this was a conversation he should be having. He liked Johan though, he seemed to be a man of integrity, and Alec respected that. The truth was, Alec could see now that Johan's agreeable, submissive nature would never have suited Cronin. Cronin needed someone to challenge him, a physical, mental, and emotional equal. Maybe Johan could see that too.

Alec smiled at him. "I didn't understand it in the beginning, but I'm getting used to it now. It is… um, like the warmth of the sun on your skin."

Johan chuckled, and Bes, still holding the stake dutifully, joined in the conversation. "I do not remember the sun."

"Do you miss it?" Alec asked, glad for the distraction.

Bes shook his head. "Not for me, no. And I do not fancy being reacquainted."

Alec laughed, and before Eleanor could finish saying, "They're on their way back," Cronin, Eiji, and Jodis appeared in the living room.

Then, in the next nanosecond, Cronin was in front of Alec, his hands to his face, Cronin's lips just a hair's breadth from his. "I missed you and you are unaffected?"

Alec chuckled at the confused sting in Cronin's eyes. "No. Not unaffected. Trying to distract myself from the ache in my chest."

Cronin seemed to finally breathe, and he pressed his lips to Alec's, despite Johan and Bes being right there. Cronin's hands skimmed Alec's face, his jaw, and his hair as though he thought he'd never touch him again. "Absence from you does not sit well with me."

Alec's sandwich was long forgotten, a new kind of hunger in its place. It was a yearning and a realization they were out of time that made something like eating food a nonessential. He whispered against Cronin's lips, "Take me to bed."

Alec's plate made a gentle clinking sound as it landed softly on the counter in an otherwise empty kitchen.

* * * *

Cronin leapt himself and Alec onto his bed, Alec beneath him while Cronin fit snugly between his thighs. He loved watching Alec's face when he realized they were in bed, that Cronin had him pinned down; his pupils blown out, his heart rate spiked, and a slow and sexy smirk played at his lips.

But it was different this time. Alec was needier, more emotional than he had been before. There was no frantic pulling at clothes or scraping fingers on skin. Alec was slower, more desperate for simple touches and holding him close. This wasn't about desire or the need for release.

This was something else. Something new.

Alec held him tighter and kissed him deeper, slower. He pulled Cronin in, wrapped his arms around his back, and held him as tight as he humanly could. Alec writhed against him, slowly, passionately, but didn't move to undress or go any further. There was no mad rush for sexual release. None at all.

But the way Alec looked at Cronin was better than unraveling in sexual pleasure.

Alec slowed the kiss, it seemed, just so he could stare at Cronin. His eyes were mostly pupil with a fine hazel ring, his swollen lips red and barely parted. He put his hand to the side of Cronin's face and not a word was spoken between them. He just stared, and Cronin knew, just knew, Alec wasn't fighting fate anymore.

He was looking at him with such complete faith and adoration, it stole Cronin's breath.

Cronin kissed him again, not even trying to hold back the purr that rumbled in his chest. But Alec stopped the kiss and cupped Cronin's face in his hands. His eyes were imploring and honest. "Cronin," he whispered. His eyes scanned Cronin's face. "I want to take in every detail. I want to remember everything." He took a shaky breath. "I don't want to forget a thing."

"Alec, what is wrong?"

Alec stared into Cronin's eyes for a long moment. "I'm scared."

"Oh, no, no," Cronin said quickly, and he rolled them over so they were both on their sides facing each other. Cronin pulled Alec tight against him, Alec's head cradled against his neck and chest. "My Alec, please do not be afraid."

"It scares me half to death to think something could happen to you."

Cronin held him tighter still and kissed the top of his head. "And me you, *m'cridhe*."

"My heart," Alec repeated. "I like it when you call me that."

"It beats only for you," Cronin whispered.

Cronin could feel Alec smile against his chest. "Stay here with me," Alec said, his voice suddenly sleepy.

"Always."

Alec fell asleep, though he never loosened his hold on Cronin. In fact, as he slept and dreamt of things Cronin could only guess at, Alec's hold on him got tighter. Every time Alec became restless and murmured his name, Cronin would whisper words long forgotten.

"*M'cridhe, m'gràdh, gu brath.*"

Words he never thought he'd say, words he never thought he'd feel.

My heart, my love, forever.

* * * *

Cronin must have dozed, because he awoke to a sharp "Cronin, wake Alec."

Jodis had called to him from the living room. She sounded worried, and Cronin knew that couldn't be good. He glanced at his watch. It was 1:00 p.m.

Dammit. He hadn't realized the time.

"Alec." Cronin gently shook him awake. "You must get up."

Alec sat up, bleary eyed and disoriented. "Wha'?"

"Something's happened," Cronin said, and Alec was suddenly very awake.

They ran to the living room, where everyone was standing, staring. Eiji was pacing with a phone to his ear. "What is it?" Cronin asked.

"The leapers," Jodis said. "They went, at one o'clock, as we'd agreed. Five went, but only four returned."

"I saw it," Eleanor said grimly. "I saw Jose, Cronin. He was set upon by horrible looking, ill-formed vampires who took him to Queen Keket. I saw her!"

"And?"

"She demanded answers about Alec. He gave none. She killed him."

Cronin instinctively pulled Alec behind him, and stared wide-eyed at Jodis. "She knows we're onto her."

Eiji disconnected the call. "Kennard's seers said they saw the same as Eleanor. Our plans have changed. We're not leaving tonight." He looked at

Jodis, then back to Cronin and Alec. "We're leaving now."

CHAPTER NINETEEN

Eleanor had described the returned mummies, just as Bes had. Blackened, sunken skin, matted hair, yellowed vampire teeth. Cronin told Alec that Jose was an American vampire from Chicago, who could leap, just as Cronin did.

Eleanor and the other seers described chambers with sandstone walls, sandy floors, and each of them described it the same. Each pyramid was like a hive.

Numbers were many, and throughout the three pyramids, there were hundreds of returned vampires at least. The information from the leapers was invaluable. It was also everything Alec expected, but at least now they knew.

"I'm sorry Jose died," Alec said quietly. He frowned. "But Cronin, that could have been you."

Cronin put his hand to Alec's face. "I know."

They were back in Cronin's room; each had changed their clothes and were dressed to go to Egypt. Alec wore black combat clothes and his boots. He wore a bulletproof vest and had holsters strapped to his shoulders, his waist, and his thighs, and his backpack as well. He needed to take as many pistols and all the ammunition he could carry. Alec had assumed inside the pyramid would be dark — vampires didn't need illumination to see — and Eleanor confirmed it. He held the night vision goggles. "If I lose these in there, I'll be blind," he said.

Cronin touched Alec's face. "I will stay with you every second."

Alec gave him the best smile he could muster, then put the goggles on the bed and picked up Cronin's bulletproof vest. He slowly slipped it over his head and fastened the clips for him. He took his time, ensuring each clip was done tightly. "You probably think it's foolish that I want you to wear this."

Cronin shook his head. "No." He looked over to the solitary shelf on the far wall at the old iron helmet and ax: the armor he wore in battle so many years ago. "I never thought those were foolish."

Alec took a moment to look over the medieval armor. "Were you scared when you put those on?"

"Yes."

Alec nodded in understanding.

"And no."

"What do you mean?"

"I was afraid, as any man would be as he dressed for war. The Pictons were moving in fast and we knew victory was not likely."

"Yet you still fought."

"Of course." Cronin gave him a sad smile. "I was also not afraid because I had nothing to lose. I had no one to live for."

"And now you do," Alec whispered.

Cronin nodded. "Aye."

Alec smiled at the Scottish term. He put his forehead to Cronin's and held his face in his hands. "Cronin, I would choose you."

Cronin smiled tentatively, looking unsure. "What?"

Alec took Cronin's hand. "I said to you on the second day I was here, I wasn't sure if it weren't for us being fated that I'd choose you. But you have to know, Cronin, I would. I would choose you."

Cronin closed his eyes, as if a flood of warmth rushed through him. "I would choose you, also."

"I know I doubted what fated meant in the beginning. I did, and I'm sorry," Alec said. "But I had to tell you, before we leave for Egypt. I had to tell you now that I know what it means. I think I always knew, I just fought it and tried to deny it, but not anymore." Alec pressed his lips to Cronin's. "If it were my choice, I would choose you. A thousand times over."

Cronin held his face and kissed him, until he broke the kiss and pressed his forehead to Alec's. He tilted his head just a fraction, obviously hearing something Alec could not, and sighed. "And I you."

Alec nodded, picked up the night vision goggles, and held out his hand. "So let's get it over with. I want to start the rest of my life, and the sooner we take out the Queen, the sooner we can do that."

Cronin smiled as he took Alec's hand, and together they walked out to the others.

Alec saw his dad first. He looked a little less shocked than before, but clearly still concerned. Alec dropped Cronin's hand so he could hug his dad. "Be careful," Kole said.

"Of course," Alec answered. "We'll be back before you know it. Eleanor is staying here; she can keep you up to speed on what's going on."

Kole looked at Eleanor, then back to Alec. "I know this is what you were supposed to do, your calling, but it doesn't make it any easier." Then Kole turned to Cronin. "You bring him back in one piece, ya hear?"

Cronin nodded. "I hear, and I promise."

Eiji, Jodis, Bes, and Johan stood waiting. Each of them wore the bulletproof vest, each armed with a crossbow and a slew of arrows on their backs. Alec fixed his night vision goggles to his face, his entire vision illuminated green. Eiji put his hands to Jodis's face and pressed his forehead to hers. What they said in the absence of words, Alec could only guess, but it was a silent, intimate conversation. Cronin looked fondly upon them and retook Alec's hand.

Then, in the middle of Cronin's luxurious apartment living room, the six of them stood in a closed circle facing outward, each with a wooden stake in their hand to be ready for whatever they would face, and Cronin leapt.

They landed in the middle of a war zone.

CHAPTER TWENTY

The humidity was like slamming into a wall, the noise was deafening, yet it was the smell Alec noticed first. The stench, rancid and foul, made him want to vomit.

The chamber was small and completely dark. Alec's only vision was eerily green and frightening, yet in those first seconds, his ability to take in details didn't let him down.

The room was twelve feet by twelve feet, the ceiling at his head and completely made of large stone blocks. There was sand under his boots, the walls had no distinct markings here—just scrapings in the stone that looked more like fingernail scratches than chisel marks.

Then he noticed movement. There were returned vampires in the room. And the sound registered in Alec's brain like a wave that held him under.

Both Bes and Eleanor had described the returned vampire perfectly: darkened, sunken skin, stretched tight and dry over a skeleton, matted hair, sunken beady eyes, vampire teeth. They reeked of embalming oils and death.

Nausea rolled in Alec's stomach.

Bes had also described the sounds, though no words could do it justice. It was a raspy, keening screech. The noise, like tortured wasps, seemed both close and far, and made by the sum of hundreds.

Alec was facing the back of the room, the farthest from danger—no doubt a deliberate ploy by Cronin to have himself, Eiji, and Jodis in front of him. Eiji and Jodis moved first, Jodis sweeping her hand out, sending a wave of freeze through the returned vampires—stunning them momentarily, still and silent, until Eiji swept through them with a stake in each hand, sending them to dust once more.

He wielded the stakes like long Japanese blades and with precise fluid arcs that were more poetry in motion than violence.

But the more vampires they killed, the more that came in through the door. Bes, Johan, Eiji, and Jodis all moved so easily, staking surprised and screeching vampires to a second death. Yet more kept coming in, getting in through the door and getting closer.

"They're not freezing," Jodis said. "They're too dry."

Alec had his pistol drawn and aimed at the door.

"Hold your fire," Cronin said.

Then, in less than the blink of an eye, Cronin was there. With a stake extended in each hand, blinking in and out of view, leaping like an automatic weapon, piercing their hearts, creating clouds of dust in his wake.

Alec knew then why all the vampires in the New York coven feared him. If he wanted you dead, he would simply leap himself to stand in front of you with a stake through your heart before you'd had time to blink.

He cleared the room in less than two seconds, and the flow of returned vampires through the door stopped.

Eiji sighed. "Show-off."

Alec took a second to process what he'd just seen. "Okay… that was… so fucking awesome."

Cronin leapt himself back to Alec's side. "There will be more. We need to move."

"Those creatures," Jodis said, "are completely dehydrated."

"What does that mean?" Alec asked.

"It means they've not fed," Jodis replied.

"She's starving them?" Eiji asked.

"So they obey her," Johan said. "If she determines who gets fed and when, they obey her every word."

"Well, I can't freeze them," Jodis went on to say. "I have no ability other than to stun them."

"That moment may be enough to save one of us," Eiji said. He sheathed the wooden stakes in his thigh holster and took the crossbow from his back.

"There are hundreds of unfed vampires down here?" Cronin hissed.

Alec understood what Cronin meant. They'd smell his blood, like ants to honey.

"We need to move," Cronin said again, though it was more of an order this time. "This way." He led them out of the room, Alec close behind him. Bes, Johan followed, and Jodis and Eiji flanked from the rear. They followed the long narrow tunnel, heading closer to the central hub, Alec knew, not from maps he'd memorized, but because the stench was getting stronger.

"The smell is putrid," Alec ground out, almost dry heaving.

A swarm of vampires rounded the corner ahead, a whole platoon of them, and Alec opened fire, his silencer doing little to snuff the sound in the echoing corridor.

He missed a few, hitting the mummified vampires in the head or torso, and their bodies just took the hits with dried skin tearing like bark, their haggard wounds doing little to stop them. One came in closer, screeching and clawing with its head half gone from where a bullet had torn through it. Yet it still moved forward. Alec fired again, this time with perfect aim, shooting it right in the heart, and the instant silence it left behind was deafening.

"Well, that wasn't disturbing at all," Alec said.

Eiji snorted out a laugh behind them. "We've got incoming from the south."

"This way." Cronin kept urging them forward. Bes now stood at the front with Cronin, his crossbow aimed at whatever came toward them. Eiji and Jodis fired arrows into the returned vampires at the rear as they walked with perfect aim, always keeping close to Alec.

They passed doorways of thankfully empty chambers, some with hieroglyphs painted above the doors, some without. Cronin never left Alec's side as the six of them crept toward the Queen's Chamber.

"My quiver is empty," Jodis said, and as though it was a prompt, Cronin led them into the next dark chamber. This room was small also, no more than eight feet square. The walls had some hieroglyphs, some Alec recognized, some he didn't. But he didn't pay too much attention as he reloaded his pistol and drew another, checking the magazine. Everyone took a moment to regroup, to replenish their quivers and holsters with arrows. Everyone but Cronin.

He stood at the door and staked countless vampire drones, who were obviously drawn in by the scent of Alec's blood. One after the other, they screeched and clawed, trying to get to their prize of fresh blood, but Cronin stopped them all.

Eiji's face, illuminated in green by the night vision goggles, was split with a grin. "You're enjoying this?" Alec asked him.

Eiji laughed. "I haven't had this much fun since the last Yersinian plague in Russia."

Jodis sighed, and Alec wondered how much self-control it took for her not to roll her eyes.

Cronin staked another vampire at the door. "Eiji, you and I need to talk about what constitutes as fun," he said, staking yet another. "Because this is not on my list."

Two more vampires stormed through the door, Cronin staked one, and Jodis fired an arrow from her crossbow, turning the other into dust. Cronin gave her a nod. "Thank you, Jodis, dear."

She shot an arrow into another drone vampire that squawked as it tried to enter. "Any time, friend."

Cronin smiled, and as the last of this swarm of vampires tried to enter the room, Cronin held a stake in each hand and, as if under strobe lights, flickered in and out of vision, staking each vampire with deadly accuracy.

When there were no more vampires, Cronin appeared, calm and collected. "Are you ready to move?"

Alec stood up, clicked a bullet into the chamber and held the gun at his thigh, and smiled at Cronin. "Your skills in decimation are both frightening and amazing."

Cronin smiled proudly. "Thank you."

He led them out again, with Bes at the front, Alec behind with Johan, and Eiji and Jodis tailing, watching from behind. The corridors got a little wider and hieroglyphics started to appear more frequently. First as random markings over doorways and down the walls, then more steadily until each stone was covered with markings. From the artwork and smooth finishes, Alec could tell these were original tunnels made some four thousand years ago.

There were noises, far off and distant but unmistakable. Screeching howls cut short and abrupt silence followed feral cries, which told Alec the other groups with leapers, the English and Italian, were slaying drone vampires by the dozen.

As Cronin led them forward, the corridor split at an intersection and Cronin took the left without hesitating. The sounds and stench were stronger to Alec's human senses, and he could only imagine what Cronin could hear.

They'd barely made it a few yards from the intersection when another platoon of blood-deprived returned vampires flooded the corridor.

This ambush hit hard. They were crazed and rabid, the scent of Alec's blood no doubt driving them mad. Screeching and clawing with teeth bared, the foul-smelling creatures came at them.

But they were not armed, fighting only with their brittle claw-like hands. The wooden stakes and arrows, and Alec's gun surprised them. It was pretty clear these vampires were unfed and uneducated.

Alec found himself behind Cronin, his back against the wall and his vampire friends in front, defending him. The corridor was narrow, the roof low, so fighting space was cramped. But the dried and rotten vampires crushed forward, driven by an unimaginable thirst for a blood they'd obviously so rarely tasted.

Alec fired over Cronin's shoulder, each shot hitting its target with a perfect aim. Arrows from bows whistled through the air, and one by one, this platoon of mummified vampires were dust.

They went forward again, starting to climb a flight of stairs, which, Alec knew from the maps Johan had drawn and from what he'd seen online, led to the Queen's Chamber, the King's Gallery, and the King's

Chamber. The stairs were narrow, the ceiling very high, the noise a constant screeching hum.

They were literally walking into a trap.

As mummified vampires came toward them, arrows turned them to dust as they filed down one by one. Alec picked up discarded arrows as they kept climbing.

They found the Queen's Chamber and, as they'd expected, the Queen was not there. A battalion of her army was, though, and as Cronin breached the door first, he was set upon.

Alec thought his heart would stop as he charged into the room with only one thought to save his mate. "Cronin!"

CHAPTER TWENTY-ONE

There must have been forty returned vampires in the Queen's Chamber, a room no bigger than eighteen square feet. The ceiling was high, some twenty feet up, and as the swarm of vampires realized Alec was in the room, they took to the walls, going high, up and over, trying to get a taste of fresh blood.

Though Alec's only fear was for Cronin.

A spray of arrows came from behind him; Eiji, Jodis, Johan, and Bes fired simultaneously and repeatedly. They shot up at the vampires that crawled the walls looking for the source of blood they craved.

It was then Alec saw Cronin, flickering in and out of view as he leapt and pierced hearts with wooden stakes to the vampires on the ground.

The room was nothing but dust in seconds.

Alec was covered in the blackened dust, and he could taste the fetid ash on his tongue. But he didn't care. He took three long strides and threw his arms around Cronin. "Jesus," he mumbled. "I thought they had you. I've never been so scared."

Cronin pulled back. He was smiling. "I'm fine."

Alec looked back to the rest of his team, knowing, not even having fired one round, he'd let them down. "I froze on that one, sorry."

Eiji clapped Alec's shoulder, sending up a plume of dust. "It's all good, my friend. You're doing just fine."

"These vampires are starving," Jodis hissed. "What kind of cruel person creates these creatures only to see them waste and starve?"

"I say we go meet her," Cronin said. "Let this be over with."

"Agreed," Eiji said, moving back to the door. He scanned the corridor. "It is clear."

"Wait," Alec said. He looked at Cronin. "Can you leap us to the King's Chamber?"

Cronin's eyes narrowed. "Yes. Why?"

"We were pretty certain she wasn't going to be in this chamber," Alec explained. "And there's a very good chance she's in the King's Chamber. It's bigger and is directly linked to the Gallery."

Cronin nodded. "Yes."

"She knows we're here now," Alec continued. "And she'll be expecting us to come up through the Gallery because it's the only entrance. She won't be expecting us to just appear in her room."

Cronin looked at the others, Alec assumed to gauge opinions.

"We know what we're dealing with now," Eiji said.

"It could work," Jodis agreed.

"I just don't fancy another few hundred yards and swarms of vampires pulling you into chambers like they did just now," Alec said, looking straight at Cronin. "You want this to be over, then let's finish it."

Cronin gave a nod. "Okay."

Each extending a hand to touch the person next to them, they disappeared from the Queen's Chamber, and landed in the King's.

The room itself was larger, about thirty-five feet by eighteen, and the ceiling some twenty feet high. The walls were covered in extravagant hieroglyphics: gold and teals, reds and greens, writings of another time.

But unlike all other chambers Alec had seen, this room was furnished. There was a large chair, a throne, Alec presumed. There were large canopic vases and a long table, and on top of the table was a mummy. It had to be Osiris. She had him ready and waiting for Alec to arrive.

It was macabre, made more gruesome by the green illumination of his night vision goggles.

His eyesight didn't betray him, though. He could see Queen Keket perfectly.

She looked just like Cleopatra from that old movie, but she wore a gold dress, and her long black hair was wavy and shiny. Her olive skin was flush and smooth, her eyes lined with black kohl, her vampire fangs were white and gleaming. She looked beautiful and equally terrifying.

She was surrounded by vampire security. They wore the traditional Ancient Egyptian *shendyt*, all returned mummies, but these looked fed and healthy, compared to her constructed army of dried and decrepit soldiers.

And to say they took Queen Keket by surprise was an understatement.

She spun around with a scream, her security guards moving in front of her, ready for attack. Her eyes were wide and a look of shock crossed her features before she spied Alec.

Her eyes stayed wide, though not in fear. Now it was desire. She murmured something in Arabic that sounded like "mistarck" before raising her hand. If her security guards were going to attack, she stopped them. She whispered again in Arabic, words Alec couldn't understand, but beside him, Cronin growled.

He stepped in front of Alec. "He is not yours," Cronin whispered eerily.

Eiji, Jodis, Johan, and Bes all moved in formation, putting themselves between Alec and the queen and her guards.

She seemed delighted by this, as though she found it funny.

"I know who you are," Alec said to her. "Tahani Shafiq."

Her eyes widened in anger this time, and she bared her teeth. She spoke in English. "I am Queen Keket."

"Not to me," Alec said.

She hissed at his defiance. "You will bow before me before this day is through. Mark my words."

"Sorry to disappoint you," Alec said with a smile. "But if it's my heart you want, you're too late. It belongs to someone else."

Her anger turned her beauty into a disturbing horror. Her face contorted and pulled back, looking more like a snarling dog than a beautiful queen. She looked straight at Cronin, then back to Alec. "Seeing me rip your heart from your chest will be the last thing your mate sees."

One of her guards sprang toward them, his speed alarming, even for a vampire. But as he was just mere feet from them, Jodis waved her hand and the vampire froze in mid-flight. He stood with only one foot on the ground, his arms out and his teeth bared, completely still.

Alec's heart was pounding, but Eiji simply put his hand to the vampire's head and flicked his fingers, shattering a hole in the vampire's head as though he was frozen with liquid nitrogen.

The Egyptian vampires all gasped in shock, obviously having never seen such a thing, before Eiji cleanly drove a stake into the frozen vampire's heart.

Keket took a step back, her guards closing in ranks, but now not so bravely. Swarms of starving vampires now squawked and clawed at the door, not game to enter their Queen's private room, but the scent of Alec's blood was too potent to ignore.

"You've been too busy creating your army," Cronin said to her. "Did you not think there were other talents more prudent than yours in our kind?"

Keket bared her teeth again. "None have the power I hold. Only I hold the power of life and death."

Cronin scoffed out a laugh. "You may be able to return the mummified vampires, yet you still cannot bring back your sister, no?"

Alec could almost feel the wrath pouring off Keket, and the guards next to her flinched from her. They looked too scared to run, too scared to stay.

Then she wailed like a madwoman. A scream of rage, a cry of pain. The blood-deprived vampires at the door went into a flurry at the sound of their Queen's anguish. Alec was sure they were waiting for the order to kill.

"You starve your army," Jodis said, over the squall of noise. "So they'll obey you and do your bidding and labor? It will be your undoing, Tahani. You underestimate the power of blood. You'll be able to control them, no more than you could hold back the rising tide."

You underestimate the power of blood.

Alec didn't know why those words rang true, but they sounded in his head like a bell.

While Keket hissed and spewed vitriol in both Arabic and English, Alec scanned the walls again. The hieroglyphs were telling him something—these walls were painted thousands of years ago, when those who buried Osiris wanted him to stay dead.

There had to be something he wasn't seeing.

He saw Anubis, the god who weighed the hearts of those he embalmed, holding scales. He saw Osiris, the green-skinned god, immune to the powers of the sun, holding a crook and flail.

The sun.

He saw Ra, god of the sun.

The sun.

He saw what Ra was holding…

Cronin growled beside him. "Can I just kill her now?"

"Wait," Alec said, still looking at the walls.

But it was too late. One of the Illyrian guards put a blow-dart to his mouth and shot at Cronin.

Like the world stopped spinning, showing everything in slow motion, Johan flew in front of him. The wooden bullet hit his bulletproof vest and fell to the floor. Johan looked up, smiling hugely. He'd just acted on instinct to save Cronin's life, yet it left him standing somewhat sideways, and this time a bullet hit him under the left arm.

Like the moment stopped all time, right in front of Alec, a look of surprise crossed Johan's face before he fell to dust.

Alec couldn't believe it. He was completely stunned, rendered useless and a complete liability.

Cronin, on the other hand, didn't waste a second.

He leapt, again and again, staking the Illyrian guards where they stood, faster than an automatic rifle.

Queen Keket stumbled backward with her arms up. "No!"

Cronin paused. "I'm sorry you were wronged in your human life," he said. "May you find peace in the next."

She cried out some word that gave the order for the returned vampires to kill, because they stormed the chamber like ants.

"Cronin!" Alec called. "The Sphinx."

Before Alec could blink, Cronin had him, Eiji, Jodis, and Bes, and they were gone.

* * * *

It took Alec only a second to get his bearings. They were in an empty corridor, and he could hear the enraged screaming from Keket and the buzz and roar of her returned vampires from afar. Though Alec knew it wouldn't be long until they hunted the scent of his blood.

He ran down the corridor, gun in one hand, stake in the other, with Cronin, Eiji, Jodis, and Bes on his heels. The air was dry and rank, though the smell of returned and rotten vampires not as bad here. Alec was farther out, under the Sphinx to be exact. They stood in a circular room with stone pillars that reminded Alec of Stonehenge, and remembering Johan's maps, he followed one shaft until he entered the small chamber he needed. Above the door, was a solitary ankh.

He couldn't read hieroglyphs, per se, but he didn't need to. The pictures said it all. The walls were marked by sphinx-looking animals, cats, each with a paw raised to shield the sun.

"Alec," Cronin whispered in a rush. "Please explain!"

Alec started to feel along the walls. He wasn't sure what he was looking for or even hoping to find, but he knew it was here. "In the King's Chamber," Alec said. "The hieroglyphs. Whoever drew them thousands of years ago was showing us what to do."

Alec had put the pieces together. The only god vampire holding an ankh, a key, was Ra, known by historians as the god of the sun. Ra was painted over and over again holding the ankh, the key, and wearing the sun-disk...

And it all fell into place. Every piece made perfect sense.

He might've been the key Keket needed to bring back Osiris, but Alec was also the key for something else.

Mikka, the vampire who saved Alec in the alley in the very beginning, said to him *it's both*. He said *it's not one, but both*. He wasn't talking about the Illyrians and the Egyptians like they'd assumed he was. And Eleanor couldn't see what Alec's real purpose was, only that he needed to be human. They'd assumed he needed his human heart to stop Keket...

It's not one, but both...

But it wasn't his heart he needed to stay human for. It was his blood.

Alec's blood was the key needed to bring back Ra. Even his father had told him it was his blood that was special.

It wasn't Anubis who would kill Osiris again. It was Ra who would kill them all.

Alec knew what he had to do.

"I'm not here to bring back Anubis," Alec said.

Eiji looked concerned. "Alec, you're not making sense."

Alec never stopped scanning the walls with his hands. "I thought I might have to bring back Anubis," Alec said, still trying to make sense of the hieroglyphs. He turned again, looking over each wall. "But that's not right."

"Alec, the room is empty," Cronin hissed. "What are you looking for?"

"Something no one wanted found, something buried..." Alec looked at the sandy stone floor. "Something buried twice." Alec went to the floor and started sweeping at the sand with his hands. He looked up at the vampires who were staring down at him. "Ra. We need to find Ra, the god of the sun."

"Stop," Cronin said, and he stood completely still and smelled the air. Then he turned to the side wall and followed his nose to it. "It is faint, but it is there."

The large stone brick Cronin stopped at, some three by two feet in size, was painted with a sphinx, like the others around the small room. But this one sphinx wasn't shielding its face from the sun. It had its head bowed; it was holding an ankh in offering. "Here, this one's holding the key. We need to get it out," Alec said. He dropped to his knees and started frantically, fruitlessly scraping at the stone wall.

"Alec?" Cronin pleaded.

"It has to be Ra," Alec said, running his fingers along the cracks between the huge stones. "They never marked where Ra was buried because they never wanted him found. He has the sun-disk. Don't you see? It's been right in front of us all along. I'm not the key for Keket to bring back Osiris. I'm the key to bring back Ra."

Cronin shook his head a little. "Alec, I do not understand."

"Just trust me," he said. "We need to get this mummy out." Which, without some C4, Alec was thinking was an impossibility.

"Stand aside," Cronin told him.

Cronin simply dug his fingers into the grout-like edges of the stone, carving it away like sand until he could get his hands between the stones. Then with a strength Alec didn't know was possible, Cronin, Eiji, and Jodis strained to bring the stone forward.

The muscles in Cronin's arms bunched and bulged, his shoulders were taut and his neck was corded. And with what Alec was certain was every ounce of strength the vampires had, they pulled the stone out.

Alec looked into the dark hole they'd created and could see there was definitely a hidden vault of some sort.

"We will stand guard," Jodis said, and she, Eiji, and Bes faced the door, stakes at the ready.

The hole the stone left was no more than three feet by two, just big enough for Alec to slide through. The chamber he found himself in was tiny: four feet by seven feet, and Alec had to stoop. Cronin was suddenly by his side.

But the sarcophagus in the middle of the tiny room was unmistakable. There were hieroglyphs carved into the stone top, the largest of them an ankh.

Alec stood at one side and shoved against the top. It was a limestone slab some few inches thick, and he couldn't move it an inch. Cronin simply put both hands against it and slid it off.

"We really need to discuss your workout routine," Alec said, looking into the stone coffin. He heard Eiji laugh from the other side of the stone wall.

The body wasn't wrapped like Alec had expected. He was expecting a bandage wrapped mummy like he'd seen in a hundred *Scooby-Doo* cartoons as a kid, but it wasn't like that at all.

The body was covered with a linen cloth sheet, in what Alec assumed was a burial for a disgraced pharaoh or a burial done in haste for a pharaoh someone never wanted found. The cloth felt like dried paper and Alec pulled it back to reveal exactly what he was hoping to find.

The body itself was dried and warped, all blackened sinew. His face looked contorted, frozen in a perpetual silent scream. His teeth were yellowed and blackened, and his vampire fangs looked too big for his mouth.

But he was holding a plate-sized disk across his chest, and that was what Alec wanted.

Ra, the god of the sun, buried within the walls of the pyramid.

Just then, there were voices on the other side of the wall where the others were, and Cronin froze. "Don't be alarmed," Bes said quickly. "It is my coven brothers." Bes leaned through the hole. "They say there are many coming this way."

Eiji spoke next. "Alec, whatever it is you're doing, you need to hurry."

"We need to take this mummy to Keket," Alec said quickly.

Cronin looked at him, stunned. "Alec, surely not."

"Now. We need to do it now," Alec said. "Bes, I need you to stay here with your friends. Tell whatever vampires come looking for me that I've gone back to the Gallery. Tell them their Queen has fresh blood for them."

Cronin growled. "Alec."

Alec carefully slid his hands underneath the mummy and lifted it, surprised by the light weight of it. "Eiji, Jodis, come in here, quickly." He looked at Cronin. "Please trust me. We need to go to the King's Gallery. Not her chamber. We need as many of those vampires in the one room as possible."

Jodis slid through first, then Eiji, both of them stopping still when they saw Alec holding the mummy. There was no room to move with the four of them squashed in the small vault-sized chamber. Cronin stood at one end, closest to Alec, of course, then Jodis and Eiji, each of them touching the person next to them.

"Be ready," Alec warned. "Because this is it."

And they were gone.

* * * *

The Gallery was about one hundred and fifty feet long, only six feet wide, but the ceiling was twenty-eight feet high. And it was a blur of movement.

Queen Keket stood inside the door to her chamber, yelling orders in Arabic to her returned army, and when Alec, Cronin, Eiji, and Jodis appeared at the end of the Gallery near her door, she flew back, keeping about twelve feet between them. Her army stood behind her, still, *still* not willing to defy her.

Her eyes trained on Alec and went wide when she saw what he held. Or rather who. She saw the disk. She knew exactly who it was.

Alec smiled at her. "I thought it was Anubis who I needed to bring back to take you down," he said. "He was, after all, the one who killed Osiris the first time. I presumed he could do it again."

"Anubis was a fool!" she cried, flinging her arms wildly. "He wasn't strong enough to do my work. Osiris will worship me. I am to life as he is to death. I shall rule over you all with him at my feet."

"You think the god of the dead will answer to you?" Cronin asked. "You are sorely mistaken."

Keket laughed wildly. "You have no idea of my power." She put her hand to the mummy of Osiris and the gallery went quiet. Her power was obviously transmitted by touch, because the returned vampires were waiting for Osiris to come to life.

But the mummy never moved. He was incomplete without his heart. When she realized her plan had failed, Keket flew into a rage.

Alec was certain this woman vampire was insane. She ranted some more, throwing up her arms, sending her swelling sea of vampires into a frenzy. They edged in, like a hive of wasps, seeming to stand on top of each other trying to get closer to Alec's blood, though they wouldn't attack without command, despite how starved for blood they were. They were truly a frightening sight. There was so many of them, so warped and deranged and misshapen…

But it was Keket who frightened Alec the most.

She was literally backed into a corner, with absolutely nothing to lose.

Without her Illyrian guards, the guards Cronin had killed earlier, she stood at the forefront of her army with a mummified Osiris she couldn't resurrect.

It was a complete stalemate.

She needed Alec's heart, yet couldn't give word to her drones to charge, because he would certainly be killed in the frenzy. One sniff of his blood and it would be an unholy carnage.

Everyone would lose.

Maybe that was her fallback plan.

Alec couldn't let it get to that. He knew what he had to do.

He knew it was his blood that was the key. It was on all the walls, in every hieroglyph. The Ancients had painted instructions on the very walls in which they stood. He needed to take out Keket and her whole returned army in one fell swoop.

He put the mummy of Ra on the ground at his feet. They were with their backs against a wall, completely surrounded. It was the only way.

Jodis had warned Keket that keeping her returned vampires underfed and isolated—her being their only provider of food—to control them would be her undoing. And so it would be. Alec knew how to get as many returned vampires into the King's Chamber at once. In fact, he knew what would bring them there in droves.

He unsheathed his knife from his thigh holster. "Cronin," he called out over the snarling sound of the wall of vampires. "Take Jodis and Eiji."

Cronin looked at the mummy on the ground, then at the knife in his hand. He seemed to understand immediately. "Alec, no!" Cronin roared; the violence in his voice stopped every vampire in the room.

"Get Jodis and Eiji out," Alec said, not taking his eyes off Keket. He needed Cronin, Jodis, and Eiji out of the room, and as many of the good vampires that were left. "Fall back," Alec yelled, knowing any good vampires on their side of the fight knew that code word meant get the fucking hell out there. "Fall back! Now!"

"Alec, no," Cronin said again, quieter this time. Begging.

"You can't be in here," Alec said.

"I won't leave you."

"I'm not giving you a choice," Alec yelled back at him. "Fall back. Now." Alec held up the knife over the sun-disk and raised his left hand to the blade.

"Alec," Cronin started to say, but Alec drew the blade across the palm of his hand, slicing it wide open.

The reaction in the room was immediate. Flooded by returned vampires, they seemed to swarm from everywhere, lured by the rusty scent of blood. The whole room seemed to moan and scream as they fought and clawed for their prize.

Cronin, Eiji, and Jodis stood around Alec, guarding him, protecting him from the rancid tide of returned vampires who sought his blood. Alec held his hand over the body of Ra and let his blood flow freely from his hand onto the sun-disk, filling it red, just like the hieroglyphs on the walls depicted.

Then Alec moved his cut hand to the mouth of Ra, letting drops of blood run over the mummy's teeth and into its mouth.

Queen Keket raged as she realized what was happening. "What have you done?" she screamed. She stood at the forefront of her army, keeping just enough distance between her and Jodis so she could not freeze her.

The body of Ra began to fuse and creak, the fetid scent of decayed flesh, camphor, and myrrh overpowering.

"Oh holy shit, holy shit," Alec said, watching in rapt horror as the mummified, dehydrated body of Ra came to life. It was one thing to imagine it, it was another thing entirely to watch it happen in front of you. Slowly, impossibly, somehow without shattering, the dried and brittle Ra stood. He was surprisingly short, his blackened, crippled body all sinew and twisted, with matted hair, and his eyeless sockets scanned the room.

He lifted the disk to his mouth and drank the blood, then he made a keening roar, a sound reserved only for the depths of hell. Everyone stood motionless and watched as Ra slowly turned the bloodstained red disk around and lifted it above his head.

Light sparked and cracked from the disk, like streaks of lightning, and Alec knew what was about to happen. He looked at Cronin and found him staring, wide-eyed back at him.

"Five seconds, huh?" Alec yelled over the dull roar of the writhing sea of vampires. "Five seconds for ultraviolet light to kill a vampire?"

Cronin gave a nod.

Alec smiled at him. "Come back and get me in six."

Then blinding sunlight ripped through the darkness.

* * * *

One second:

Sunlight, pure and warm, engulfed the room like fire, and harrowing screams filled the air. A parched and screeching roar came from Ra.

Cronin gave a final wide-eyed glance at Alec as he grabbed Eiji and Jodis. There was a struggle between them, and Eiji ripped his arm free just as Cronin and Jodis disappeared.

Two seconds:

Eiji spun away, his long black hair like flowing ribbons around his head as he picked up a wooden stake from the ground in one swift, fluid movement.

Alec noticed then that Keket was in full flight toward him, almost upon him, her arms raised, her teeth bared.

Three seconds:

Eiji struck Keket in the chest with a stake, a look of horror on her face, her rabid scream cut silent, and her body seemed to explode into dust.

Four seconds:

Eiji spun to look at Alec, his face shockingly calm and at peace. He smiled.

Alec turned to Ra, who stood, brown and mummified, yet returned. His mouth bore horrid teeth and fangs, and his bony hands still held the sun-disk above his head. Alec threw the wooden stake he was holding as hard as could at Ra's chest.

Five seconds:

Alec launched himself at Eiji, scooping up the small Japanese vampire, shielding him from the sunlight, and with all the strength he had left in him, screamed out, "Cronin!"

The room went dark.

* * * *

Encased in darkness, Alec found himself in familiar arms, and he welcomed the pain of leaping. He *welcomed* it.

Then he was on the floor of Cronin's apartment, holding Eiji against his chest like a child with Cronin's arms around them both.

Jodis fell to her knees before him, a silent tortured pain across her face, and she put her shaking hands to her lover's face. "My Eiji," she whispered. Kole stood some yards away, white-faced and wide-eyed, his hand to his mouth.

Alec pulled his night vision goggles off and threw them away. He ripped the Velcro tabs on Eiji's bulletproof vest, exposing his burned torso. That vest had no doubt saved his life.

Eiji went rigid and sucked in a ragged breath, only to let out a scream. Alec had never heard anything so painful, so heartbreaking. Eiji fought against Alec, and Jodis quickly took him in her arms. Alec did the only thing he could think of.

He pulled at the cut on his hand, stretching and ripping it open until blood pooled in his palm, then put his hand to Eiji's mouth. "He needs to feed," Alec said. "It will help him heal."

At first the blood just ran into Eiji's mouth, but after a few seconds, he began to suck. "He's taking it," he told them, flooded with relief.

It was then Alec realized Cronin was growling. He was still kneeling behind him and had his head down against Alec's shoulder, and his grip on Alec was tight.

Alec turned the best he could in Cronin's arms without moving his hand from Eiji's mouth. "He's not hurting me," Alec told him.

Cronin lifted his face, his eyes a haunted, *haunted* black. "I know."

"He saved my life."

"I know," Cronin said again, his voice trembling as he spoke.

Jodis sucked back a sob, and white snow-like tears ran down her face. She put her forehead to Eiji's. "My sweet Eiji," she cried.

"We need to get him more blood," Alec said. He was starting to feel woozy.

Cronin shook his head. "I cannot leave you."

"You have to," Alec said. He knew he was paling.

Cronin pulled Alec away, removing his hand from Eiji's mouth. "It will mean bringing a human back here…"

"He will die if you don't," Alec urged him. "Please."

"Get him into the shower," Cronin said quietly. He then turned to Kole. "Please go to the theater room.

Close the doors, turn the volume up, and stay there until we tell you it's safe." Cronin looked to the floor. "You will not wish to witness this."

Kole nodded and did as he was asked. Jodis carried Eiji into the first bathroom, and Alec quickly followed. They had Eiji on the floor in the shower under the stream of cool water immediately, shirtless but otherwise fully dressed and trying to cool any damage the burning sunlight had done to him. He screamed again through gritted teeth, and his whole body shook.

Alec knelt beside them and brushed Eiji's hair from his forehead, then a burst of shouting came from the living room.

Alec jumped up just as Cronin came through the door. He had his hand to the throat of a man who was struggling against him. The man, with wide, feral eyes and a shaved, tattooed head, was shouting obscenities, which Alec knew to be Russian. His Russian prison garb and tattoos left no doubt as to where Cronin had plucked him from.

The man yelled again, his neck corded and his face an angry shade of red. He thrashed against Cronin, but the vampire held him easily. Cronin lifted his free hand, and with a simple tap to the head, the man was quiet. Unconscious, he slumped in Cronin's hold.

"Alec, you need to leave," Cronin said.

Alec didn't argue. He simply walked out of the bathroom, not even stopping to see if the door closed behind him. He found himself in the kitchen, wet, dazed, overwhelmed, and shaking. Only then did his hand start to hurt.

He wrapped a dishcloth around his injured palm, though the bleeding was now almost stopped. Realizing he needed sugar or something to replenish his own system, he opened the fridge door and pulled out the orange juice. When his hand shook too much to pour any into a cup, he drank it straight from the bottle.

Then Cronin was behind him. "I'm sorry you had to witness that," he said.

Alec wiped his mouth and shook his head. He didn't think he could speak.

"If it rests your conscious, the vile human was imprisoned in the worst of prisons in the depths of Russia, reserved for crimes that don't bear repeating."

"Will Eiji be okay?" Alec asked. He didn't care about the Russian guy. He just simply… didn't.

Cronin took Alec's shaking hands and held them softly. He looked him all over, over every square inch as if to make sure he was okay. "You were brave today."

Alec's eyes filled with tears, the shock of what he'd witnessed and what he'd done starting to take hold of him.

"You risked your life today," Cronin said. His tone was impassive, but Alec could tell he wasn't happy.

"I did what I had to do," Alec said. "Is Eiji okay?"

Cronin nodded. "He is getting stronger already."

Alec let out a relieved breath, and his tears finally fell. "Oh, thank god."

Cronin wrapped his arms around him, and each man held on as tight as they dared. Alec ignored how the skin on his hand protested, he simply let himself cry and let himself be held in the strongest, safest arms he'd ever known.

Eventually Alec pulled back and wiped at his face. "Who else made it out?"

"I don't know," Cronin said, putting his hand to Alec's face. "You were my first concern."

"Thank you for coming back for me."

Cronin barked out a hard laugh. "Like you gave me any choice."

"I didn't..." Alec shook his head. "I didn't make you leave me there—"

"That is *exactly* what you did," Cronin countered.

"I just needed you to be safe," Alec said. "I knew what I had to do. As soon as I saw the hieroglyphs of Ra... He held the ankh—the key—in every painting, and the sun-disk was always painted red like blood. I don't know how I didn't see it sooner, but as soon as it all clicked into place, I knew what I had to do." Alec swallowed hard and wiped his face again. "I would never send you away if it weren't to save you."

"You asked me to leave you behind," Cronin said. "Is it difficult to believe that those six seconds seemed longer than a century?" He shook his head and looked at their joined hands between them.

"I will never ask you to leave me again," Alec whispered.

Cronin looked up at him then. "Do you promise?"

"Yes," Alec swore to him. Then he shrugged. "Unless I need to bring an Egyptian god back to life with my blood and he can make sunlight from a round dinner plate. Then yes, I'll need you to leave."

Cronin almost smiled. He reached up and swept Alec's wet hair off his forehead. "I'm still mad at you for making me leave you."

"For what it's worth, I am glad you did," Alec told him. He put his hands to Cronin's face and leaned in to kiss him, but Cronin pulled his face away.

He quickly took Alec's cut hand. "Probably best not to put that hand so close to my face," Cronin said quietly.

"Cronin." Jodis spoke from the hall, and when Alec turned around, he saw that she was carrying Eiji. "He's done."

Cronin gave a nod, and whispered to Alec, "I must dispose of the body. I won't be gone for long."

Alec nodded. "Okay," he whispered back, then leaned in and pressed his lips to Cronin's before he disappeared. Alec smiled into thin air, but followed Jodis down the hall and into the bedroom he'd slept in the first night.

Jodis lay Eiji on the bed, his hair wet and swept back off his face. She pulled the sheet to his waist then kissed his forehead before sitting beside him on the bed, holding his hand. Alec gave a soft knock. "Can I come in?"

Jodis smiled, only briefly taking her eyes off Eiji to look at Alec. "Yes of course."

Alec stepped tentatively into the room. Eiji opened his eyes and tried to smile. "Hey," Alec said. "You saved my life."

"And you mine," Eiji said, his voice just a whisper.

"You feeling okay?"

"Been better," Eiji said, his voice quiet and harsh. "The blood helped."

Alec nodded. "You'll need a lot more, yes?"

Jodis nodded. "Yes. But it was your quick thinking, Alec, to let him feed from your hand that in all likelihood saved his life." She gently rubbed Eiji's arm. "And by association, mine as well."

Alec smiled at them both and touched Eiji's hand. "Well, it was worth it, even if Cronin's really pissed at me," Alec said, shrugging one shoulder.

Jodis gave a laugh that sounded more like a sob. She wiped her eyes, and her lip trembled as she spoke. "You both left us! You have no idea what it was like to leap back here without either of you." She looked at Eiji and slowly shook her head. "I had my hand on you, then you were gone... We got back here and our hands were empty of both of you... I thought I'd lost you. And Cronin," she said, looking at Alec, "he was—"

"Distraught," a voice said from the door. Alec looked up to see Cronin leaning casually against the door frame. Cronin never took his eyes off Alec. "Upset. Angry. Hurt." He took a deep breath and added a quiet but profound, "Helpless."

Alec quickly got to his feet and stepped in front of Cronin. "I never meant to hurt you. I did it to save you."

Cronin gave a small smile and he shook his head. "I was also proud and honored that you would sacrifice yourself for us. But mostly I was pissed off."

Alec put his non-injured hand to Cronin's face, then ran his fingers through his rust-colored hair. He never said anything, just leaned in and kissed his temple before sliding his arm around Cronin's waist and staying there.

Cronin put his arm around Alec as well, but he looked at Eiji. "You saved my Alec, and I will be forever grateful."

"You've saved us countless times, brother," Eiji said weakly. "It was the least I could do."

Cronin gave a nod. "You need to rest. I will bring you more blood in a few hours."

"Thank you, Cronin," Jodis whispered. "We'd be at a loss without you."

Cronin smiled. "It is the least I could do."

Smiling and grimacing at the same time, Eiji slowly closed his eyes. Jodis lay down beside him, their hands joined on his chest, and Sammy the cat was now purring beside them. Cronin pulled Alec out the door to the hall and gave a small nod toward his bedroom door with a hopeful, suggestive smirk, but Alec shook his head and walked out to the living room. He picked up the four wooden stakes that were thrown on the sofa.

"What are you doing?" Cronin asked, his eyes wide.

"We need to go back to Egypt," Alec said simply.

Cronin blinked. "What on earth for?"

"To make sure it's done properly," Alec said. "No loose ends, no stragglers left to take up the cause. It ends today."

Cronin shook his head. "There was no one left in the chamber when I leapt back to collect you."

"There were others," Alec said. "The ones who didn't make it into the chamber when they smelled my blood, or maybe they fled when they saw the sun, I don't know. But we need to make sure." Alec shoved the stakes into the waistband of his jeans and reclipped a fresh magazine of wooden bullets into his pistol and slid it into his shoulder holster. "Will you take me?"

Cronin's jaw bulged, his words spoken through clenched teeth. "You are impossibly frustrating."

Alec grinned at him. "You're welcome." With a black glare from Cronin that was clearly supposed to menacing but only made Alec smile harder, Cronin slid his arms around Alec. Just before they leapt, Alec chuckled and said, "Stay behind me."

Cronin was still growling when they arrived in complete darkness, though the familiar putrid air told

Alec they were back in the Gallery. There was also only silence.

"Shit. I forgot my goggles. I can't see," Alec whispered.

"The room is empty," Cronin replied, but he took Alec's hand and led him just a few feet. "Your knapsack."

Alec was handed the canvas backpack. Going by feel alone, he found the zipper and rummaged through the bag until he found what he was after. He put the backpack on, held out the flare, striking it to illuminate the chamber.

The room was empty, just as Cronin had said, except for piles of blackened sand covering most of the floor and the bloodstained sun-disk laying disregarded amongst the mess. Alec picked it up and slid it inside the backpack.

"What are you doing?" Cronin asked quietly.

"Figure I'll start adding my own things to your wall of memorabilia," Alec said. "So in a thousand years, we can look at them and say 'Do you remember when?' like the old folks do."

Cronin's grin was immediate and warm, just as someone far off called out his name. "Cronin?"

Alec had the flare in his injured left hand, his pistol drawn in his right, and he instinctively stood in front of Cronin. "Stay the fuck where you are."

Alec could see three figures coming toward them, hands raised. "It is I, Bes," the first man said.

Cronin stepped around Alec, and putting his hand to Alec's raised gun, he pushed it down. "It is Bes."

As they approached and walked into the light of the flare, Alec could see Bes and two of his coven members. The smile Bes wore was huge. Despite the fact Alec was holding a gun, Bes drew him in for a quick embrace, kissing both cheeks before letting him go. "We owe much to you, Alec. A human who would save vampires! One would never believe it!" he cried.

Cronin smiled, but stood protectively close to Alec, as the three Egyptian vampires all thanked Alec, touching him. "Who remains?" Cronin asked.

"We spoke to the English vampire, Kennard," Bes said. "I told him I fought with you. He said they had no losses on his team, that redcoats were always better. I don't know what that means."

Cronin snorted a laugh. "Thank you for that news."

"What about the mummy-vampires?" Alec asked. "Did any survive?"

"There were a few dozen returned vampires who were trying to get out," Bes explained. "But we stopped them. When the returned ones all ran to this room, like them, we smelled the blood, but there were so many and we were at the entrance when the sunlight beamed out," he said, using his hands as he spoke. "We ran back, away from the light, and some returned vampires ran too, but we found them. They were mad with hunger, and they were—" Bes swirled his hands as he searched for the right words. "—wild and lost, confused. Those poor creatures."

Cronin's brow creased. "Did any survive?"

Bes shook his head. "We put them out of their miserable ways. We lost some of our own today, though."

"I'm sorry to hear that," Alec said softly.

Bes put his hand on Alec's arm. "But we fought well and we will honor their bravery." Then he asked. "And you? What of Eiji and Jodis?"

"Jodis is safe and well, Eiji was injured," Cronin said. "He's safe now and healing. He was exposed to the light of Ra."

Bes's eyes went wide. "And he yet lives?"

Alec nodded. "Barely, but yes. We must be getting back to him. I just wanted to come back and see that this was truly over, that none of them remained."

Bes brightened once more. "They are gone, and we have our lands back!" he said. His jubilation was contagious. "We can never thank you enough, and we are forever in your debt." Bes bowed his head to Alec. "It's been an honor and a privilege to have worked with you."

Alec found himself smiling back at him. He reholstered his gun and shook Bes's hand. "You are a good man."

Bes bowed his head again, still holding Alec's hand. "You will be remembered always."

Alec found himself looking at the hieroglyphs, and in particular the ankh. "Yeah, I guess I will." He turned to Cronin. "I want to go home now." He threw

345

the dying flare into the sand, put his arms around Cronin, and they were gone.

* * * *

Alec wasn't sure when the effects of leaping stopped ripping him to shreds. Maybe it was the events of the last day, of the last week, but when they leapt back to Cronin's apartment after leaving Bes and Egypt that last time, Alec didn't even flinch.

He just stood there, his arms still firmly around Cronin, with no intention of letting him go. Neither of them moved, but something was different between them.

Something unspoken. Something profound.

The danger was over. The fight, the battles, the planning, the stress, all of it was gone. They were free to be themselves, to start over.

"Are you well?" Cronin whispered.

"Yeah," Alec answered, just as quietly. "You?"

Alec could feel Cronin smile against his collarbone. "Yes." Cronin pulled back just a little, so he could look up and into Alec's eyes. "Do you need sleep or food?" He reached up and touched Alec's dust-filled hair. "A shower?"

"Yes."

"Which one?"

"All of them," Alec answered. "But I need something else more than any of those things."

346

Cronin grew concerned. His eyebrows furrowed. "What is it?"

"You."

"Oh." Cronin laughed quietly and ducked his head. "Maybe we should check on your father —"

"Shit," Alec said with a laugh. He ran to the home theater. "Dad!"

Kole stood up, still pale faced and wide-eyed. He looked like he'd aged a decade in a day. "Alec?"

Alec crossed the room and hugged his dad, hard. "You okay?"

Kole nodded, but didn't let go in a hurry. When he eventually pulled back, Alec saw his dad had tears in his eyes. "I was worried about you, son."

"I was worried too, Dad," he said honestly. "It was scary as hell."

"But you did it?" he asked.

Alec nodded, but it was Cronin who answered. "He figured it all out and saved us all."

Kole looked at Cronin and swallowed hard. "When you came back without him…"

Alec put his arm around his dad. "Let's go out to the living room, and I can tell you everything."

Alec sat his father down and gave him a brief rundown of what happened in Egypt, telling him how it all ended, how Eiji was injured, and of how Johan was killed.

As they talked, Cronin collected the wooden stakes and bulletproof vests, tidying as he went. Then he lowered the metal wall, revealing the most remarkable

New York City skyline. "We have no reason to be in lockdown anymore," Cronin said.

Kole stared out the window for a good few seconds. "Oh."

Alec took in the beautiful lights against the peaceful blackened sky, then looked at his father's face and laughed. "I told you it was something, huh?"

"I had no idea," Kole mumbled. "I mean, you said it was nice."

Cronin smiled warmly at Alec. "If you'll excuse me, I need to shower. The smell of mummified flesh lingers longer than I care for."

Kole scrunched his nose up. "Is that what stinks?"

Alec laughed. "Yeah, we must smell, sorry. I'll get cleaned up after Cronin. Then we can take you home if you want?"

Kole sighed deeply. "So Johan died, huh?"

"Yes," Alec said softly. "He died defending Cronin. He didn't need to, but he acted on instinct, I guess. He had his left arm up at the wrong angle and a second wooden bullet got him in the heart through his armpit." Alec sighed again. "If it was a deliberate aim or just a freak shot, I don't know."

Kole was quiet for a long second. "I have to tell ya, son, when Cronin and Jodis came back here and you weren't with 'em." He shook his head. "I thought you were dead."

"I'm sorry, I didn't think of you being here and seeing that."

Kole looked at Alec. He put his hand over his son's and whispered, "I ain't seen anything sadder. Poor Jodis screamed and was clutchin' at the air like she dropped something, but Cronin…" He shook his head again. "Well, the sound he made… I'll never forget it."

Even though his dad tried to whisper, Alec knew Cronin could hear every word. He spoke with a smile. "Yeah, I think I have some making up to do for that one."

Kole squeezed Alec's hand. "He's in love with you, Alec."

There was a metal clanging noise from the bathroom, like Cronin had just broken the shelf in the shower. Then Eiji's pained laugh sounded from the bedroom.

"Someone's sounding better," Alec said, trying not to smile or die from blushing to death.

Kole smiled widely. "From the look on your face, Alec, I'd say you're in love with him too."

Another clanging noise came from the bathroom, and another bark of tortured laughter came from Eiji. "Ow. Stop it," Eiji cried.

"They can hear me?" Kole whispered.

"Every word," Alec said.

Cronin walked into the living room, all clean and even better smelling. He wore simple dark blue jeans, a dark blue sweater, and a smirk that made Alec's heart beat out of rhythm.

"I, uh, I, uh…" Alec needed to swallow so he could speak apparently. "I better go get cleaned up too."

Eiji laughed again, and this time Alec said, "Oh, shut up, Eiji."

Cronin let out a nervous laugh. "You're supposed to be resting," he said toward the hall. Alec didn't hear exactly what Jodis replied with, but Cronin grinned and smiled at the floor.

Instead of dying of embarrassment, Alec stood up and made his way up the hall toward Cronin's bedroom. He stripped off his shirt and caught sight of himself in the mirror. He was a blackened, sooty mess. Well, he was white where his night vision goggles had been, and his torso was kind of white, but he was smeared black everywhere else.

He looked like an unshaven, un-slept chimney sweep.

He pulled the makeshift bandage off his hand and inspected the cut on his palm. It was dirty and deep, and Alec wondered if he should have a doctor look at it. He wondered what would happen if he walked into a hospital. Would he be arrested? Jesus, he'd gone from a cop to a felon in a week.

Alec tried not to let that thought bother him as he walked into the huge double shower, and he burst out laughing when he saw the now-broken shower shelf in two parts on the floor in the shower. At least Cronin had put the shelf parts and soaps in a neat row.

But showered and shaved, Alec felt so much better, despite the fact that hunger and exhaustion were now slowly creeping in. He went through Cronin's extravagant wardrobe and found himself some jeans and a shirt that fit, and when he walked out, Cronin's dark eyes smoldered, spreading warmth and want though his body. He was sitting on the sofa with a purring Sammy on his lap, and Alec had to look away from him. His stare—which Alec could only describe as eye-fucking—was intense, to say the least.

"Right, then," Kole said, standing up. He looked a little flustered and a whole lot of embarrassed. "I guess I should be going home."

Alec was about to object, but then thought twice. He really didn't want his dad here, privy to what he and Cronin would surely be doing in the bedroom. "Only if you're sure," Alec said.

Kole nodded quickly. "I, uh, I think you two need some time to… get acquainted."

Again, Eiji laughed from the bedroom.

Alec could feel his whole face and neck flush with mortification. He laughed it off and nodded toward the bedroom. "Eiji must be feeling much better."

"Yes," Cronin said. He looked as humiliated as Alec felt.

Kole took Sammy the cat and held him tight. "I'm ready when you are."

Alec put one arm snugly around Cronin's waist and put his injured hand on his dad's arm, and they leapt.

Kole's house was dark and quiet. Cronin sniffed the air. "There's been no one here since the vampire that broke in when we took you with us last time."

Alec flipped on the lights and did a search of all rooms and closets. He knew Cronin would have smelled another person or vampire, but Alec wanted to see it with his own eyes. "Okay, Dad. It's clear. No one here but us."

Alec knew his father was still shaking off the effects of leaping, though the silence from the older man spoke volumes. He put the cat down on the old sofa.

"What is it, Dad?"

"Is this the last time I'll see you?"

"No," Alec said quickly.

"Is it the last time I'll see you... human?"

"Oh."

"That's what I thought."

"Dad," Alec started to say.

Kole put his hand up to stop him. "It's okay, Alec." His dad nodded pointedly at Cronin, then back at Alec and looked him square in the eye and said, "If you get forever with someone you love, then you should take it."

Oh.

"Just promise me you'll call in on your old man every now and then?" Kole said. "Just so I know you're doin' all right."

Alec nodded. His voice was quiet. "Okay." He hugged his dad, knowing it would probably be the last time he did so as a human. "I promise."

Kole pulled back and gave Alec a teary smile. "I'm proud of you, Alec, and I'll be proud of you as a vampire too. You'll do great things, I know it."

Alec didn't know what to say to that. He wasn't sure there was anything he could say. So instead, he just hugged his father even tighter.

When Kole pulled back this time, he smiled. Then he looked to Cronin. "I trust you to look after him. Teach him right."

Cronin gave a hard nod, a promise. "Of course."

"Okay, then," Kole said, looking again at Alec. "I better get some shut-eye."

Alec knew his dad was trying to say goodbye without saying the actual word.

"I'll only ever be a phone call away," Alec told him. "Then we'll be here in a second, okay?"

"'Course," Kole said. He walked into the kitchen and called out, "You boys want a cup of tea?"

Alec knew his father didn't want an answer. He watched him for a second as Kole reached for his teapot, and Alec gave Cronin a small nod. This time when Cronin leapt, Alec smiled.

* * * *

Alec stood in Cronin's apartment with both arms wound tight around Cronin. He didn't ever want to let go. He'd never felt anything so right, so perfectly just for him.

"Are you well?" Cronin asked.

The customary formal way Cronin asked if he was okay made Alec smile. He nodded. "Yeah. You?"

Cronin's reply was just as formal. "I am."

"I will see my father again," Alec whispered with conviction.

Cronin pulled back and put his hand to Alec's face. "Yes. Anything you want."

"Anything?" Alec asked suggestively, before he very softly pressed his lips to Cronin's. And then his very human stomach growled for food.

Cronin laughed and, taking his hand, led him into the kitchen. "You need food."

Alec couldn't deny it. He was flagging, and the thought of food made him even hungrier. He opened the fridge door and started collecting food. "I can't tell you how happy I am just to be able to make myself a sandwich," Alec said. "Every meal this week's been takeout." He looked at Cronin and quickly amended, "Which is fine, but real food made at home's good too." He piled up bread, mayo, cold cuts, cheese, tomatoes, and pickles. As he was about to add lettuce to his burden and was struggling to hold them with his sore hand, Cronin took them from him.

"Allow me," Cronin said, putting the sandwich items on the kitchen counter. He spread everything out and cautiously took the bread first. Then he went to touch the deli bag of meat and pulled back his hand. Alec had never seen him so unsure about anything.

Alec smiled. "You've never done this before, have you?"

"Uh, no," Cronin said, shaking his head. He picked up the bag of deli meats like it was a pair of dirty socks.

Alec laughed, and when Cronin got embarrassed, Alec took the bag and kissed his cheek.

"I'm hardly to blame." Cronin shook his head slowly. "I've never exactly had a need for such things."

"I guess you didn't even butter bread in 744, huh?" Alec said.

Cronin looked at him and smiled. "No. I am sure I'm capable of such a simple task. I managed your coffee just fine."

"You did!" Alec said. "Though it came with instructions. Making sandwiches doesn't."

Cronin picked up the butter knife, and Alec couldn't waste the opportunity. He stood behind him, slid his arms around him, and put his hand over Cronin's hand that held the knife. "I'll show you how it's done," Alec said, dipping the knife into the mayo first, then spreading it across the bread. "Just like that."

Alec pressed himself against Cronin's back and ass, and Cronin started to purr. Or growl. It was kind of loud.

"Then we take this," Alec said, picking up the meat.

Jodis cleared her throat. She was standing at the edge of the hall. "I do apologize," she said. "I'm not interrupting deliberately this time. Eiji needs to feed again. He's feeling pain, and quite frankly, I can't stand it."

Alec stood back just a little and turned Cronin around to face him. He held his face and kissed him.

"Go get him something to eat while I get me something to eat." He pressed his hips into Cronin's, feeling how turned-on he was.

Cronin gave a growly-sigh. "Then it'll be just us for a few hours, yes?"

Alec nodded. "Yes. A few hours. Forever. Same thing."

Cronin smiled, and he was gone.

"I hate to take him away from you," Jodis said. She looked sad and shaken.

Alec piled on his sandwich ingredients. "Think nothing of it," he said, trying to act blasé about it all. "I just want Eiji to get better. I'm really sorry he got hurt, and I'm sorry he's in pain." Alec shrugged. "I mean, he *has* to get better. I still have to give him and Cronin driving lessons yet, and there's about a thousand years of funny stories he has to tell me."

Jodis smiled then. "Alec, fate couldn't have chosen better for Cronin. I am thankful for you. So very thankful."

Alec grinned back at her. "Me too."

CHAPTER TWENTY-TWO

When Cronin came back from disposing of Eiji's supper, he found Alec packing a bag. He was alarmed. "What are you doing?"

Alec spun around to face him and grinned. "What time is it in Scotland?"

Cronin didn't even have to look at the time. "It's 4:00 a.m."

"Perfect."

"Why?"

Alec put on the heaviest coat he could find, picked up the bag, and took a blanket from the linen closet. "Okay, that's everything, I think."

"Alec?"

He gave Cronin a smile that set fire to his blood. Alec walked up to him and kissed him. "Take me to the moor."

Cronin didn't argue, he just thought of the moor at Dún Ad, the very battlefield where he'd died, and with his arm firmly around Alec, he took him there.

As soon as their feet hit the ground, Alec kissed him. It was a sweet kiss, but it held a promise of what was to come. The night sky was impeded by mist, the air was cool, though Alec didn't seem bothered. "Do you notice how you don't even flinch at leaping now?" Cronin whispered, then kissed him again.

"I don't feel it anymore," Alec said with a shrug. "Well, that's not entirely true. I feel it. I just concentrate on the energy of it instead. And being pressed against you helps."

Cronin chuckled. "You're remarkable, you know that?"

Alec handed him the blanket. "Here, help me spread this out." When the long grass was pushed down and the blanket spread out, Alec sat himself down and patted the blanket next to him. "Sit with me."

Cronin did, but he couldn't help the feeling that Alec was planning something. "Alec, why here?"

"Privacy," Alec answered. "Jodis and Eiji can't hear us here."

"No, why *here*?"

Alec swallowed hard. "Your human life ended here. I thought if we have sex and you bite me, then maybe it should be where mine ends too."

Cronin blinked. "You what?"

Alec shrugged, suddenly nervous. "It's what you want, isn't it?"

"Of course it is, but, Alec, it has to be what you want. Not me."

Alec swung his leg over Cronin's and straddled him. He tried to push him back to lay down, but it was like pushing a concrete wall. "Can you at least pretend I have the strength to push you backward?"

Cronin laughed and fell back, taking Alec with him.

Alec put his hand to Cronin's face, and stared into his eyes. "I want to make love with you."

Cronin's black eyes caught fire. "Alec."

"I want you inside me," Alec whispered. "I want your cock in my ass and your teeth in my neck."

Cronin flipped Alec so fast it took a second for him to realize what had happened. Cronin was over him now, between his legs and his face just an inch from Alec's. Cronin's fangs were glistening in the moonlight. "You shouldn't say such things to me."

Alec smiled. "I want you to fuck me. And I want you to bite me."

Cronin snapped out a growl and pressed himself harder against Alec, pinning him to the blanket completely. He whisper-purred, "You said I needed your permission."

"You have it. You have all of me." Alec writhed underneath him, still fully dressed and wanting. "Please."

Cronin seemed to hesitate, so Alec reached between them and started to undo his own jeans. Then in less time it took to blink, Alec was bare-chested, his shirt torn right down the middle. Cronin growled again as he leaned down and licked a stripe from Alec's sternum to his chin.

"Jesus," Alec whispered, fumbling with his jeans fly. Then with a loud ripping sound, his jeans were gone. He yelped in surprise and shivered.

"Are you cold?" Cronin asked, starting to pull away.

Alec quickly held Cronin to him, and shook his head. "No."

Cronin held his stare for a long moment. "Are you sure of this?"

Alec held Cronin's face in both hands. "I've never been more sure of anything." Alec reached over and grabbed the bag he'd brought with them and took out the bottle of lubrication. "I'm also very sure we'll need this."

Cronin ducked his head and chuckled, but he soon ripped his own jeans off like he was tearing tissue paper, then reached over and flicked the edge of the blanket over them both, wrapping them like a sleeping bag. When he settled back on top of Alec, their hard cocks aligned.

Even in the darkness, Alec could see Cronin's eyes roll. But when he opened his eyes and looked at Alec again, he knew there was no going back.

He pulled Cronin in for a kiss, and Cronin rolled them onto their sides with Alec's leg hitched over Cronin's thigh, leaving his legs opened, his hole exposed. Alec smeared his fingers with lube and started to prep himself, sliding a slickened finger inside himself. But Cronin soon took over, growling into Alec's mouth as he kissed him.

And Alec was lost. Lost in every touch, every sound, every taste of tongues, every slide of fingers, everything. He was moaning without shame, bucking onto Cronin's fingers, precome dripping freely from his cock. Alec had never been this close, this fast.

"Cronin, please," Alec begged. "I need you inside me."

Then at a human pace, Cronin rolled them over again so Alec was pinned underneath him. Alec wrapped his legs around Cronin the best he could, his knees up near their chests.

Cronin pressed his cock against Alec's ready hole, and he paused. "*M'cridhe. M'gràdh.*"

Alec whispered his words back to him, "My heart. My love."

Cronin closed his eyes at the words, his chest heaving. Alec held Cronin's face once more, making him look at him. Alec wanted to see every flicker of emotion, every ounce of love that sparked in Cronin's eyes.

"Cronin," Alec murmured. "Give yourself to me."

And with that, Cronin pushed inside him.

It took Alec's breath away. Not in pain, no, this was something different. As the blunt head of Cronin's cock breached him, every nerve in Alec's body burst with pleasure. It was instantaneous. It was like a bomb detonated without warning, exploding ecstasy through every cell in his body.

And he came.

Wave after wave of orgasm rolled through him, emptying his cock between them. Cronin snapped a growl in Alec's ear, sending another roll of pleasure through him.

Alec's eyes widened, his still-hard cock pulsed again and again, and he came again. He screamed, a hoarse sound, his whole body wracked with a pleasure too huge to contain. He was unable to move his body, a bliss so intense, so pure, that Alec was spent, completely pliable like a ragdoll in Cronin's arms. All he could do was crane his neck, exposing the pale skin. He wanted it. He wanted to belong to Cronin in every way. "Make me yours."

Cronin thrust up into him once more, hard and deep, and his release, half-physical, half-emotional, poured into Alec.

Cronin bared his fangs, and he growled a sound Alec had never heard. It was a primal sound, a growl that said *mine*.

* * * *

Cronin ran his nose along the thrumming pulse in Alec's neck, he tasted the salt on his skin, and he sunk his teeth into his flesh.

Mouthfuls of the sweetest blood he'd ever tasted filled his mouth. It was Alec's scent, his taste, his very essence that he drank, and in all his years, Cronin had never tasted anything like it.

Alec writhed and moaned underneath him, and when his hands found Cronin's hair, he thought Alec was about to push him away. But he didn't. He gripped his face and lifted it from his neck, then brought their mouths together.

Cronin's cock was still buried in him, and this renewed vigor from Alec sent a surge of passion through Cronin. Being inside him, coupling with him, making love with him, combined with deep and bloodied kisses was more than Cronin could take.

It was frantic and primal, savage almost, and Alec dug his fingers in deeper and moaned louder. The sounds, the blood, the sex, sent Cronin's second orgasm into a tailspin, and he came again, deep inside Alec.

Their kisses slowed somewhat, and Cronin tore his mouth from Alec's, expecting him to start feeling the effects of change. He should be feeling discomfort, pain even. There should be heat and fire in his blood, and the fear of the unknown in his eyes.

But Alec looked intoxicated, and instead of screaming in pain, he laughed. His face was smeared with blood, his lips swollen from kissing, and his eyes were hazy and unfocused.

"Wow," he said with a laugh. "Jesus. If I had of known it was gonna be that good, I wouldn't have held out all week."

Cronin didn't laugh. "Alec, how do you feel?"

He bucked his hips and gripped Cronin's ass. "I feel so good right now."

Cronin slowly slid out of Alec. "Are you sure?"

Alec looked a little hurt by the question. "Why? Was that not good for you?"

"Alec we need to get dressed and go home."

"Well, you kinda tore our jeans to shreds—"

* * * *

Alec suddenly found himself lying on Cronin's bed, still wrapped in the blanket, still with Cronin on top of him. But that's not what shocked him. It was the look on his face. "Cronin, what is it? You're starting to scare me."

"Are you sure you feel okay?"

"Yes, great actually. And I thought you said you'd end up biting me."

Cronin dragged Alec to the bathroom, walking instead of leaping, and stood in front of the mirror. It was then Alec saw himself. There was dried blood, smeared over his face and lips, and two very distinct puncture marks in his neck.

"You did bite me," Alec whispered, lightly touching the bite mark.

"I did." Cronin looked at Alec in the reflection of the mirror. "You should be…"

"Changing?" Alec finished for him.

Cronin nodded. "And you're not."

"What does that mean?" Alec asked him.

"I don't know." Cronin swallowed hard. "Take a shower, get cleaned up. I'll consult with the others."

Alec nodded woodenly. "Okay."

Before Cronin walked out, he stopped and put his hand to Alec's face. "For what it's worth, what we did, was everything to me."

He kissed him softly before he walked out, meeting Jodis in the hall. She'd obviously heard their conversation. "Cronin?"

"I bit him," Cronin said quickly. "He wanted it. He asked me to, but it didn't work. He's not feeling any ill effects."

When Alec got out of the shower he put on new jeans and a simple shirt that showed off his bite marks clearly. The more he'd stared at the two puncture wounds in the mirror, the more he'd liked them. He was proud of them. When he walked out into the living room, he found Cronin was sitting with Jodis, a bundled-up Eiji, and most surprising of all, Eleanor. Cronin stood up and quickly took Alec's hand. He could feel all eyes on his neck, but instead he looked at Eiji. "Hey. How're you feeling?"

Eiji gave a nod. "I will be okay."

"Shouldn't you be resting?"

"I think something else is more important, no?"

Alec looked at Cronin his eyes wide and searching. "What is it?"

Cronin looked at Eleanor. The blind woman swayed her head a little. "You are a surprising one, Alec."

Alec squeezed Cronin's hand. "What does that mean?" Alec asked her. He turned to Cronin. "What does that mean?"

"It would seem your birthright is not yet fulfilled," Eleanor said.

"What?" Alec shook his head. "We defeated the Egyptian psycho-woman. We went back. There was no one left."

Eleanor shook her head again, this time as a no. "You're still the Key, Alec. You are Cronin's Key. Now you have mated, I can see that much more clearly."

"I don't understand," Alec said, looking at each of the vampires in the room. "What does that mean?"

"I saw your being linked to Cronin," Eleanor explained. "As we all did. You are fated, that cannot change. But this is different. You are linked in ways I cannot explain, nor can I see. Not yet."

"So, something else has to happen, something no one can tell us about, before I can be turned into a vampire?" Alec asked incredulously.

Eleanor smiled. "It means you will stay human for a greater purpose, yes. Your blood is something special, isn't it?"

Alec shook his head. "I don't know."

"It healed Eiji when he should have died," Eleanor said. "And Cronin said it was not like anything he's ever tasted. There is a strength in it. A power."

Alec looked at Cronin. "A power?"

"I never said that," Cronin objected. "I said it tasted different, yes."

"*I* said it has a power," Eleanor said. "A power needed to help Cronin. I can't see to what purpose yet, Alec, but I am sure you will stay human, whether you want to or not. Your blood has more work to do yet."

"So I'm still the Key?"

Eleanor nodded. "Yes."

Alec turned to Eiji. "You tasted my blood. Did you see my DNA? Is my lifespan different to what it was before?"

Eiji shook his head slowly, and he smiled. "I still see many years for you. You will be vampire, Alec. I am sure of it. You and Cronin have a millennia in front of you."

Alec sighed, and the relief that flooded through him was immense. He took Cronin's hand. "So, you can bite me all you like and it won't change me?"

"So it would seem."

"And we have an indeterminate length of time before whatever we need my blood for happens, right?"

"A few months," Eleanor said. "No more than a year."

Alec laughed and dragged Cronin back toward the bedroom. "You guys might wanna get yourselves some earplugs or something," he said, knowing they'd all hear everything he was about to do to Cronin. "We're gonna be a while."

~End

About the Author

Who am I?
Good question…
I am many things: a mother, a wife, a sister, a writer.
I have pretty, pretty boys who live in my head, who don't
let me sleep at night unless I give them life with words.
I like it when they do dirty, dirty things… but I like it even
more when they fall in love.
I used to think having people in my head talking to me was
weird, until one day I happened across other writers who
told me it was normal.
I've been writing ever since…

Website:
nrwalker.net

Email:
nrwalker2103@gmail.com

Also by N.R. Walker

Blind Faith
Through These Eyes (Blind Faith 2)
Blindside: Mark's Story (Blind Faith 3)
Ten in the Bin
Point of No Return – Turning Point #1
Breaking Point – Turning Point #2
Starting Point – Turning Point #3
Element of Retrofit – Thomas Elkin Series #1
Clarity of Lines – Thomas Elkin Series #2
Sense of Place – Thomas Elkin Series #3
Taxes and TARDIS
Three's Company
Red Dirt Heart
Red Dirt Heart 2
Red Dirt Heart 3
Red Dirt Heart 4
Cronin's Key
Cronin's Key II

Free Reads
Sixty Five Hours
Learning to Feel
His Grandfather's Watch (And The Story of Billy and Hale)

Translated Titles

Fiducia Cieca (Italian translation of Blind Faith)
Attraverso Questi Occhi (Italian translation of
Through These Eyes)
Confiance Aveugle (French translation of Blind Faith)
A travers ces yeux: Confiance Aveugle 2 (French

translation of Through These Eyes)

Coming Soon

The Spencer Cohen Series: Book 1
Exchange of Hearts

46187910R00209

Made in the USA
San Bernardino, CA
28 February 2017